Love in the
Time of Affluenza

Love in the
Time of Affluenza

Shunali Khullar Shroff

BLOOMSBURY
NEW DELHI • LONDON • OXFORD • NEW YORK • SYDNEY

BLOOMSBURY INDIA
Bloomsbury Publishing India Pvt. Ltd
Second Floor, LSC Building No. 4, DDA Complex, Pocket C - 6 & 7 Vasant Kunj,
New Delhi 110070

BLOOMSBURY, BLOOMSBURY INDIA and the Diana logo are trademarks of
Bloomsbury Publishing Plc

First published in India 2019
This edition published 2019

ISBN: PB: 978-93-86826-03-9; eBook: 978-93-86826-05-3

Typeset in Palatino by Manipal Digital Systems
Printed and bound in India by Thomson Press India Ltd.

To find out more about our authors and books visit www.bloomsbury.com
and sign up for our newsletters

To my wonderful mother Shobna

Contents

Chapter 1

I nearly fall face-first into the meat section at the supermarket today. As a vegetarian, it's especially surprising. But I see I've gotten ahead of myself here, so let me start at the beginning.

The driver is off sick, so I have groggily done the school run at the crack of dawn. While I'm driving back experiencing a glow of pride at having managed to not kill myself and my three children, the cook – who thinks I work for him – rings to dictate an urgently needed list of provisions. I turn into the first mall I see near their school and head towards Green Bazaar to find arborio rice and shiitake mushrooms and just as I'm walking in, I see someone who looks exactly like my friend Trisha.

Spotting a friend at a supermarket isn't usually this suspicious a happening, only Plaza Mall isn't anywhere near Trisha's house and also Trisha is to domestic errands what Donald Trump is to environmental conservation. In addition, while she's given to a bit of bling, why on earth is she wearing red lipstick with her Lulu Lemons this early in the morning? I wave to say hello, but she doesn't see me and turns into another aisle. I go towards the aisle and am about to call out when I see a man in a checked shirt – quite possibly made from a French tablecloth – move towards her, put his hand on her back and whisper something into her ear. Trisha responds by throwing her head back and letting out a volley of such merry giggles that either he's the funniest man on earth or she's flirting with him. The man taps her jokily on her head with the baguette he is carrying and that unleashes another torrent of giggles. And then when I see Trisha turn in my direction, I do the only thing I can – I dive behind the closest aisle where I find myself nose to nose with a bag of frozen chicken thighs. I realise I haven't missed meat, having left it about five years earlier. I peer out to see Trisha and the mystery man's back walking down the Bath & Shampoo aisle, with him trying to hold her hand and she, belatedly remembering that she is married, yanking it away and looking left and right in the manner of a woman who's really bad at having an affair.

I make a dash for the tills to pay and leave before being spotted by Trisha and Tablecloth Man but on seeing them emerging from the baked goods aisle facing me, I'm left with no choice but to abandon my basket, shiitake mushrooms and all, pull out my phone as if receiving an important call and run out of the supermarket. As I scurry to my car, heart thumping loudly, it occurs to me that it's a bit much that I'm the one hiding and not the woman cheating on her husband. And also, how dare she does not tell me? I mean, it's one thing to lie to your partner but to the person you call your best friend?

Driving out of the mall, I take a deep breath on hitting the main road and ring her from the first traffic light I hit. I'm not especially surprised when she does not respond – too busy giggling, I'm sure. God, I wonder how long this has been going on. Or if she just randomly met this man at the supermarket. No, that would be too weird. I have theorised to the point of exploding by the time a message from her flashes on my screen five minutes later.

Can't talk, at the dentist. xx

The dentist? Really Trisha, is that the best you can do? I take another deep breath. I'm going to wait for her to tell me. There's no point getting involved, no good can come of it. The next thing I know I've pulled up on the side of the road.

No problem. Just wondering if that man that I saw you getting cosy with at the supermarket was your dentist???

No response. I think of the colour draining from her face and while I'm still totally bewildered, I have a little smile on my face.

I get home and ask Shambhu to bring me a cup of coffee. Clearly, this is a situation that demands drugs, and caffeine is about as exciting as it gets in my house. Shambhu asks if he should take the groceries out of the car. I have no idea what he's talking about till I remember the basket abandoned at Green Bazaar. 'No groceries,' I tell him, 'there was an emergency.' I can't believe he's bothering me with questions about food at a time like this. He brings the coffee out on a tray and I'm about to ask him why he hasn't served my almond milk along with the coffee when I remember that it too was sitting in that basket that got left behind. Damn you, Trisha!

She eventually rings some twenty minutes later.

'Hello?' I say, icily.

'Natasha don't be mad at me. I...I can explain,' voice faltering.

'What's left to explain? I saw everything with my own eyes. And then you tell me you are at the dentist's! Why would you lie to me, Trisha? Why, Trisha, why?' I say. I know I'm prone to being a little dramatic sometimes but I think this conversation calls for it.

'I have yoga in forty-five minutes. Meet me for coffee at Yoga House and I'll tell you everything,' she says enigmatically. I so badly want to know that it doesn't even occur to me to say, 'No, adulteress, I don't have a driver today, you come here and tell me.'

Draining my coffee, I make a dash for Yoga House, feeling light-headed with anticipation. I wedge the car into the only free spot I can find, praying that it's actually intended as a parking space. Driving around the narrow lanes of Bandra without running a life form over is in itself an achievement. Besides, I have bigger things to worry about.

Trisha is at the organic café on the second floor. Expecting to find her filled with contrition, if not outright panic, I'm quite surprised to be greeted by an utterly sanguine woman who appears to have just reapplied her lipstick. Not even French women wear red lipstick this early. Madam is insouciantly sipping carrot juice and asks me to sit on the sofa next to her. One glass of beetroot juice and two cups of coffee later, I still can't make head nor tail of it.

Not only has Trisha – one half of what I thought is the loveliest couple I know – been cheating on Nakul for eight months now, but who has she found worth risking twelve years of marriage and the happiness of two lovely children for? Guneet from Vasant Kunj.

They'd met at a coffee shop in Istanbul last October. Trisha had been to see her cousin in Crete and was availing of the free Turkish Airlines stopover in Istanbul to buy affordable fur and carpets from the Grand Bazaar on her way back. Cupid struck at a sidewalk café in the upscale neighbourhood of Nishantashi. Only Trisha could go to the threshold of Europe and find herself mesmerised by a Punjabi from Delhi.

She glows as she tells me about their first meeting and the moment when she decided that she was willing to take that next step. 'He lives in Delhi with his wife, their marriage sucks, you know,' she says as if that justifies everything. 'But we are making it work, he keeps coming to Bombay for work and now also to see me,' Trisha adds coyly. I listen to their love story with a sentiment that can be best described as nausea. The only time she looks worried while sharing details of her romance with me is when I mention her twins.

'They're my world,' Trisha says, 'but I only have this one life and at the moment I want to do this for me. You'll love him when you meet him!' she gushes, ignoring the disapproval writ large on my face.

'Meet him?' I say, aghast. 'I'm going to do no such thing, Trisha,' I say, 'what's more, this ends here.'

'I can't guarantee that,' she says shrugging her shoulders as if she cannot guarantee whether or not she can accompany me to a morning walk on Juhu beach. I look on bewildered. 'Promise me you won't tell anyone,' she says.

I look at her blankly. If Varun had been at home and not out playing polo, I might already have told him.

'I know you won't say anything, I trust you implicitly,' she says, the manipulative so-and-so. 'I've been wanting to tell you about him for so long, Natty,' she says, 'I just didn't know how to. I think the universe wanted you to know and that's why it sent you to the supermarket to find us sneaking around there!'

'I was at the supermarket because Varun has been asking for risotto for dinner and we didn't have any arborio rice, Trisha,' I say but she continues to look at me as if she was the teacher in *The Karate Kid* and I was the naïve disciple, unable to process the cosmic wonder that is life. When she's done, she laughs and, planting a scarlet adulterer's kiss on my cheek, disappears into her Ashtanga class.

I leave the cafe to find that my car has been towed. It's divine justice for my having agreed without protest to be complicit in Trisha's adultery. God has towed my car.

As I head home in an auto, bumping my way over the potholes, I think about Trisha and the complexity of my relationship with her. In life, you choose some friends and some friends are thrust upon you. I had many misgivings about Trisha when Nakul had first introduced me to her as his prospective bride. She seemed ambitious, had borderline tacky dress sense right from the start and came across as someone who was born with the singular intention of always being the belle of the ball, even when there wasn't a ball. After her marriage to Nakul, we started seeing so much of each other that I had to just accept her for what she was, warts and all. She has her redeeming qualities, but I'm in no mood to go into them while being tossed around inside an auto.

Not when I am worried about the school pick-up. If it wasn't hard enough already to ferry the kids to and from school without a driver, I realise it's going to be even harder without a car. There is also the stress of planning how to get the car back without Varun discovering what happened. He gets this look on his face, you see, when I make a mistake – it's this little knowing smile. I adore my Varun, don't get me wrong, but that little my-wife-is-such-a-flake smile of his makes me want to claw his eyes out.

❋ ❋ ❋

Well, the children have been fetched in an Uber, I nearly forgot my son Sumer though, what with my mind still disturbed after what I have witnessed this morning. I kept thinking of Trisha and Tablecloth Man having sex. It was a revolting thought, let me tell you. Thankfully, Ria reminded me to wait for her brother, just as I was walking towards the school gate with her and Sofie, my oldest and most temperamental child.

Anyway, after attending to my brood's après-school needs, I'm now sitting in front of my laptop, going over the details of this eventful day, letting it all sink in. I'm also trying to get a start on my weekly column that I do for *City Reflections*. Unfortunately, while inspiration doesn't strike, my awful mother-in-law, Rani Devika Kumari, does, in the form of a phone call.

'Natasha', she begins, without hellos, imperious from the get-go. 'I need you to go to Ravissant for me to pick up a gift for Bhabhisa's birthday. Can you do that by tomorrow?'

'I'm afraid it'll be hard for me to make it all the way to South Bombay today, Ma,' I say, as evenly as possible.

'Oh, I understand, the thing is that I don't want to ask Varun, knowing how busy he is. So, I thought, why not ask you since you are mostly free.'

The unhappy realisation dawns on me yet again that I will never, ever, be able to outmanoeuvre my mother-in-law. I blame my upbringing. My parents are softies; decent, kind and utterly devoid of Machiavellian tendencies, all of which has left me with a clear disadvantage against Her Ladyship.

I know what you're thinking – I'm overreacting to Varun's mother asking me to do a spot of shopping for her. That's because you don't know her like I do. Let me see if I can help.

My mother-in-law, Devika Kumari, is a natural born princess. Even today she is an arresting beauty. In her youth, she was famous for her looks and featured in more than a few coffee table books about India's glamorous royals. Beneath her Ming dynasty cheekbones, her almond eyes and her still lustrous hair though, lurks Nietzsche's abyss.

When she was eighteen, she could have married anyone – she was deluged with proposals from princes and assorted titans. But the heart – or whatever it is she carries in her chest – wants what it wants, and she chose my dashing father-in-law, the heir of a minor principality. They met at a polo match and the aristocratic beauty fell for him right away. Bhairon Singh's good looks and Etonian education enchanted her into turning her back on her immense fortune and vast property to move to the far humbler Srilampur. She's been in a foul mood since. This isn't to say that she has lived in penury as Bhairon Singh's wife. They lived well – travelling in style, often buying beautiful things wherever they went, living between tastefully done family-owned havelis and hobnobbing with the chic set in well-appointed living rooms, both in India and abroad. They gave their son the best education money could buy. But compared to the wealth and lifestyle of the rest of her family, such a life always stuck like a thorn in her side. And then when she lost her husband it not only broke her heart but also occluded her from many a social opportunity.

Rani Devika Kumari has not stopped competing with the royals higher up in the pecking order, and her sense of being hard done by was only heightened by her failure to forge an alliance between her beloved son and a princess from a relevant blue-blooded clan like the Gaekwads of Baroda or some pretty thing from the Mewar dynasty.

As a non-royal, I'm ideal for her lost prestige target practice, and she misses no opportunity in making herself feel grand by trying to make me feel like something she scraped off her shoe. She articulated her horror at me joining the family the very first time she invited me over to tea after Varun proposed.

'Your background,' she said, uttering the word as if it were a dead rat she was holding by the tail, 'is somewhat different from ours. I had rather thought Varun might marry someone more like us. Still, perhaps you can adapt to our ways,' she had said, sounding as if she thought this was hugely unlikely. I'll give her something, her complete lack of respect for me has at least been perfectly consistent. Just last month I went to a family wedding with her and she saw my necklace, diamonds borrowed from my mother, put both her hands on her cheeks in horror and started shrieking, rather like she was trying to re-enact *The Scream*. 'Your set is SO bright, Natasha. I can't even look at it with my naked eye!'

'It's my mother's, and I happen to love it,' I had snapped back in the hope of shaming her into silence but I am more a fool for not realising after all these years that insults fell from my mother-in-law's mouth as the indifference of rain in England.

'Now that you are a part of our family, it's high time you started grooming yourself like one of us and left the loud pieces to the nouveau riche!' Small mercy then that Devika Kumari lives far away from us with her mother, Nanisa, in Jhalakpur. If she lived any closer, I might have left Varun by now.

Still, my mother-in-law had been the one blip on the glowing horizon of wonderfulness that has been my life with Varun. We met at Heathrow where I had been in the middle of an angry exchange with the staff at the check-in-desk at the British Airways counter. The London-Mumbai flight that I was heading home on, after a wonderful holiday largely spent shopping, was overbooked and I had unceremoniously been bumped off. The duty manager was trying his hardest to get rid of me till Varun, a business-class passenger on the same flight, stepped in and managed to convince him otherwise. Once we'd boarded, he found me and invited me to join him at the bar, and we sat there chatting and laughing all night till we were forced to return to our seats to buckle up for the descent into Bombay. I was in love before we even touched down in India. And who could blame me? Varun was every bit the prince you read about in fairy tales – upright, decent, chivalrous and hardworking, which was virtually unheard of among India's famously indolent royals.

When I met him, he'd just started his architectural firm, Paradigm Design. Turning his family havelis and palace into heritage hotels, done with his sense of ingenuity and strong work ethic, has kept his family afloat while his royal peers struggle to keep up appearances. Then he partnered with his dearest childhood friend Nakul and started another successful vertical called V&N Consultants. Poor Nakul! Someone has to tell him about Trisha. God! I hope it doesn't have to be me.

Chapter 2

I have arrived at the conclusion that a happy marriage is one where the wife is daft and has no opinions of her own on anything except what moisturising cream to use and where to buy bed linen. Men, as long as you agree wholeheartedly with everything they say and toe the line, are happy creatures, their egos sated and sense of power intact. But say anything to contradict them, and their world goes off balance. Submissive = good wife = happy marriage.

The editor's assistant from *City Reflections* has sent me a politely worded email to remind me that she is expecting my fortnightly column today. To misquote Anaïs Nin, my desire to surf the internet expands and contracts directly in proportion to the urgency of my deadline. The tighter the deadline, the more I'm drawn to Twitter and Facebook.

I know Varun thinks I lie around all day wondering what I'll wear to dinner, but the truth is that there's always something sucking up all my time. It's either the driver taking off when he fancies or the cook who seems to have an unending supply of dying relatives that all require long trips back to his village. If Sylvia Plath's cook had a death in the family every time she was due to throw a dinner party, I bet she would have stuck her head in the oven sooner. These last few weeks were especially bad with little Sofie coming down with dengue. It was so awful! And then the cleaning lady came down with it too, God help me – that was worse.

Coming back to my column, after days of discussing platelet counts and fever, I had planned to write about the scourge that is dengue and how it must be the most inelegant-sounding disease in the English language – like a Punjabi swear word. But when I sat down to do it, I couldn't face the thought of more dengue, even on paper. Besides, all I really wanted to write about was homemakers having affairs and whether this was a trend or just my friends being slutty. I couldn't possibly write it, of course. For one thing, absolutely everyone would be after me wanting to know who I was talking about and secondly, Trisha would be devastated. While I think she deserves to be exposed, she's my friend and even though she's behaving like an idiot, I have to be decent about it. All this agonising meant that my deadline had come and gone and I had produced, oh let's see, nothing.

And are my children grateful that they have a mother who spends her time sacrificing what's left of her career and throwing herself into traffic for them? You'd certainly not know it. For example, regardless of how demanding my day has been, Ria, our six-year-old, won't spare me until I've given her her nightly bath, even if I have to do it in a coma.

Varun is no better than the kids when it comes to a little appreciation. When I remind him, and I often do, that I need to be physically there to raise psychologically sound and secure children in a house that runs smoothly, he tells me I have a warped notion of what gives children security. He's a man of many contradictions, my Varun. The modern man in him wants me to speak my mind but sometimes the feudal DNA takes over and suddenly he knows better than me on everything under the sun. Still, he has a wonderful heart and he loves me no end which is why after spending so many years with him I don't take his criticism seriously.

He had promised to be home early today but since it seems increasingly clear that that shan't happen, I go ahead and bathe Ria.

Minutes later she and Sumer start fighting loudly over bedtime stories. Sumer says he's had it with fairies and princesses and Ria, who's partial to them, gets out of bed and decisively pulls a handful of her brother's hair. Sumer turns around and tugs at her hair in return, not terribly hard I must say, and she starts to bawl her lungs out. Seeing her father standing in the doorway, I understand that the waterworks have been turned on in his honour.

On cue, Varun rushes to save his beloved from her brother's clutches. The crying stops instantaneously and is replaced by a gloating expression. You never know how happy you should be when you discover that your children are incredibly manipulative.

Leaving their father to tend to the younger two for once, I pop in on Sofie. She may not need me to read her a bedtime story but at twelve she very much still wants her mother around. Only not tonight it seems, as she has her nose stuck in a love story about vampires and answers questions about her day with thinly veiled, monosyllabic annoyance.

With the children finally asleep, and Varun bathed, changed and positively glowing with the joy of having been a hands-on father for all of twenty minutes, we have convened at the dinner table. I've decided against lying or making excuses about the towing of my car. I'm a grown woman for God's sake. Varun isn't my father; he's my partner, my equal. Why should I have to cover up the occasional entirely human error? I should be sitting here expecting compassion and sympathy rather than worrying about being made fun of.

'Natasha, I wanted to speak to you about something…'

'Varun, I know, and I don't really think it's even worth bringing up. I'm sorry, but the driver keeps leaving me in the lurch, and you know how difficult this city is to navigate.'

'I meant your credit card statement; it arrived today.'

'Oh,' I say.

It had to be today, of course. It must be stated that any man expecting not to be mildly alarmed by his family's credit card statement after a six-week vacation is a man estranged from reality, a man with a utopian bent of mind and my Varun, bless him, is one such man. He wants to know what I have to say about 'it'.

I'm a child again, being confronted by my parents about a disappointing report card. I tell him that I think 'it' isn't bad at all and that 'it' includes my shopping as well as things for our children. One's children generally cannot be emphasised enough in such situations. I also remind him that I had purchased new upholstery for the whole house two weeks ago and that it was for us.

'And why am I having to explain these expenses to you anyway?' I say. 'If you think that you go off to work in the morning and I sit around watching Netflix or shopping then I'm afraid you don't understand my life. I'm here making sure your children don't accidentally kill themselves and that everyone returns from school and walk into to a beautiful home and a delicious supper every night.' Of course, the cook would take that moment to undermine my argument by placing tonight's repast of daal chawal before us.

Varun looks at it and then at me. I remember this deadpan routine from when we first started seeing each other. His poker-faced humour was so charming, I used to smile till my jaw ached. Thirteen years later, I'm glowering at him over a steaming tureen. 'At least I'm not out and about bonking,' I mutter.

'I'm sorry, what was that?' Varun asks.

Had I just said that out loud? I flushed high red. 'I said…I said…At least I'm not into Birkins. I've saved us a fortune.' It was a masterful save.

'Birkins,' Varun says, looking around incredulously. 'What do Birkins have to do with any of this?'

'I'm just saying I could have been into them. The exotic skin ones. Imagine what the credit card statement would look like then.'

Varun is gaping at me.

'Why do my bills go through you anyway, as if I'm your child and I have to ask you for permission? I used to have a job and my own credit cards, you know, before I gave it all up.' I hope Varun realises that he is violating my privacy and, in some countries, this could be sufficient ground for divorce.

'Alright, Natty,' he says, smiling with a hint of exasperation, 'We don't have to do this every time. I shall delink my number and give the bank your phone number instead. Just go through it though and confirm your expenses. Happy now?'

'Varun,' I say, smiling across the table at my handsome and eminently wonderful husband, 'I love you.'

'Natasha,' he says, returning my smile, 'I believe the car got towed again.'

Chapter 3

The things that make a woman happy vary through the different stages of her adult life. But as one grows older one realises that it isn't only the big things like finding the dream job, the perfect man or hearing your baby's first heartbeat that make you happy, but it's the simpler, smaller things you never imagined that hold your life together. Many of these seemingly insignificant events we take for granted, but we only have to look closer to realise that it's the ordinary that we truly count on to make our lives extraordinary. At twenty, finding a flattering outfit to wear to parties or getting a good haircut is enough to keep a girl in high spirits for days. When you fall in love for the first time and you find out that the object of your affections likes you just as much, isn't just happiness, it's heaven. Finding the right recipe to bake a sponge cake or a nanny high on hygiene are the kind of blessings that add to your happiness quotient when you become a mother. It gets more and more basic as the years roll on...the blood report that wasn't malaria, the cook who came back when his leave was over, the school report with no negative remarks, the visas that arrived on time, the friend who looked you up when you were lonely...

The driver has returned, thank goodness, but God gives with one hand and takes with another and in the morning,

Shambhu tells me he needs to go to his village in Nepal for a month. I remind him that he has already used up his leave on his last trip home and that he's been off sick with dengue for most of last month. His mother had died before his last trip and while I thought he'd completed her last rites, he informs me that there is one essential ritual that remains. Along with his leave, he'd also like another loan. I'm to add it onto the tab of his previous loan. I have a sign on my forehead inviting people to keep asking me for money that they have no intention of paying back.

He needs the money, he says, to gift cows for his mother's salvation to the village priest or her soul will not be granted permission to reincarnate.

I'm happy to help him with the money, but I urge him to please wire the money to his father and stay on in Mumbai where three little mouths needed him. 'I think your mom's soul would prefer it too,' I say with conviction.

He says that his father would never forgive him and that his village would talk about his unfilial behaviour for generations to come.

There's no arguing with that kind of logic. It's time to accept that I shall now be cooking for the three bottomless pits I gave birth to, along with Varun, whose aristocratic roots sometimes start to show themselves at the dinner table. And speaking of aristocratic roots, I'm filled with instantaneous despair at the thought of what I may have to do to make the next two weeks less trying. Please don't let it get so bad that I have to call my mother-in-law and ask her to lend me one of her cooks, I whisper to the gods, bowing my head and hoping they'll have mercy.

Luckily, these domestic anxieties fill me with all the energy I need to tear across town to my new kick-boxing class. Varun had appeared pleased last week when I had told him I was taking kick-boxing lessons – he thought it would be a good example for the girls to see their mother being able to defend herself. I smiled and nodded and didn't want to say that it was to get the wobble out of my thighs.

'Gigi Hadid also does kick-boxing,' Sofie said, visibly impressed. 'I know!' I said, confidently, before quickly looking her up. I would not mind kick-boxing three times a day if it meant Hadid's litheness, I thought. Some people spend their lifetime in pursuit of love – I spend mine in pursuit of weight loss. At 5 feet 3 inches, one has to be careful, especially if one has produced a litter of children.

The class was intense, but I survived partly by pretending I was kicking Trisha, her boyfriend, the cop who'd had my car towed, and the woman who pulled a beautiful primrose yellow cashmere sweater out of my hands at the Harrods sale a few months ago.

I'm munching on a rice cake that tastes like polystyrene in the back of the car while shifting about trying to find a sitting position that doesn't hurt when my phone rings. It's Ananya, South Bombay's high priestess of gossip and dispenser of other people's secrets. Even though Ananya isn't somebody I'd ever confide in, she has her redeeming qualities. She is consistent in her affections with me and always ready to help, be it with things like helping me find new staff when the last cleaning lady vanished or taking all my kids out for a movie when I need a break from being around them. Her love for gossip, I'd say, stems from being rich and bored with no abiding interest to save her, other than her interest in the lives of other people. We move in the same circles, more or less, and because her daughter Tara and Sofie have been classmates and friends since they were at kindergarten, we have come to understand each other.

I answer her call with my mouth full of the rubbish rice cake. Ananya asks if I'm doing well, but before I can answer that question, she seemingly innocently mentions that she has just seen Trisha having lunch at Hunan Kitchen with a man she didn't know and that they seemed to be 'rather good friends' in a manner that left little room for misinterpretation.

'Trisha?' I say, as if I've never heard the name before. 'Oh, Trisha! Oh! I haven't seen her for a few days, she's busy with her cousin from Chandigarh. I guess that's who she was with.' Ananya sounds disappointed and not entirely convinced. 'How was the food at Hunan Kitchen – I just read a really great review,' I say breezily, in spite of the cold trickle of fear in my stomach. Ananya tells me about the mock chicken with red peppers with an edge of irritability before quickly getting off the phone. All the frustration I got rid of in kick-boxing is pushing me down again. I'm furious with Trisha for her carelessness, angry with Ananya for her nosiness and angry with the cardboard diet biscuits for not being mock red pepper chicken instead. I punch out Trisha's number in a rage.

'Why don't you just put an advert in the papers, Trisha?' I say.

'What are you talking about, Nattie?'

'What do you think? I just had a call from Ananya dying to know who you were having lunch with at Hunan Kitchen.'

'Oh my God, what did you tell her?'

'I told her that you'd taken a lover,' I said in a whisper, worrying now about the driver. In one afternoon, I had worried more about Trisha's marriage than she had in the last eight months.

'Please tell me you are joking,' she says, sounding panicked.

'Obviously, Trisha. I told her that it was your cousin!' I snap.

'So typical of that nosey bitch to see me having lunch with a man and assume I MUST be sleeping with him!'

'But Trisha, you ARE sleeping with HIM!' I hiss.

'Yeah, but she doesn't know that,' Trisha responds, with flawless logic. 'And Natty, I get claustrophobic inside hotels. It all seems sordid if you just stick to hotel rooms.'

'Well, here's a thought, Trisha, why don't you stop doing it if it seems sordid?'

'You don't understand. We have been together eight months – clearly, it isn't only about sex. I think…it's possible Guneet is the one. I think I've known it from the moment I met him.'

'What do you mean Guneet is the one? How many ones do you have? When you married Nakul you felt he was the one. There is only one "The One",' I say, breathless with rage at the ease and urgency with which she has replaced Nakul. It's one thing to have an affair but quite another to declare that you are so in love that what you felt for your husband never counted.

Trisha, though, is listening to the sound of her own voice and barrels on with her love story. 'Why do you think I was at the supermarket that day? We wanted to do small normal things together, do you get it?'

'No,' I said, 'I don't get it. At all.'

'Well then let me tell you, Nakul and I stopped doing normal, everyday stuff a long time ago. I want to do all of that with Guneet. We enjoy spending time with each other…,' Trisha starts to tell me.

Varun is as busy as Nakul, I think, you don't see me running into the arms of the first man I see on holiday because of it.

'Okay Trisha, I have to go, my husband,' I say, with all the emphasis I can manage, 'is on call-waiting.' I click off. 'Hey hon,' I coo into the phone, being extra loving.

'Nats, listen, I've decided to visit Nanisa over the weekend. Thought I should let you know.'

'But Varun, you promised to take the kids swimming and to lunch, remember? And on Friday we're dining at Nomad with Anoop and Sheila.'

'I know we had plans Nats, I'm sorry, but I spoke to Nanisa earlier today and she sounded lonely. She's really getting on, you know, she needs me. Please cancel with Sheila, we'll do it another day. And I'm sure the kids will be just as happy to go swimming with you.'

'I see,' I say icily.

'Hon, don't get upset,' he says, as sweetly as he can manage. 'I'm only free to see Nanisa over the weekend. For you, weekdays and the weekend are all the same. We'll go out another weekend. Bye, honey. I'll see you at home soon,' he says, hanging up.

I clench my hand into a fist.

The truth is that Varun is off to Jhalakpur not only to see his old and lonely grandmother as he claims but to play polo with his cousins. His two great loves are his grandmother and his children. I probably come in third. God knows where I rank.

To add insult to injury, my harridan mother-in-law rings me a little later to thank me for 'allowing' Varun to come and visit them. The thought of seeing him has made Nanisa very happy, apparently. And if that isn't enough, she asks me if she can send some food back with him, 'He likes the cooking in this house so much, you know. Sometimes, I think he comes here just for the food,' she titters.

Universe, are you listening to this conversation? Don't you have a plan in place for people like this? Can a flash of lightning not strike her down? These things aren't unheard of – people drop dead all the time, don't they?

'By the way, I have asked Varun to bring the kids also the next time he visits. Nanisa is getting old, and also, Natasha, it's important for them to learn family values,' she says before hanging up.

Chapter 4

'I'm off to Goa for the opening of that new casino next week – want to join?'

Nafisa, one of my closest friends, and the much-sought-after editor-in-chief of *La Beau Monde*, asks me. Thanks to her job and her good looks, she has people virtually throwing free clothes and travel at her. It's the best life a girl on the wrong side of her thirties could aspire to. We'd started out in journalism together and used to work at the same magazine till I met Varun. I went on to marry him and produce a litter of children while Nafisa is still in search of that man who will fulfil her. Having seen her go through a series of relationships however, I personally feel looking for a unicorn might be a lot easier.

'Don't tempt me Nafisa. I don't have a proper cook, and Varun will find a way to bail out of fatherly duties because of his work,' I say with resignation.

'Aww, you sound upset Nats. What can I do to cheer you up?'

'You could take me out to dinner. Varun is not in town and, more importantly, I haven't seen you since forever.'

'I had love to take you out Nats, but I have a dinner at the Italian ambassador's tonight. Pray, I meet a dashing Italian hunk!' she says, laughing.

Listening to the kids fighting in the background, I wonder why she doesn't pray for me instead.

'But I will leave office early one of these days just to come home to see you. Sounds good?'

'Don't leave it too late, I might have died of boredom by next week.'

'I promise we will make a plan the week after next. I'm not in Bombay next week remember? Oh God, I need to start my meeting now. See you!'

'Don't sound so important. Not like I have nothing to do myself. I'm a very busy woman, FYI,' I say with mock seriousness. I hear her giggle as she hangs up.

I sit down to sort out the children's medical files and start putting them in order. This kind of work is tedious and something only a peon or a clerk should be doing, but then such is a homemaker's life. A glorified peon who does not get a salary nor any credit.

I'm only halfway through Sumer's vaccine records when I see Nakul's number flash on my phone. A shot of fear jolts through me. Oh God, please let him not be calling to ask if I know something about Trisha that I haven't told him. But no, from his customarily jaunty and warm hello, it's clear that Nakul is blissfully ignorant. I sink into myself in relief.

'I was just telling Trisha that Varun was away which meant you would be alone and hopefully bored. That way we could convince you to come with us for dinner to Soho House.'

'Oh, Nakul, you're so thoughtful!' I say and mean it. He truly is such a kind man. One of those wonderful men whose good nature radiates off him.

'Natasha don't be formal. I know how busy Varun and I have been. I'm just trying to make it up to you girls. Now, throw something on quickly, we're coming to get you,' he says.

Sofie is having a sleepover at her friend Diya's place and with both Ria and Sumer bowed in front of the television reverentially as if in the presence of the Buddha, I might as well go out and get a drink.

Throwing a burgundy off-shoulder blouse over my skinny jeans, I lovingly pull my brand new Gianvito Rossi shoes out of their box. Who needs an exciting lover on the side when you can have shoes like these? Nafisa was right, the prospect of a night out with friends is making me feel better.

When I hear the car at the gate though I'm filled with panic. How can I face Nakul knowing what I do? I've always been a terrible actress. I kept auditioning for the college play for years, but they wouldn't let me near it. What if Nakul can see right through me? What if he does know everything and this is all a test? I reach for my Bach flower remedy, praying it'll rescue my nerves, but what kind of a God would consider the prayers of a lying woman, I wonder.

When I step out into the drive, Nakul gets out of the car to give me a big hug before opening the door for me. Trisha is beaming from ear-to-ear flashing her extra white, orthodontically enhanced teeth in the dark. Dressed in a silver bustier and an elegant white jacket over her leggings, she is looking chic for a change. It's easy to be around Nakul so long as I don't have to look at him but once we step out of the car and take the elevator to the rooftop restaurant, I wish I had my sunglasses on.

Trisha's brazenness, on the other hand, is truly awe-inspiring. She is completely at ease with Nakul, enjoying herself, paying attention to him when it's required, giggling girlishly and holding his arm warmly. Who knew she was this unflappable? I'd be super impressed with her if I wasn't so appalled.

'Are you okay?' he asks me. 'You seem a bit restless.'

I realise I must be frowning because of the thoughts racing through my mind. Instead of helping me out with a response, Trisha makes it worse by saying, 'You do look pale, Nats. Have you done your vitamin tests lately?'

'It's the lethal combination of boredom and heat,' I lie, taking a large gulp of wine. I have to constantly stop myself from imagining Nakul confronting me. It's only after some alcohol has passed through my veins that I begin to feel more relaxed.

'I'm glad Varun could go to meet Nanisa. He takes on too much, you know. I've been telling him to learn to let go a bit, but he just won't. I think this break will do him a lot of good,' Nakul says. 'In fact, it's been a while since we went to Jhalakpur. Why don't we all go there with the kids over the next long weekend? Aunty Devika keeps asking us to come, and I promise her each time that I will make a plan soon,' he suggests.

'Why don't you and Varun just take the kids and go on the long weekend after next? Natasha and I could do with a nice break right here in Bombay, "a staycation".' Trisha suggests slyly. I can guess her motives behind this eagerly volunteered suggestion only too well.

I dart a disapproving look in her direction and to my amazement, she winks at me. Love is blind but it's also pathologically selfish.

Chapter 5

At a party bursting with glamorous people recently, I couldn't help but notice the Botox — Botox everywhere. Even young girls who didn't need it had gone in for filled up kissers and plumped up their cheeks with fillers. An actress who'd quit after marrying a young restaurateur had had so much work done to her face that most of us thought that the man was openly dating another woman. Is this what living in tinsel town does to you?

When did duck mouths and paralysed foreheads in women become the norm?

And excuse me if I sound old-fashioned, but I increasingly find young girls today dressing trashily and calling it sexy. Plunging necklines and short hemlines with six-inch heels leave little to the imagination. Sexy is good, be sexy by all means, but the importance of elegance cannot be stated enough.

Coco Chanel, the high-priestess of timeless style, had famously said, 'A girl should be two things, classy and fabulous.' Why then is everybody looking trashy and fake?

I'm pleased with myself this morning. First, I sent off my column and now I'm herding my children along with Trisha's twins to a musical that has been put together by a team from Broadway. The highlight of the show is that it has cast children from poor backgrounds to give them the experience of a lifetime. Trisha and I were supposed to go together but, surprise, surprise! She messaged to say that 'G' was in town and Nakul was looking for land in Alibaug and could I please do this for her.

'Surely Aarna and Aaditya would like to see you there too, Trisha. It's one thing to cheat on your husband but quite another to start shortchanging your children.'

'My babies love you and the kids, you know that. Your taking them along is as good as me taking them. Do this for me please Nattie.'

And that is that.

The stalls at the theatre are brimming with entitled children in Armani Junior, Ralph Lauren and Dior. Trisha's twins are in Burberry. My girls are wearing frocks from Zara and Sumer is in an old polo shirt, and I'm beaming at how comparatively unspoilt they are but, during the interval, Sofie and Sumer turn to me and say in unison that it's the most boring play that they have watched.

'This isn't like Shrek or Matilda! You said it was like the Broadway musicals,' Sofie says sulkily.

The twins are yawning with boredom too but Aarna says, 'I like it verrrry much Tasha maasi,' because they're always happy to be around Ria and Sofie didi. My heart flutters with love for these sweet little children and the possibility of their lives being turned upside down by Trisha's indiscretions.

I drop the whole brood off outside our house and head to Priyanka Chokesy's brunch where I run into Ananya who tells me she is going to the fashion awards party tonight that I have sent my regrets to already. Our common friend Sheila, waves at us from a distance and then walks towards us, glass of mimosa in hand.

Sheila is not only a practising corporate lawyer but also a bit of a fixture on the high-profile social circuit of the city. She joins our conversation briefly. 'Why would you not attend an event like that Natasha? One goes to these events for people watching, you must go.'

'It's too tiring to take the trouble to travel that far, plus I have sent my regrets already,' I tell her.

'So un-regret it. Just show up, as if anybody will remember.'

'But I'm neither receiving nor presenting an award, and I'm not sure it's worth my while to get myself into an evening gown to just look at what other people are wearing, fun as that sounds.'

'Natasha, you're nearly forty, aren't you? All those clothes that you have been hoarding, when will you put those to use? After forty your window for sassy, sexy dressing shrinks dramatically.' Sheila can afford to say that, she is only thirty-seven herself.

I feel something behind my rib cage breaking as I hear 'nearly forty' said aloud. Must be my heart. 'Nearly forty, yes. Not terminal, Sheila. You make it sound so morbid. And I'll always wear beautiful clothes. Look at Diya Malhotra. She is forty-seven and in such good shape that she can wear dresses that you and I haven't even looked at since our twenties.'

'Oh please, she's on the lookout for a rich husband,' Ananya chimes in. 'If I had that sort of motivation, I could live on a few salad leaves a day too,' she adds.

Diya has been married more than once and is dating a billionaire from London presently. Her lifestyle and svelte figure have generated much envy over the years and her name crops up regularly wherever fashionable people meet.

And here I'm, just growing older quietly, never giving anybody anything to talk about.

Maybe I will go to that event after all. But to travel an hour from home, by myself…

As if reading my mind Ananya offers to fetch me. 'Varun isn't in town, right? I can fetch you if you like. My husband may decide to join us, but more the merrier, I say.'

I accept Ananya's offer and head back home in a hurry to fix my hair and lie in bed with a face pack on for about two hours.

***

Sheila was right. I have too many clothes and too little time left. This could well be the name of my autobiography I realise…with an accompanying image of my shrinking life and expanding closet. I ring my mother on the way and ask her opinion on this matter. I was over-mothered as a child, and I'm convinced this has incapacitated me as an adult to take any major life-altering decision by myself.

'Yes, please go. You are approaching forty, not sixty. And forty is the new twenty Natasha,' she says reassuringly. I'm pleased to hear my mother is up-to-date with all the new clichés. If only Nafisa was in town, I'd have gone to the party with her and perhaps Parthiv, her literary lover. The importance of having a best friend by your side at a society event such as tonight's cannot be overemphasised.

I put my sweetest voice on and call up Michelle, celebrity hairstylist who gives you magazine cover-girl hair in exchange for a small fortune. Luckily for me, she has just had a cancellation and she says she can see me in an hour.

At times like these, I realise just how demanding a woman's life can be and that the phrase 'Lady of Leisure' is terribly misleading. There is nothing leisurely about coordinating clothes, bags, shoes, hair and jewellery for soiree after soiree. To be beautifully put together always while retaining one's pre-teen figure is by no means less demanding than running a successful business. Make a mental note to never dismiss socialites ever again.

At home, with Sofie helping me with the zipper, I manage to get into my unforgiving floor-length red Valentino gown that I picked up at the Neiman Marcus sale. I consider my reflection in the mirror hoping to be pleased by it, but I find that standing in front of me is a woman who has completed the first trimester of her pregnancy and is ready to announce this happy news to the world.

What else was I expecting after delivering children the old-fashioned way? I should have taken Trisha's advice and asked Dr Loonawalla to do a C-section and give me a tummy tuck at the same time. Three kids later, my abdominal muscles have no memory of the time when they were firm and in place and my bladder – well, let's just say that I have to rush to the washroom every time I sneeze. At this moment, I cannot comfort myself with the thought of how unequivocally fulfilling the experience of motherhood is.

I hold my breath and somehow squeeze into my Spanx – may the abundance of the universe be upon its inventor – and try the dress once again. With my internal organs screaming murder, I'm certain to be irritable all evening but at least now I don't look pregnant any more, I just look like a woman who likes her carbs.

Michelle spends over an hour working her magic on me with tongs, hidden pins and sprays and when I finally hand over my kidneys' worth in cash to her, I feel the expense has been worth it.

Between the pins in my head and the Spanx digging into my skin, I feel like a soldier in a Stanley Kubrick film, but I do look, well, staggering, if I may say so myself. Only saying so myself isn't half as satisfying as clicking a selfie and posting it on Instagram so other people can say it too.

My friend Sukh Thakran is delighted to hear that I'm going to make it to the ceremony. He tells me that his date for the evening is a Jordanian model by the name of Mayara 'You should Google her and check her out. Smokin' hot.' Sukh is a sworn bachelor, the éminence grise of the advertising world and one of the most entertaining men that I know personally. He always manages to get some model type thing to hang off his arm, particularly at parties where photo-ops are plentiful. 'I'll make sure you're at my table,' he says, with his usual air of complete confidence.

Varun would have loathed every minute of this sort of evening and sneered at my enthusiasm. Knowing him, he would not have even accompanied me to something like this in the first place and stayed at home reading a book about the Great Chinese Famine or some other similarly light subject. It's all a great shame, not least because the man looks divine in black tie.

I do believe that inconvenient as it can get for me sometimes, it's great for our marriage that we're not joined at the hip. He's always there when it comes to the big stuff, but we aren't that annoying couple that has to do everything together. Even when we go to the same party, we don't stand with each other all night. Sometimes, when I catch his eye across the room at a party and he smiles at me to say 'I'm here', I can still feel some of the old fluttering of excitement.

Ananya and her husband fetch me in their spacious SUV and when we arrive at the venue, the press photographers at the Taj entrance, poor things, assume that we are movie stars and come running towards our car and then unceremoniously withdraw with a *'star nahin hai, star nahin hai'*.

The fashion photographers near the red carpet, however, are more respectful and request for solo photographs. Before I know it, Ananya is proudly posing in front of the big sponsor cutout in the backdrop, her green sequinned gown reflecting the flashlights from the shutterbugs positioned right outside the Crystal Room. I oblige them without smiling too much because it brings out my crow's feet. I just hope I don't come off looking constipated, if at all the photos get published somewhere.

'Did you look at THAT,' Ananya says to me conspiratorially as we wade through the crowd inside the Crystal Room. 'Not there, THERE,' she adds nudging me in the direction of Alisha Choudhary, a buxom actress who married a successful restaurateur and a politician's son, and gave up acting after a short-lived career in the industry. I gasp. Alisha couldn't be a day older than thirty, but she has been rendered unrecognisable by some bad cosmetic surgery. 'See that? Who would spend money to make a perfectly cherubic face look like someone from the *Night of the Living Dead*?' Ananya whispers. I feel bad for the girl. Yes, she'd had a really big nose before her surgery but she was pretty, very pretty. Now she sadly looks like Picasso's Dora Maar from his Cubist phase.

Someone else whose face doesn't match up to her reputation that evening is Sukh's model, Mayara. If Sukh is disappointed with the way she looks in bright light, he's not hiding it. 'I think I had too much to drink last night when I met her,' he offers by way of an explanation as he hands me over a champagne flute. 'Jordanian supermodel, my ass, she is herself the size of Jordan,' he turns towards me and says sotto voce.

'Hush Sukh! That is just rude. And sexist!'

'Oh, come on Natasha, it's getting harder and harder to say anything even in jest without it being called a misogynist, a racist or an anti-nationalist,' he says. 'Now don't you go and write about it.'

Sukh is a pig and scolding him is almost entirely pointless but he is also warm and entertaining; so I've learnt to just blank out his more obnoxious pronouncements. Tonight, that's the most of what's come out of his mouth. Bored, I drink faster than usual and down my flute in record time before telling Sukh to point out his table so I can take my seat and slow down a bit. It's going to be a long night and I can't drink too much, for one thing, if I need to go to the loo, there's a real chance I may never fit myself back into my Spanx.

On the way to the table, I catch my reflection in a glass door and realise I'm much too hard on myself. I'm not some forty-year-old has-been. Today, I look the same in my eyes as the girl who could make heads turn all those years ago, the one boys would step outside to punch each other over. Yes, yes, no one likes to be objectified blah blah blah but before Varun and I got married, I was a staple on Bombay wish lists. There's nothing wrong with being beautiful, is there? I give myself a little wink for all the credit I've stopped giving myself since I got married. I'm not just a wife and a mother, I'm a beautiful woman, and I deserve to remember it.

With a new spring in my step, I walk towards the table, wiggling my hips just a little, looking left and right with a secret smile like a girl in a shampoo ad. I check out my designated table. Some of my companions for the evening are already there. There's a well-known designer, a catty socialite and her rather timid boyfriend, two gorgeous models and the achingly handsome film director Riyad Siddiqui. He is, I cannot help but notice, even more attractive in person than in photographs. A chiselled face, dark hair, Raghavendra Rathore-type bandh gala...the man is gorgeous. I hope he doesn't think I'm staring at him. I look down with a smile playing on my lips, and when I look up again, he's smiling at me, revealing a perfect set of pearly whites. Not some polite 'you're smiling, so I'll smile' thing. He's giving me a big grin – I think it even borders on the suggestive. My insides light up with warmth. I'm not Trisha, but let's face it there are few things nicer than the attention of a desirable man, more so at a gathering like this where all the women have been airbrushed to perfection.

I look up at him again. Oh my God, he's waving at me! Ooh, I think, a bit forward isn't he, a bit presumptuous – I could be married, and what sort of woman does he think I am? Still, it seems rude and indeed gauche not to respond. So I wave back at him and give him my best Madhuri Dixit hundred-watt smile. He gets up and walks towards me in long steps. I panic. I'm not sure what to do now – it's all moving a little faster than I had thought. I smile and lean in, preparing to introduce myself and break the sad news that I'm taken as he approaches me. He gives me a puzzled look and backs away. Walking past me he stops at a chit of a girl in a gold sequined dress ending just below her crotch. I know her through friends – she's not just young and nearly naked, she's also an heiress. She looks at me and smirks as if to say, 'In your dreams, granny.' She has the sort of self-confidence I used to walk into parties with once. But I can bet she is dumb. She has to be.

I'm sure everyone at the table has seen this humiliating debacle, and I'm rooted to the spot, blushing and pretending to look at my phone with great urgency. I can still just go home and not have to face this table after all. As I turn to leave, Sukh, who's been watching, loudly calls me over saying, 'Darling! This is our table, not that one. Stop being a butterfly and come take your seat.'

My cheeks burning with embarrassment, I self-consciously walk towards my saviour. Sukh has Mayara seated to his right and rises to pull the chair on his other side for me, hands me a glass of champagne and starts making loud, rude and delightfully inappropriate jokes about everyone present. Tonight, I could kiss him in gratitude.

'This is the brightest woman in the room,' he bellows to everyone at the table, and I blush with pleasure. We start chatting about mutual friends and ignore everyone else to such an extent that I have to ultimately remind him about his date, rudely ignored and obviously bored, downing glass after glass of champagne. Sukh, for all his kindness towards me, poses cheek to cheek with a starlet at his table as a photographer passes by, ignoring the look on Mayara's face. The starlet seems to be aware that Sukh can help her further her career and pulls her dress down further to show off some more skin, batting her eyelids at him at the same time. Poor Mayara, ignored and entirely on her own now, isn't upset because her heart is breaking so much as because she's losing her chance to get on Page 3. Still, whatever she wanted out of the night, this must be humiliating.

Sukh is now telling the starlet that he will recommend her name to his movie producer friends. It's hard to say who's using whom at this point. The relief of not being a single woman in this hell is so immense I take my phone out and message Varun.

I miss you baby, come home soon.

I sit there for a minute just holding my phone, and it vibrates in my hand. It's my beloved husband.

Can you check if my blue polo shirt got left behind in my cupboard? Otherwise, I'll make them take another look for it here.

I catch Mayara's eye and give her a warm smile because it's hard to be a woman, it truly is.

Chapter 6

Varun surprises me this morning by coming home straight from the airport instead of going to the office. I'm watering the plants in the garden in my tracks (this week it's the gardener's turn to be sick), when in walks Varun, bright-eyed and bushy-tailed. Spending time at his grandmother's has him looking more relaxed than I've seen him in a long time, I think with a twinge of envy, wanting naturally to be the principal source of happiness in his life, even though Nanisa is in fact lovely.

'Hello husband, it's so good to see you. How long will you be visiting us for?'

'It's lovely to come back home to the loving arms of my sarcastic wife,' he says smiling.

'And it's lovely to be married to someone who has no time for me any more,' I shoot back.

'Natasha, love, are you sure we are doing this?'

'Doing what, Varun? Speaking the truth?'

'Are you seriously upset I spent a weekend visiting my grandmother?'

'No, I'm just upset that we don't do anything together any more. The last time you took me to dinner was on our anniversary because you had to.'

'I told you this was going to be a tough year. And why are you fighting with me anyway? I have something for you – let me show it to you at least. Then you can fight all you want,' he says softly.

'Kachoris and other rich things I don't eat?' I say laughing.

'Just shut your mouth for a few seconds and close your eyes,' he says, raising a warning brow and smiling.

I close my eyes and Varun takes my hand, stretches my palm out and places a velvet box in it.

I open my eyes and squeal with delight when I open the box to find a massive heart-shaped emerald pendant in a gorgeous shade of translucent green inside.

'Like it?'

I throw my arms around him. 'Love it.'

'But whose is it? Your mother's? Has she decided to pass it on to me? I have never seen it before,' I say.

'Natasha this is from me. It isn't from mom and now don't ask me about the hows and wheres, just enjoy it,' he says, kissing my forehead.

I'm so happy that I need a vitamin shot to steady myself. I mean, I have been so upset of late that I could easily throttle Varun, but then what is a woman to do when he goes and does something like this?

'Still want to fight?' he teases.

'Have you had breakfast?' I ask. Moments like these call for some fussing over the man, so he realises that every penny spent on his wife is worth it.

'No, no, I have to head to work now,' he says, turning towards the bedroom door.

'Stay, skip work today. Please.'

'One of us has to work to pay off the EMI of that pendant, Natasha,' he says, patting me on my cheek gently and goes off into the house to change for work.

After Varun leaves for the office, I open my locker and take out a thin gold chain that was presented to Ria by my mother-in-law, and string the pendant through it. It has so much luminescence, it seems to make my skin glow. I try to take it off before leaving for my workout, I really do. I reach for the clasp on the chain but it sits there glowing at me, sparkling Morse code for 'don't leave me'. Who am I to argue?

I still have it on, tucked into my t-shirt, when I finish my kick-boxing class and Trisha calls. She wants to know what I'm doing at four.

'I'll be home for the kids to get back from school,' I tell her.

'Okay, well I want to take you somewhere at 5 pm. You need to help me select something important, so don't ask too many questions,' Trisha says. 'And I know you're irritated with me – you made it evident at dinner, but you're still my closest friend, and just for that you have to say yes.'

'Sorry, Trisha, I can't.' I am about to hang up when settling into the car, I spot my pendant in the rear-view mirror. It flashes at me, demanding attention from more people. 'Okay, Trisha,' I say, 'but it had better not take too long.'

At home, I spend an hour trying to get the kids to answer the question 'how was school' with something a little more descriptive than a sullen 'okay' like they are fed up with me. What was the point of waiting around for them?

Trisha duly arrives to collect me at 5 pm.

She's looking beautiful, I think with a slight pang of envy, in a salmon off-shoulder top and distressed white jeans.

'You're glowing,' I say and then wish I hadn't when she answers, 'It's the you-know-what!'

'BTW what do you do for vaginal tightening?' Trisha follows.

'Good Lord, Trish! You can't be serious?'

Trisha used to be such a prude. The few times that I brought up something private with her, she looked so visibly uncomfortable that I felt embarrassed and have steered clear since. Cut to Trisha describing her muscular elasticity in some detail and recommending me something called yoni eggs. Why is it that women in love blab constantly, sharing too much information about their relationships, whereas men in love go quiet?

The last thing I want to discuss with Trisha are my nether regions.

'I'm serious Nats, your face isn't the only thing that goes loose with age,' she goes on.

'Trisha, please!' I snap, stroking my emerald which she has yet to comment on. 'You haven't even told me where we're going, at least tell me when we'll get there.'

'I can't,' she says, 'but it won't be long.'

'What am I going to select for you. Give me some background. Is it jewellery? Clothing? Is it art?' I'm now mired in regret at having agreed to do this, remembering an exhausting afternoon been dragged through Knightsbridge by Trisha one summer in search of the perfect stilettos.

'I can't tell you,' she says.

'Will there be food there?' I ask, hopefully, remembering that I had missed my post-kick-boxing snack.

'I can't say.'

'Am I going to come back from this alive, Trisha?' I ask, only half joking now.

She laughs enigmatically.

We drive through Bandra Kurla Complex till we finally reach the Trident Hotel. Trisha ushers me into the elevator from the lobby.

'Why are we going to a hotel room? What am I going to pick there?'

'We're going to the lounge on the club floor. There is something you must see.'

'Is it a designer exhibit? For God's sake, Trisha, why this secrecy? Have you become a spy now along with...,' I don't finish my sentence.

'Patience, my dear, all will be explained.'

The lounge is deserted except for an undistinguished-looking man perched on the edge of the sofa by the window. A sickening feeling flutters in my stomach. His jeans, the polo shirt worn with the collar up, the dark glasses and the seriously dandy shoes, flashing the LV logo, all have Vasant Kunj, New Money, New Delhi written all over them. The rest of him belongs to Punjabi Bagh. He isn't entirely unattractive, you can see him appealing to Emraan Hashmi's fan base for example. He's the same height as Hashmi too, I note.

Other than the momentary sense of having my curiosity sated, seeing Guneet there is a 9.5 on the Richter scale of bad surprises. How utterly daft of me to not have seen through Trisha's plan to get me on board for her affair. Oh, I'm going to be in so much trouble if this gets out. I dart a nervous look around the room feeling ridiculous as there was only Guneet in it when we entered, and the door hasn't opened since.

Preparing to shake hands coldly and making a quick escape, with or without Trisha, I see that Guneet is awkward about meeting me too. His voice trembles on introducing himself. I can't bear to be cold – God, I hate how soft I'm. I not just smile brightly at him but the next thing you know, I'm making conversation.

'Where in Delhi do you live?' I ask, mentally high-fiving myself for my finely tuned skill at matching shoes to postcodes when he confirms my suspicions of Vasant Kunj.

'And how often are you in Bombay?' I ask, only realising after the sentence is out of my mouth that I'm basically asking him how often he bonks Trisha.

'I'd say about once a month, but now after meeting her,' he says, shooting Trisha a meaningful look, 'I've started coming more frequently.' Then he smiles and Trisha smiles too and I feel unwell.

'And is your work hectic?' I ask, keen to keep to this one topic.

'Well, I'm an exporter, so it depends on the season.'

He apparently has nothing to ask me and I daren't ask a question to which the answer might somehow be 'having sex with Trisha'. So the conversation languishes and is replaced by benign smiles as we sit there looking at the carpet as though it were a Gaitonde painting. What does one talk about under these circumstances anyway? I can't ask about his family in New Delhi. I can't tell him what a fine man Nakul is. So, I sit there, annoyed, playing absent-mindedly with my gold chain.

'Trisha speaks very highly of you,' he suddenly says to me, turning towards Trisha to seek acknowledgement from her. She gives him an approving smile, almost like a mother encouraging her child to go on with his poetry recitation in front of her club friends.

'I tell her she is lucky to have a confidante in you,' he adds sincerely.

I smile nervously, really not wanting to inhabit that role.

Tea is served, and though I usually don't touch caffeine after noon, stirring and sipping at least gives me something to do and is less awkward than just sitting there smiling. After the server leaves, Guneet reaches out for Trisha's hand and casually caresses her slender manicured fingers with one hand while sipping his coffee with the other. Oh my God, is he going to just mount her right there, in front of me? I gulp a mouthful of tea which is still far too hot and burns the roof of my mouth. He's sweet enough but let's face it, he isn't half the man Nakul is.

Unable to bear their hideous foreplay I start to shuffle my legs as if making a bid to leave. 'Oh, you're leaving already?' Guneet asks weakly, pretending to be disappointed at the prospect. 'Aww, you must be wanting to rush back to the kids,' Trisha says in an annoyingly empathetic tone. 'See you then Natty,' she waves goodbye, unfazed by the fact that she brought me here but now I have to get an Uber back. No one offers to walk me to the lobby. In fact, I could see them leaning in towards each other before the doors had even slid closed after me.

I had seen Nakul through a break-up before he met Trisha. Soon after I got married, Sheena left Nakul and he had the most terrible time – morose for months, not wanting to be involved in anything. Varun and I encouraged him back to life, really, insisting he join us at social gatherings, even to the cinema. I introduced him to all my single women friends as it was clear he was a great catch but while he went on a couple of dates with them, no one caught his fancy like Trisha. An interior decorator by profession, Trisha met Nakul while working on his new office site in Delhi. What followed was high-octane drama. They fell in love, and Trisha called off her engagement, leaving her fiancée broken-hearted and suicidal. Her father, a proud Sikh gentleman, was mortified by what his daughter had done and, as expected, he opposed the marriage. Trisha and Nakul waited a year before her father gave in to his beloved daughter's entreaties and the two were finally married in a quiet ceremony at a friend's farm not far from Kasauli.

Stepping out of the elevator, I scan the hotel lobby quickly to ascertain that I'm not recognised by somebody I know. Imagine having to exercise caution for someone else's affair!

When I get home, I find Nakul and Varun at the porch. I almost have a cardiac arrest. What are they doing at home at this hour? And where shall I say I'm returning from in an Uber? It's unlike me to take a taxi with the cars parked in the compound and the driver neither sick or away. Anxiety is playing havoc with my ability to think of a plausible excuse.

Nakul turns around to greet me immediately with a warm hug with an even warmer intonation of my name. 'Natashaaaaaa…I'm so happy to see you.'

Just look at the way he is smiling at me with such warmth. I hate myself.

I will have enough time for self-flagellation later, I tell myself, but right now I must do my best to present a happy and guilt-free face.

'Where have you been, hon?' Varun asks walking into the house. The dogs come running downstairs to greet us.

'Oh, I was just having coffee with Trisha and … me,' I say as I pet our needy dogs turn by turn.

'Oh, that must have been a crowd then, you, Trisha and you,' he pats my back and chuckles. 'But why were you using Uber?' Varun says with a hint of surprise.

'Oh, she had to run an errand and I just wanted to be home, for the kids.'

Upstairs, I ask Shambhu to send us coffee on the terrace, it's cool and breezy for a change.

'Beautiful pendant, Nats!' Nakul says, sitting down and stretching his arms upwards. As if I needed any further confirmation that he was the better of the two men in Trisha's life.

'I see you wasted no time in putting it on,' Varun says, smiling.

'Did you want me to save it for Ria's dahej?' I retort with a smile.

'So what's cooking between you and my wife?' Nakul asks with a grin. 'The two of you are meeting all the time, aren't you? She's always on the phone with you these days... It's all rather mysterious to me'

'Oh, haha, we have been busy planning Varun's surprise birthday party!' I say, suddenly inspired, my guilt getting the better of me. 'And clearly ... this isn't a surprise any longer,' I laugh settling into my chair.

'Really? So early? But my birthday is months away!' says Varun leaning over to place his cup of coffee on the table.

'But it'll be your fortieth after all Varun, it will need planning. Caterers get booked months ahead, as you know.' *Why did I just say that?*

'Alright, in that case, I'm very flattered. Thank you Nats,' he smiles and then looks behind me and says, 'Ah, you are here early.'

I can hardly believe my eyes as I find a peachy Trisha stepping onto the terrace. Why is she here? Is today Friday the 13th?

'Hello Trisha darling,' Varun says, getting up to hug her.

'Why are you here?' I hear myself say.

'Nakul rang me and asked me to come over, and I was just running errands, so I came directly from there,' she says with a straight face.

'We had work to discuss and we decided we could do it from home so that we can spend some time with our favourite ladies later,' Nakul says.

I lunge towards her to hug her too, which I realise later must have looked strange given that I was supposed to be with her minutes ago. 'Trisha, good you could join us, I just told Varun about the party you and I have been planning for him,' I blurt out.

'Party?' she says blankly as I scream, 'Trisha, you stupid cow', inside my head.

'Yes, I can't believe it slipped out of my mouth,' I say, making eye contact with her in my effort to urge her to play along.

She stands there looking dumbfounded. Her salmon pink top, I notice, is looking crumpled perhaps from too much anaerobic activity with Gurinder.

'I still don't know why you both are doing this. I mean, it's very sweet, of course,' Varun says.

The daft woman just looks at me. 'Trisha, don't be upset, it just slipped out,' I carry on beckoning her to sit down.

'Oh, why did you tell him?' she says finally, with exaggerated annoyance as she slowly settles into the chair.

Acting isn't a talent that we can both be proud of at this moment.

'How special are you Varun?' Nakul teases as he bends over to oblige Chester who has been lying on the floor wiggling his paws with his belly facing up, begging for a tummy rub. 'So tell me girls, aside from Varun's surprise party, just what are you two so busy bonding over these days? Trisha seems to be on the phone with you or going to lunches and coffees with you all the time of late,' he asks casually.

'Ah, the truth is that Trisha is in love,' I say. I see all the muscles in her face clench beneath her smile, and I relish the moment before adding, 'She is in love with me since both you and Varun don't have the time for either of us.'

'Here we go again,' Varun says running his fingers through his hair with a theatrical sigh. And then I hear Ria's voice saying, 'Vroom vroom,' and I see his eyes light up. She's sitting inside her toy car and showing off to Uncle Nakul and her daddy.

'Daddy, Daddy … look I made Peppa Pig sit behind me,' she squeals with delight riding straight past me and stopping in front of her father, climbing out her car and jumping into his lap.

Trish plants a kiss on Ria's head and excusing herself disappears into the powder room, where I hope she's actually using the toilet and not sending objectionable texts or, God forbid, naughty selfies.

'Come here, baby girl,' Nakul says to Ria with affection, arms stretching forward, urging her to sit on his lap.

'No, my daddy first,' the brat replies, bouncing around on her father's lap to prove how much she enjoys it there. 'Natasha, now that there is no chance of us discussing work with you and Trisha and this monkey around, should we perhaps ask you all to excuse us for a little while? Give us twenty minutes and then you can bring out some chilled white for us,' says Varun.

'Can you organise the wine yourself when you are done Varun? I need to go check on the dinner and also Sumer's homework,' I say visibly irritated. What's with all this ordering around that men feel so comfortable doing?

'Alright, alright,' Varun says with a shrug and a placatory smile, 'I'll organise the wine, you go do the rest.'

Trisha comes looking for me just as I'm finishing up with Sumer. By his age, I was acing the spelling bee contests but children today are barely even managing to spell their own name correctly. So much for the phonetic method of teaching!

Trisha tells me tetchily that she wants to speak with me. 'Sure, let's go inside then,' I say, pointing towards my bedroom.

Shutting the door behind us, she charges at me 'That was very mean, what you did to me outside today, Natasha.'

'Lighten up Trisha, I was just having fun with you.'

'I didn't think it was fun at all,' she says with, hands on hips in a combative position.

'Oh, you didn't? Well, perhaps you shouldn't have ambushed me into meeting *your lover*,' I hiss, stung again by how she embroiled me in this awful situation. 'And perhaps you shouldn't be sleeping with him to begin with.'

'And perhaps you should stop being so judgemental and preachy and start accepting people for who they are. Especially people who love you.'

With that Trisha plonks herself on my bed and picking up the lip balm pot on my bedside starts rubbing it on her sulky mouth. 'So, what do you think?' she asks, her voice suddenly soft.

'Well, I guess I need to start planning the party for real and you need to help me do that. We could set it up in the garden…'

'Not about Varun's birthday!' she says. 'What do you think of Guneet?' she asks, lowering her voice. 'Isn't he…?'

'For God's sake, Nakul is downstairs! We are all just about to have dinner together. I can't do this, he's my friend!' Guneet's shoes flash unbidden to my mind, the checkerboard LVs with the black strip running through them.

'But you're my friend too,' she says tenderly, and I have no answer to that.

'You do realise we will actually have to throw a big party for Varun now,' I say edgily.

'Okay, so we'll throw a party,' she says. 'Although that was a silly thing to say Natasha.'

'Look, unlike you, I'm no good at lying. I had to think on my feet when your husband asked me why we were meeting so much and chatting on the phone so much lately,' I bluster. 'I think you need to stop using me as your alibi. I'm just not comfortable with it, Trisha.'

'Natasha, calm down. I did not go looking for another man. This just happened and I'll die if I have to leave him. I cannot do it, please don't act difficult,' she wails. 'You are like a sister to me, who else can I turn to for help.'

Looking at her like that, I can't help but feel a little overwhelmed with her life and this crazy situation that she has dragged us both into.

'And yes, yes, I know, I'm being unfair on Nakul? Don't you think I think about that all the time? But our marriage...' She stops and takes a deep breath. 'It might seem perfect on the outside but trust me it isn't.'

I open my mouth to remind her that marriages aren't perfect, ever, and especially not a decade in but Trisha holds up her hand registering that she knows what I'm about to say and doesn't want to hear it.

'He never wants to touch me any longer, Natasha. It's like he's impotent or something.'

'That's not impotence, that's marriage!' I cut in and regret it when Trisha shoots me a look that suggests this is no time to mess with her. She continues as if I hadn't spoken.

'He's fond of me, we are used to each other, but there's something missing. It's been missing for a long time and it's not just that spark of a new relationship, believe me. I've thought about this. To him, I'm just the mother of his children and the housekeeper whose cleavage he's allowed to check out. He never talks to me the way Varun talks to you. I know it doesn't seem like that because he's fine around other people, but when I'm alone with him … he's the most unresponsive man on the planet. It's hard trying to share your life with someone who treats you like an idiot or as the most boring woman alive.'

'Our life has a sameness to it that was almost making me suicidal. I know you're worrying about what'll happen now that I'm doing this. I'm still worried about what would have happened to me if Guneet hadn't come along.' Her eyes, I notice, are moist.

I don't jump in telling her to speak to Nakul or telling her to try to understand that their work has been awfully demanding lately. I don't say anything. I wonder for a fleeting moment if Trisha has just described my marriage, but I dismiss the suspicion. Varun does not find me boring, for one. The moisture in Trisha's eyes has condensed into teardrops. I stand up and walk over to her wanting to hug her but Nakul calls out from outside, 'Girls, come on, time for a drink! Varun and I are moving to the bar downstairs.'

I put an arm around Trisha and ask her to cheer up and offer her a tissue to wipe her tears. We then head to the drawing room downstairs.

A round of drinks later, it's like the good old times again when the four of us got together all the time for impromptu dinners. Varun is in a fabulous mood and making us all laugh with his pointed wit. It has been a while since I watched him unwind like this. Nakul too is his affable, endearing self, teasing Trisha and me, blissfully unaware of the lie that he is living.

I smile weakly as I reflect on the wonderful camaraderie between us and am reminded of the fact that Nakul is family in every possible way.

If Trisha's deception continues, things may change between us forever. We will never be like this again. The four of us have spent so many happy moments together over the years and not once did I think that I'd be the unfortunate intersecting part between the two Venn diagrams of Nakul-Trisha and Trisha-Guneet relationship.

While I get busy working myself up, Varun goes upstairs and disappears into the children's bedrooms to kiss them all goodnight.

Later, he is in the study on his laptop when I lie down to sleep, my mind restless but exhausted. I feel a dumbbell has been placed over my heart. When I do fall asleep, I have terrible dreams – of Nakul ringing the doorbell in the middle of the night, looking at me accusingly and saying nothing when I answer. The fact that I'm having nightmares over someone else's affair also pretty much kills the dream I had always secretly nurtured of having my own *The Bridges of Madison County* moment in my autumn years. Not that I'm surrounded by exciting candidates for an affair but still, to know that one will never have the nerve is just depressing. That's not the only thing depressing me after speaking to Trisha last night. Some things are best not dwelled on though.

Chapter 7

It's getting more and more difficult for us common mortals to liberate ourselves from the snares of the material world. With everything around us – not least the internet – relentlessly enticing us into buying more, who wouldn't be tempted? So many of us unsuspecting women, living with this void that rises like the sun within us just as the kids leave for school, are sitting ducks for these e-commerce sites. Then those alerts pop up on your phone, announcing the arrival of your little bundle of joy. When the parcel arrives like a surprise gift from the universe, you feel thrilled, but only momentarily, because you soon realise that it doesn't look half as good as it did on that model on the website. But you'll soldier on and buy something else in a few days. I see this happening to women around me, and I hope it makes them happy. I, for one, have realised the shelf life of happiness purchased online is limited, but now and then, I slip. The road to minimalism may be long and hard but I'm determined to walk on it one day.

Today's column is taking a lot out of me. It's been nothing but an exercise in self-restraint. With Net-a-Porter doing a flash sale it is nearly impossible to not wander off for a spot of online shopping. Maybe, I should try and be a minimalist starting next season when the sales are over. Had she seen some of the discounted shoes with her keen scientific eyes, even Madame Curie would have interrupted her research on radium and said, 'Sure, radium's great but do you have those in a five and a half?'

And so, I succumb. I had to. Still, I only ever shop during a sale, and it is money saved after all. I have also ordered a beautiful electric-blue chiffon dress by Marchesa, electric-blue is the colour of the season. Thank God Varun doesn't get my shopping alerts any more and I don't feel spied on.

I'm basking in the afterglow of my bargain shopping and staring into space, imagining the reaction my shoes would get from Nafisa, when my phone rings. It is her.

'Nafisa, you have to see what a fabulous purchase I have just made, I got such a good deal on it,' I exclaim.

'Your idea of a good deal and my idea of one vary. We have different disposable incomes, just in case you've forgotten,' she says wearily. This isn't like Nafisa at all!

'Is something the matter? You don't sound good Naf.'

'Oh, it's nothing, I think I need a new romance and I'm just bored.'

'Oh! I see, did Parthiv just die?'

Parthiv is Nafisa's boyfriend and a self-obsessed but successful author of books that I personally find unreadable.

'I'm irritated with him. He's too full of himself. I don't think I can bear him much longer'

'And how is it that you realised that suddenly? You have been with each other for a whole four months. It's the longest you have seen someone in the past few years!'

'Stop it Nats. I cannot help it if I'm not good at relationships like you. Sometimes, I wonder if I have set a very high expectation of standards from men and that everyone comes short, sooner or later. At this rate, I will just die an old, broke maid unless, of course, I inherit some of your wealth.'

'This will need to be analysed by the Number #1 relationships expert, that is, yours truly when we meet personally. And I will tell Varun to remember you in his will. Now, let me go. My column is getting held up.'

'Alright, alright, go. But do you want to try the new dim sum house Zen Den near my office over lunch tomorrow, say one-ish? I hear their dim sums are like Dim Thai Fung. I have been dying to go there. I could get away for a bit if you are keen,' Nafisa suggests.

***

In the evening, Varun is home in time for an early dinner, but he appears worked up. The children and I are sitting around the dining table and eating and eagerly waiting for him to join us, but he has other plans, like speaking with his mother on the phone.

'Maa, now that is a bit harsh…' I hear him say as he gets up from the couch and walks towards the terrace.

A bit harsh? What, even by her standards? What could they be discussing? No doubt, me. He steps outside so I don't get to overhear the rest of it.

The children have finished eating by the time he returns to the living room, and when I ask him if all is well with Maa, Varun says 'Oh, ya. All good.'

'And Natasha, maybe you can call her on your own sometimes to see how she is,' he adds, a little curtly.

I'm now certain the witch has cribbed about me. This is the tone Varun takes with me every time his mother has something not nice to say about me to him.

Still, I pretend not to have noticed it until he says something about the grilled chicken on our table tasting like 'tribal food'.

'Maybe your mother could send us one of her battery of khansamas,' I say bitterly, before excusing myself from the table and leaving him to finish the meal by himself.

Gone are the days when he would come home and tell me he is taking me out to dinner, just the two of us. Gone are the days when he would ask me to let Shambhu off early because he wanted to cook for the five of us. Is this the same man who used to be so interested in talking to me every day after work? No, he isn't, I think bitterly. Varun, like all men, has changed.

Later, when he joins me in our room after cuddling up with the kids in theirs, he appears guilty. Varun knows I'm seething and he tries to diffuse the tension by asking me if he should sleep on the couch, a smile forming around the corners of his mouth. 'Don't take the trouble, I'm sleeping with the kids,' I retort rising from the bed as I walk towards the door. 'Come on Natasha, don't do this please,' he pleads, offering me his hand from the other side of the bed. I hand over the AC remote to him. 'Here. All yours. And goodnight,' I say, before slamming the door behind me.

Too irritated to sleep, I decide to sit in the living room and flip channels. As I am absently pressing the buttons on the remote, my mind drifts towards Trisha's conversation with me about Nakul not being interested in her. Today, for the first time, it has struck me that Varun too has changed. Well, I noticed it before but today it struck me that I just wasn't enjoying this. What if he finds me boring and predictable? And what if domesticity, all our children and this routine of our lives have eroded all feelings of love and passion towards me?

In an effort to snap out of these anxieties, I try to focus on the image on the television screen and find Shri Shri Parivartan Prasad, draped in a maroon robe, talking about emotions through his thick soda-bottle glasses. 'All emotions arise from the mind. Meditation is important to calm the mind and to balance these emotions,' he is saying to a devoted audience in front of him. 'When we bring dogs home, don't we train them? We train them not to pee indoors, we train them not to bark at our guests...In the same manner, we must train our mind because we only ever suffer from our mind. That is the only way to be happy.'

I realise at that moment that there might be some truth to what Parivartan Prasad is saying. Not all of it though, on second thought. I haven't trained our pet dogs very much, for example. The two of them can still be found peeing on the carpets and sniffing guests' crotches and barking at poorly dressed visitors. But what he is saying about learning to calm the mind to find happiness makes perfect sense. I dwell on his words as I drag myself to Sofie's room shortly after. Maybe, I should train my mind dog to be happy, no matter what. I go to sleep determined to sign up with the local Art of Joy centre run by Shri Shri Parivartan Prasad at Pali Hill.

✿ ✿ ✿

Varun puts *The Daily News* away and greets me with uncharacteristic politeness accompanied with a broad smile when I stumble into the living room in the morning.

I mutter a frosty 'morning' back at him and ask the maid to bring my tea to our small terrace, making my desire to sit far away from him amply known.

Over my second cup of tea, I look up the Art of Joy website. 'Hello Inner Peace,' it boldly announces. 'Life will never be perfect, but you can be perfectly happy,' it reads further.

This is exactly what I need. My life is begging for it. I feed in the number of the centre on my phone and get back to the newspapers.

Varun appears on the terrace shortly and pulls up a chair close to me. 'So what compelling gossip are you reading?' he asks with a grin the size of a sliced cantaloupe.

'Sometimes I also need to be left alone, Varun.' I'm in no mood to be teased. He continues to look at me seriously for some time and then unable to hold it in much longer, bursts into paroxysms of laughter.

'Okay, stop. Sometimes you behave like Ria. Now I know where she gets her petulance,' he says, chortling at his own excellent observation.

'And you Varun, you are cold and unfeeling like your mother,' I say, rising up from my chair to get away from him. I watch him recoil in shock. 'Now, I know where you get it from. It isn't your fault. The ice in your veins is inherited,' I say angrily as I turn to leave.

'Woah! Woah! Woah! What happened here?' he says. 'And please let's finish this conversation. There is no need to say your bit and storm out. And can you please grow up and not drag our mothers into it?'

'Didn't your mother start it? And aren't you are always comparing whatever it is that we serve you to your mother's food? And if you like her so much, go live with her. In any case, you are never around, you will hardly be missed.' I realise that I'm, in fact, crying as I say this.

Varun rises from the chair and walks up to me and pulls me towards himself. 'Don't touch me,' I say, pulling his hands away from me.

'Natasha, first of all, Maa wasn't complaining about you exclusively. She was mad at me for not being able to call her. She feels lonely and left out. I assumed you and the kids were speaking to her regularly and then I found out even you hadn't bothered. That's all.'

'That's not all! Why should keeping your mother in the loop be my responsibility too over and above all that I do already? And what about the tribal chicken?' I hiss.

'Ah that,' he smiles. 'That chicken was undercooked. I was criticising the cook, not you! I didn't think it would upset you so much. Anyway, I will be careful, I promise. Don't be so touchy, darling. I love you,' he says softly.

'I'm not being touchy. I'm being quite fed up, Varun,' I retort. 'This family is no longer your priority. We used to be so close, we used to watch movies, chat for hours, go out to dinners…we never do that any more. You are hardly ever home and when you are, you bring work home. You snap at me all the time…' I trail off.

'You know what I'm trying to build here is for all of us. I want to be able to give you all a better life. I need time, once we have raised enough money and some of the properties are off the ground, things will go back to the way they were before, I promise.'

He holds me closer and I lean against him as I sob. 'Next weekend, I promise I will keep myself absolutely free, so we can do something fun together,' he says stroking my hair. 'But since we are speaking, may I say something?'

'Say,' I wipe my nose on his T-shirt sleeve as he continues to hold me. 'Sit down first,' he says taking my hand and weaving his fingers into mine.

'Do you remember a few months ago we had spoken about you going back to working full-time? I think it's time.'

'But I cannot be in an office Varun till 10 pm every night. With you being as busy as you are the kids will feel neglected,' I say.

'How about I speak to Nirav Sinha for you? You do remember he had told me not long ago that he was looking for a copywriter. You could work at his agency part-time. How about that?'

'But what is wrong with me being here at home and doing my column? I have enough on my plate at home as it is. This house does not run by itself.'

'Nothing wrong with it except that the girl I had fallen in love with was a busy girl with her own career and now that the kids are older, she has more time to spare and she doesn't have enough to do with it,' he says tenderly, as if speaking to a child again.

I haven't the energy to fight any more and so I just accept his offer.

'Alright. So, I will meet Nirav. You let me know when,' I say with resignation. Varun decides to delay his morning meeting and takes me to our bedroom. There are only two types of sex after so many years of marriage – there is make-up sex and then there is drunken-after-an-occasion sex. And make-up sex is decidedly the better of the two.

***

After Varun leaves for work, I quickly shower and leave for Nafisa's office, today being our lunch date.

I find her sitting on a cluttered desk with brochures, a pile of magazines and some other paraphernalia lying on the floor of her cabin. 'Hello darling, ignore this mess in my room. I have so much to do that I haven't had the time to clear it all up!' she sighs.

'How can I help you with all the things that burden you Nafisa?' I say melodramatically.

'You can. By seriously taking on the responsibility of doing a supplement we are working on, but we shall discuss this at length once the advertisers are confirmed.'

'Sure,' I say, although I'm already feeling stressed and burdened with all the work I'm going to be doing for Nafisa and Nirav Sinha in the future.

Presently, we arrive for lunch at Zen Den, right next door from her office building, and we talk about Parthiv at length. 'So when did you begin to feel this disenchanted with him?' I ask after we have ordered an assortment of dishes.

'So before I get to what happened last week, let me tell you, it's not like I haven't noticed how most of our conversations always veer towards him. At times, I have even felt that he wasn't paying attention to anything that I was saying unless it was about him or his book. Even after sex, it was always about himself, his work, some column he was going to write to oppose a point made by other columnists, all of whom according to him are creatures of inferior intelligence…'

'Any surprise then that smart women don't date male writers. Padma Lakshmi and Salman Rushdie broke up all those years ago; it must have been the same for her too.'

'Well, now that I'm experiencing it first hand, I can tell you they are fit for nothing but shagging, that too if one is going through a desperate dry spell.' She begins to mix all the dim sum sauces in a dish to make her own sauce, a typical Nafisa thing to do.

'So tell me quickly, what happened last week?' I ask impatiently.

'Hmm, so last week Parthiv was away at the Edinburgh International Book Festival. For starters, I felt a little mad at him for not asking me to come along. Not that I'd have gone…I have too much to do here, but still, it would have been nice to have been asked,' she says holding up her palms. The dim sums begin to arrive.

'But it's his work. You do not ask him to travel with you on every work trip, do you?' I help myself to the chive and chestnut dumplings and extend my arm and place two of them on Nafisa's plate.

'I do. When I know I can squeeze in a day of leisure, I ask him to come along and he happily obliges,' she says with a shrug. Realising that the turnip cakes haven't been ordered, she waves her hand at the waiter and asks him for a portion of the same.

'So maybe he knew he would be busy enjoying the adulation from foreign media after the success of *The Forest of Remembrance*. You know how well it has done internationally! He may have anticipated he would be busy with interviews and what not,' I offer.

'Fair enough. But listen to this exchange between us on WhatsApp. It was late in the night – booty-call time basically, when two days after going to Edinburg he decided he was missing me. He had returned drunk after some lit-fest party.'

'And what did it say…'

'Oh, the usual sexting. You will know nothing about it, grandma. You are old-fashioned but it was nice and flirty. It's still early days after all…'

'Sure, so then what is the problem with that?'

'Oh, he was basically telling me he wished I was there with him in his big bed etc. and then some other stuff.'

'Aww, that's sexy…' I say, shoving a crystal dumpling into my mouth and feeling sorry for my unexciting life, and the fact that I'd die without ever experiencing first hand, the joys of sexting.

'Wait, don't get excited. There is more,' Nafisa says dismissing my comment with a wave of her chopsticks.

'He then goes on to tell me – the next time I want to see you in that purple and yellow kaftan you wore in Bali. I have never seen you in it again, but when we are away, I imagine you in it…then he moved to my toes. Red toe-polish when I return please.'

'And then?' I'm enjoying this exchange vicariously.

'So I told him that I was taking notes and that I was passing out. I had just returned from Cochin and it was draining to be outdoors in that heat for the photo shoot. So, he says, alright, you go to bed. I will keep making more notes for you to read when you wake up in the morning.'

'And then the next morning, I realised that I was running a temperature and I had a splitting headache. Even so, I texted him – Don't want to kill our vibe from last night or anything but I'm running a temperature from a possible heat stroke and will have to miss work,' she puts her chopsticks aside as her story approaches its climax.

'And I want to show you what he wrote back Natty,' she reaches for her mobile and hands the conversation over to me.

Parthiv has shared a photo of mist and rain from the window of his hotel in the Highlands.

You think I'm getting too old to appreciate this weather that poets dream of?

There is not one message acknowledging her illness or enquiring after her.

'So what do you think?' Nafisa asks, folding her hands across her chest and leaning back into her chair.

'Dump the bastard,' I say casually.

Nafisa says she will give him some more time and then make a decision about the fate of their relationship. 'He is still in the UK. Let him return from his holiday, and let my party be over, then we shall see,' she says, as though she was talking about changing her laundromat.

'Did you just say party? What party? Why haven't you invited me?'

'Because I want to discuss it with you before sending out the invitations. You forget Natasha, my bestie, that my birthday is coming up.'

'Of course, I haven't forgotten,' I lie.

'Right! So anyway, I want to have a sit-down dinner. Think candlelight, think printed menus, think silver service, think poached lobster, think return presents…Nice?'

'Very nice, Nafisa. Sounds perfect. Who are we inviting?'

'I don't want to do the usual thing. This time I'm thinking of inviting an entirely different mix of people to make the evening interesting for myself.'

Natasha takes me through her list of high-profile guests, mostly from the world of publishing and media. 'Sounds like an eclectic bunch of people,' I say with a pang, realising that my world is much smaller in comparison to Nafia's. How fortunate she is to be meeting interesting people with exciting careers, unlike me, who only ever meets people who are related to me biologically.

'Don't worry,' Nafisa says, waving her hand as if to dispel my worries that she knows little about. 'You know Parthiv, of course, but you haven't met most of them before and you will love them. I hope your busy husband will be in town. I'd love to show him off to everybody on the table,' she laughs.

'Oh, I'm not worried Nafisa. I'm looking forward to it. Varun has promised to be with me this weekend – no work, just family time. Don't ask me how I got him to commit, but he is going to be around and I shall bring him to your party.'

Nafisa claps joyfully.

'Now I'm really excited. Varun's presence at the table will be the best thing. You see, I'm not calling too many people. I just owed most of the people on my guest list a dinner and I thought why not do it on a Saturday before my birthday. That way we don't technically call it my birthday dinner. So nobody who isn't invited feels resentful about being left out. Correct?'

'Agreed. Do you need any help?'

'Not at all. I am getting the catering done by Saffron Palate and I just need to figure out what to wear. Will send you some photos, you help me choose.'

'Your birthday is in two weeks. What are you going to do on your actual birthday?'

'Two months ago I was daydreaming about doing something romantic with Parthiv. But now I will just go to the Moscow Food Week,' she says with exaggerated sadness.

'Oh, poor you, I feel terrible about your bleak life.'

❋ ❋ ❋

On my way back home, I think about Nafisa's relationships and how they all come with a short 'sell-by' date. Sooner or later they all go south. Shortly before Parthiv, she was dating a marketing maven by the name of Matthew Kurien, who at first was all adoring, charming and chatty, but a few months into the relationship he became inconsistent. At first, we both assumed he had found another woman, but then we realised he was just emotionally stunted, a common condition afflicting millennial men.

At least Nafisa got to say it was she who dumped him. I felt bad for her then. She had seemed very smitten to me while they were together. It wasn't long before Parthiv came along and she bounced back very quickly. She always does.

I don't lead Nafisa's action-packed single life and am a sexting virgin, but at least I don't have to suffer dysfunctional men like Parthiv and Matthew. Varun and I are married, and that's what marriage is supposed to be like after three kids, isn't it?

Chapter 8

There is so much talk about mindfulness and spirituality among people my age these days. A still, calm and content mind is something that everybody is coveting along with the new house, car, shoes and bags. Nobody is talking about fitness coaches – life coaches are the ones having their moment in the sun. My mailbox now receives mindfulness and spirituality spam mail along with all the other shopping deal spam. This is all a happy sign. As such our collective consciousness is moving towards a higher state of being. I do wonder though if this spiritual quest of our generation's is, in fact, a midlife crisis masquerading itself as 'the search for a higher meaning and liberation'?

As much as we all want peace and happiness it isn't easy to get, like something one can order off a catalogue. It's harder still for women my age who, like, the multi-limbed goddess Durga, are trying to do it all. In my opinion, an executioner at the gallows is more likely to find inner peace and a still mind than some of us women. As it is, with the best milestones of your youth behind you, your life begins to appear a little dreary. Then to be a mother and a homemaker means you have signed up for a job that never gets over. How does one acquire a thought-free state when there is constantly so much on one's mind? Over and above the maternal tasks, one has to find time for fitness, read books, manage a happy marriage, be a devoted daughter, a loving wife, a sincere friend and, at times, a happy hostess. Much like God, a mother's work is never complete. Thankless jobs, both, God's and ours. And then there are sworn atheists like Christopher Hitchens who argued that God is not great and Dawkins who calls God a delusion. If even the maker does not get his due, then we had better not expect any acknowledgement from our families either.

I have my first trial session of Art of Joy meditation class tomorrow morning. After my emotional outburst yesterday, which I know was a long time coming, I feel even more certain that I need to meditate. Maybe this is my opportunity to embrace my higher consciousness and be like those people with a powerful aura who are forever smiling. I think I might have just described the Dalai Lama but who knows, I may well be like him one day. I can picture myself in one of those monasteries in Dharamsala chanting Om Mani Padme Hum and walking slowly in red robes with a beatific smile on my face. Also, people who do yoga and meditate don't wrinkle, so I will still look good even though my children will be older by the time I give up secular life. Who knows I might meet somebody like Richard Gere in the monastery and then...I'd never do this to my Varun though. Richard Gere-type guy and I will just be friends, like spiritual comrades.

I'm still daydreaming about my life as a monk when I get a message from Varun asking me to check my email. He has copied me on an exchange between him and Nirav Sinha, who has written to say that he cannot wait to work with me.

'I'm not ready to work yet. I just said yes to Varun because he was being very loving to me then and we were patching up,' I'm telling my mother on a phone minutes later when she rings me.

'How can you work full-time? Bachey kaun dekhega?' Mummy asks. I can hear my father's muffled voice in the background.

'That is what I'm saying too. Anyway, now I will have to meet Nirav and see how I can get away with doing the least.'

'She is going to meet Nirav and try and do very little work,' Mummy is relaying everything to Daddy.

'You father is saying it will be good if you go back to work,' she tells me. 'Maybe you should seriously consider it then.'

'Mummy, just give Daddy the phone, will you,' I snap. This relaying business is annoying me no end. 'And how can you be so fickle and change your mind so quickly after asking me to stay at home and take care of the kids first?'

'Why are you taking out your anger on me Natasha? I did not call you to be insulted!' She is sounding hurt. I apologise to her and then speak to my father who sweetly counsels me. Both the men in my life do not know what it takes to raise children. It takes a village to raise a child. And here I'm, doing this pretty much by myself and if even I disappear, my poor children will grow up to be psychopathic criminals because of neglect.

I check my mail again after lunch and Nirav has written to me to confirm our meeting at two on Monday next week.

Shambhu presents his usual bewildered face to me along with my coffee in the evening. If there is anything I hate more than cooking, it's to have to tell this man what is to be cooked. Menu after menu has been handed over to the dolt, but no, he must ask every day. I'm still speaking with him when Nakul's call comes through.

'Natasha, are you busy?'

'No Nakul, I'm home. All good?'

'I was just craving the laal maas you make. So I have told Trish that I'm stopping by to have a chat with Varun and I'm hoping that I won't be eating at home tonight.'

I laugh over the fact that not only has Nakul sweetly invited himself over for dinner, but he has also fixed the menu for tonight. 'Oh, of course! Come over for dinner! This is your home you know that.'

'I was coming anyway. Varun and I have some work to discuss, and I thought this was my chance to ask you for my favourite food ever.'

It's a given that Nakul and Varun intend to talk shop, and this bodes well for me, as I can then make myself scarce after dinner.

Nakul walks in with a big bunch of liliums for me and a shopping bag full of ice-cream tubs for the children.

'Nakul, this is very sweet of you,' I say as I receive the bouquet from him. 'But you didn't have to.'

'I felt like it,' he says with a warm smile.

I don't deserve Nakul's warmth or his flowers. I'm a cheating, lying fraud.

I walk him into the living room and ask about Varun. 'Where is my husband? I thought the two of you would arrive together, as usual.'

'He should be here shortly. He was wrapping up a meeting when we last spoke,' he says. 'I want to go see the kids first. May I?'

Nakul then barges into the children's room to say hello to the three of them, trading kisses with a Magnum lolly from the bag. Knowing how much he adores our kids, I allow them this treat even though it's their bedtime.

Varun too arrives shortly after and joins Nakul in the kids' room.

A little later he comes to the living room and sinks into the sofa. 'Oh man, I'm tired. Glad that Nakul Uncle has been roped in to read the kids their story,' he says, putting his hands behind his head and stretches.

'Nafisa rang me today to invite me personally to her dinner along with you. I told her there was no need for formality and that when it came to being there for Nafisa's party my wife wouldn't leave me with a choice, would she?' he chuckles.

'She really wants you there Varun. It's going to be a fun evening,' I say, feeling excited.

'Any evening where my wife is happy is fun for me, Nats,' he grins, unbuttoning the top two buttons of his shirt. 'I'm happy to spend this weekend with you, whichever way you want it.' I feel a rush of love for him. I knew we were different from Nakul and Trisha.

Later as the three of us are sitting around the dinner table and chatting Nakul asks me if I remember Sasha, his American friend from university. 'Natty, she was the one who was walking around at our wedding with a garland in hand, in search of an Indian man?'

'Hmm, yes,' I say recalling his comical friend who did not want to leave India without finding a prince for herself.

'So she has just given birth to triplets, from an Indian father. And at least one of them is going to be named Nakul,' he says proudly.

'Poor boy, his future is going to be blighted in that case,' quips Varun. 'He will be a bleeding heart, the patron saint of all those who get conned easily.'

'Oh please, just because I'm asking you to be reasonable with Maharaja Bhupinder Singh?' Nakul takes an extra helping of the mutton and says. 'And that does not make me a bleeding heart. It's somebody's home, after all, that we are taking over.'

'Speaking of which, thank God we did not sign an agreement with Zorawar Singh for his kothi in Bhatinda,' Varun looks at me and says.

'And why is that?' I ask.

'Because he took off the face of this earth after doing multiple deals and taking signing amounts on fake papers with another party. Last we heard, he was in London, possibly playing bridge with all the other famous fugitives from India! There has been no response from him. It has been a year,' Nakul answers for Varun.

I eventually leave Varun and Nakul to their conversation about crumbling castles, fusty maharajas, ancient havelis and hedge funds and I slip under the covers with Ria and Sumer, wondering if we'll have nights like this again or if everything is about to change.

❈ ❈ ❈

We are chanting Om Namah Shivaya at my first Art of Joy class after a short yoga session. We are about to start meditation by focusing on our breath.

Most people at the centre appear to be professionals, no doubt in creative jobs that allow them the luxury of strolling into work at 11 am. There is also a skinny model in the class, all cheekbones and a high ponytail who has definitely had work done on her lips. There is also a new socialite who has smartly constructed her image in the art world via Instagram to make herself appear as more than a rich housewife.

She is speaking to a long-haired man about Rupi Kaur in the veranda of the centre. I'm purchasing a yoga mat from a small counter, just adjacent to the two, when I overhear her tell him that Rupi is the new Rumi. I nearly gasp in disbelief when I hear that and turn back to look at her face. The man looks at me and smiles.

I realise that while I'm busy judging and sizing people up, the rest of them have taken their seats and are sitting with their hands on their knees in yoga-mudra.

'If thoughts come...ignore them and bring your mind again to your breaths,' the yogacharya says.

It's hard to focus on my breath when there is so much on my mind. Instead of calming me down, this breathing technique is bringing up worries. I begin to wonder about Varun and me. What if we are still together, going through the motions but our relationship is dead? I feel my heart sink at the thought.

'Inhale slowly from your right nostril, count to eight... exhale your negative thoughts away.'

'Don't fight your thoughts, but do not engage with them either.' I can hear yogacharya saying.

Finally, as we wind up the session, I realise that I'm indeed feeling lighter. The yogacharya asks us to spend the rest of our day in a state of awareness of our inner selves. 'And keep a diary where you honestly document your reactions through the day,' he says.

At home, I do my best to retain my newly acquired equanimity. I don't react when the maid irons the logo of my track pants. I don't react when Sumer pulls Sofie's hair and she slaps him in return.

Then Trisha drops in to meet me in a gorgeous cotton summer dress made by Guneet's factory for the brand Alice and Olivia. I tell her seriously that I'd love to be able to buy his export surplus and I'm hoping she will tell me there is no need to buy anything, and that Guneet will gladly gift it to me for free. But she tells me instead that he discusses his new orders with her and often sends her photos to let her know how wonderful he thinks she will look in the clothes. 'It's our thing now,' she says. 'I feel personally invested in these designs that he discusses with me. And so, I feel a bit possessive about what he stitches. He stitches, I wear,' she smiles with that besotted look in her eyes.

I'm aghast at her pettiness. I mean these clothes are exported and worn by half of Europe and Americas and she is feeling possessive about giving a piece or two of these dresses to me, her closest friend and the sufferer of her dirty secrets?

This is ridiculous! I find some silliness has crept into her already somewhat silly personality ever since her new romance, but I say nothing. I surprise myself by listening to my higher self and I tell her that I understand where she is coming from when, in fact, I should be wanting to slap her hard.

It's a trial by fire when Varun comes home from work and announces that he is to leave for Singapore and Hongkong for a series of important meetings that have come through.

'But you'll be back the next weekend for Nafisa's party, right?' I ask in a small voice.

'Probably not, depends on how the meetings go,' he says without remorse. 'Nats, with investors one cannot say. If they are interested in your company, they want to meet again a few times,' he says, pausing his unpacking to look at me with consternation. 'You are looking upset. Are you upset?' he looks up in surprise.

Upset? I feel like Muhammad Ali in front of an opponent in the boxing ring and I struggle hard to overcome a pugilist's urge to punch him in his face. I'm disappointed but not surprised that Varun hasn't been able to keep his word to me once again. Managing my disappointments has become a way of life for me of late. I continue to sit on the chaise lounge of our bedroom watching him pack his formal shoes in a shoe bag without a mention of his promise to spend the weekend with me. I remind myself to keep my emotions in check by focusing on the journey of my breath. In. Out. In. Out.

'What are you doing Nats? Why are you breathing so heavily?' he says looking at me in amusement.

'Just trying to control my anger Varun, by focusing on my breath. You are just lucky I'm not reacting and giving you a hard time about this you know?' I say, restraining my voice. 'You not only promised me, but you also promised Nafisa that you will be there! I was looking forward to us spending the weekend together and then going for her dinner. I miss you and enjoy having you by my side when we go out. But that doesn't happen lately, and now, after promising me, without an apology you are taking off because work comes first!'

'When did I say I'm not sorry? Of course, I'm sorry. I'm just preoccupied and unable to commit. So I don't know what to say Natasha,' he shrugs his shoulders and chucks a whole bunch of shirts into the suitcase.

Before I can say anything else, Ria walks into my room in Sumer's Shrek night suit. 'Can I sleep here tonight?' she asks, clambering on to our bed. 'Sumer will make me remove this night suit if I sleep in our room Mummy,' says the cunning child.

'Come here to Daddy,' Varun says, picking her up and kissing her. I'm surprised by the twinge of envy I'm suddenly feeling watching him dote on her in this manner when he should be fussing over me instead.

He comes looking for me in the study before leaving. I say bye to him formally. 'Enough ya, Natasha, you have got to understand. Otherwise, we will both be miserable,' he says, putting his arms around my waist. I break away from his arms and walk away. 'Have a good trip Varun,' I say. I see him wince briefly and then he leaves without a goodbye.

I watch him close the door of the study behind him, my eyes welling up with tears. Am I going mad?

Not wanting to be left alone with my thoughts, I ring Nafisa to inform her that Varun is unlikely to return in time for her party. 'You sound upset darling. Don't be. We will miss him, but I will make sure you have a good time,' she says in a soothing voice. I weep silently.

'He is always doing this to me,' I whisper.

'That isn't true. Varun is ONLY doing this to you since he got busy with his new project and surely you can understand the amount of time and commitment it requires of him Natasha.'

'I think this is how it's always going to be. I feel I'm losing him.'

'Don't talk nonsense. He is doing this for you, right? Varun has to afford three kids and a wife who believes in online shopping more than the Jehovah's witnesses believe in Christ,' she laughs. 'So cheer up. I will place you next to the most interesting people on the table.'

'I hope one of them won't be Parthiv Mehta,' I say dryly.

'No, it won't be unless you want to spend the evening listening to his yet unwritten autobiography,' Nafisa giggles. 'But would you like to bring Trisha along instead since I have one person less on the table?'

'No way, Nafisa,' I say emphatically. 'She is being very petty. And I want a change. I see her enough already.' I hear myself snap.

'Oh, you are angry at her too now?' Nafisa chuckles.

'Trisha is having an affair and I'm her confidant, by the way. And then she acts petty with me about the clothes her boyfriend is exporting to the world. Says they are special, I feel possessive blah blah when I ask her to get some for me. I had even offered to pay for them...' I hear myself blurt.

There is a stunned silence at the other end of the line. Then I hear Nafisa clear her throat. 'How long have you known?'

'Not too long, and I wasn't the one who encouraged her but...'

'I don't need the details, but I hope you are not involved in any way,' she cuts in.

'No, I'm not. But it's complicated. And I did not want to tell you, but I cannot bear the burden of her secret much longer.'

'Well, her secret is safe with me, but I'm not feeling good about this. Varun will be livid if he finds out that you know,' she warns me.

'Yes, yes, but he won't find out. I'm not involved anyway. But I will tell you one thing. It isn't a frivolous distraction for Trish, she is in love. There were problems between her and Nakul,' I find myself justifying Trisha's affair. And defending my silently consenting to being witness to it, perhaps.

'Oh well, you worry about your own marriage and stop fighting with poor Varun,' Nafisa says. 'And see you soon!'

In the morning, I receive a flower delivery from Varun, a box of two dozen red roses along with a note – *My darling, I feel terrible I had to go. I realised on my way to the airport how let down you must feel. I promise to make it up to you. Love, Varun.*

I hold his note and weep for some time. Love is a wonderful thing after all. A small gesture from Varun has made me so happy that all my previous grievances against him have eroded in an instant.

There was a time in our lives, not long ago, when Varun would make me special in so many little ways that I took it for granted that things would never change. On our ninth wedding anniversary, I received nine flower deliveries from him throughout the day. Sometimes, after a fight, a tub of ice-cream would arrive at my door with a note asking me to 'Cool down because I love you'.

Varun even flew my parents down to Croatia for my thirty-fifth birthday. I wasn't expecting them there and screamed with mad joy when I opened the door of our hotel room in Zagreb and found Mummy and Daddy outside. Then there was this other time he plotted with Trisha and took me away to Bali after telling me that we were going to the movies with her and Nakul. How special had I felt then when he drove me into the airport instead! I remember Trisha telling me that there were men and then there was Varun. Little did I know then that it wasn't just a passing observation that she was making. It was to her, perhaps, a realisation of what she was missing in her relationship with Nakul. The greater surprise for me on that trip though was that Varun had managed to pack in one suitcase everything from my wardrobe that I was never likely to wear. Anyway, there was no Instagram in those days, so I survived the trip without any ignominy.

My eyes well up with tears as I go through this flashback of all the special moments of my life with him. Can anybody blame me then for missing him so terribly? The Varun I see at home has indeed changed so much from the romantic man I used to know. I send him a long emotional message thanking him for the flowers and spend the rest of the day with a smile on my face. He does love me after all. Nothing has changed.

The meditation session this morning followed by yoga has had a transformative effect on me. A rare inner calm is taking over my entire being and I'm learning to shed my ego.

My new-found spirituality is helping me in other spheres of my life as well. Not only have I not lost my temper on my infernally ungrateful children today, what has really given Art of Joy a real run for their money is that I picked up not one but three calls in one day from my mother-in-law asking after Varun who is now not only too busy for me but also for his mother. In fact, I can hardly believe that he has forgotten to inform her that he is going away overseas. *That* is seriously busy. She is aghast about being kept out of the loop by her adoring son and even though this has given me some pleasure, I'm trying my best not to feel too thrilled about it.

'It's not like him to not tell you. He has been really busy, I guess it slipped his mind,' I tell her to reassure her of her importance in Varun's life.

'Then you should have called me yourself and told me,' she says haughtily. Hearing her speak to me in that offensive tone when I'm struggling internally to keep an equable temper makes me want to strangle her with one of her leheriya sarees. But I take a deep breath and remind myself to keep my ego out of this communication.

'How was I to know he hadn't told you Maa?' I manage to say calmly. This is called conquering your lesser self.

But just as I'm congratulating myself on my zen attitude, my mother-in-law changes the subject to my children's riding lessons. I tell her that the children's schedules are getting too demanding for them at school for them to keep up with the lessons.

'I know you have completely stopped sending them for their riding lessons Natasha. I spoke to Sumer this morning,' she says edgily.

'So then why are you cross-checking, if I may ask?' I retort sharply. I'm done being saintly with her.

'I'm doing no such thing,' she says to me tersely. 'I have noticed this isn't a priority for you because every so often I have to nudge you in the direction of the stables at the Turf Club all the way from Jhalakpur. Look, Natasha, we sent our children to school too, but we always found time for their riding lessons.'

I'm itching to tell Maa that we are living in the 21st century and that there are enough cars and buses on the roads to make riding lessons completely unnecessary.

Instead, I tell her firmly that I no longer deem horse riding a necessity in their lives and view it as a luxury that my children haven't the time for at present.

Varun's mother has been keen that her grandchildren learn to play polo, especially Sumer, so he can play for the Jhalakpur Royals polo team when he grows up. Her maternal family is the proud owner of the team, and Varun too is a 'visiting faculty' on that team; he plays for them from time to time. Well, if she is so keen, she can ask her son to take charge. I'm done pleasing everybody in this family.

❈❈❈

I'm reminded about my meeting with Nirav today by a calendar alert on my phone. I had forgotten that our meeting was fixed for this afternoon and now I barely have any time to put myself together and show up at his office looking like a human being. I do manage to throw a linen salwar kameez on and get to his posh agency on time. Nirav seems like a sharp guy, full of energy and enthusiasm. He sounds eager to work with me for some reason. 'Your writing has a spark in it. We need that in our brochures,' he says. Something within me dies when I hear the word 'brochure'.

He must have some other work in mind for me too. Surely it cannot just be brochures? There must have been a misunderstanding. Perhaps Varun hasn't given him a proper background of my work as a writer.

'Of course, but there are ads to be written as well, aren't there? That is the work I'd really be interested in frankly. I'd love to work on some good ad copy and work on storyboards for ad films,' I clarify.

He tells me he has a big enough team in that department already and it's the brochure writing that requires my 'vast talent'.

When I ask him about the clients he wishes me to write for, some extremely uninspiring FMCG organisation names come up. Who wants to write the brochure for a dehumidifier or washing machine? Not me for sure. I cannot bring myself to tell him that though, and I leave his office promising to think it over. 'I look forward to working with you soon Natasha,' he tells me cheerfully as he sees me off till the door, as though my offer to think it over was a mere formality.

At home, I receive some mildly pleasant news from the Rotary Club.

An email from the Rotary Club of Mumbai Sea Face informs me that an award is to be bestowed upon me for vocational excellence as a writer/columnist and that the club president is 'sincerely hoping that I can make myself available for the same' on such and such date. I confirm my presence. It isn't like I receive awards every day. The last time I got feted for my work was possibly in a previous life, perhaps, for discovering some special variety of fungus.

Given how bleak my professional life in the last decade has been, even if I were having a lobotomy performed on me the same day, I'd have excused myself from the operation theatre, and gone hobbling under anaesthesia to receive this Rotary trophy.

I have interesting reactions when I share this news with my loved ones. Nafisa is pleased with the news. 'See, you have so much talent and I'm happy to see it getting recognised. Quickly tell me when it is so I can make sure I'm in town for it,' she says.

Unable to contain her excitement, my mother wants to know if she can fly down for the event and I tell her she absolutely cannot; I'm not getting a Pulitzer after all.

Sofie is thrilled too and looking at me with unqualified admiration for a change.

When Varun rings me in the evening to ask me about my day, I talk about general things and then let it slip in gently that I'm to be awarded by the Rotary people. I don't want to sound too pompous and make a big deal of it, Varun will think me silly. He has been collecting awards throughout his professional life and he has never given his own awards too much importance, so it's best that I downplay mine. 'Wow, congratulations honey,' Varun says. 'Maybe this will give you the incentive to start writing more often now like proper writers do,' he adds.

I realise that any minute now he will ask me about my meeting with Nirav and I don't want to tell him now, when he's away, that I'm happier squatting flies than writing brochures. So I quickly change the subject by asking him about his meetings with the venture capitalists instead.

Chapter 9

Most of us will remember the story of the well-known media executive who allegedly murdered her own daughter a few years ago. When the story first broke, each one of us was consumed with discussing the sordid details of her crime and the possible participation of her long line of husbands in it.

More recently, a successful businessman's wife, a society diva, is embroiled in a bitter divorce with him, details of which have been routinely splashed on the front page of the local editions. I refuse to believe that there is even one person who does not secretly enjoy a scandal. They bring us solace and remind us that our own lives aren't so abysmally dull after all.

We might have moved away from being spectators at gladiator fights and guillotine executions during medieval times, but deep down we are still voyeurs…We are the people who give reality shows about couples breaking up high TRPs, and we are the people who relish the bickering that goes on during primetime news. In many ways, perhaps, we are still stuck in the dark ages inside our heads.

My own life may be all about a phantom husband, depressing brochures and inquisitions from a demanding in-law right now, but at least Art of Joy is there to bring peace and calm, I think to myself, as I enthusiastically slip on my yoga linens and head towards Pali Hill after a light breakfast. There have been new enrolments and the room is packed with yoga mats, there are nearly twenty-five of us in the hall today and no air-conditioning. God help us!

About twenty minutes into the class, we are holding our downward dog poses for twenty counts when the yogacharya's wife walks in and starts hurling abuse at him.

The crisis, of course, is whether to hold our pose and remain on all fours with our butts pushed out or to release it so we can comfortably watch the high drama unfolding before us.

'You shameless man,' Mrs Yogacharya is screaming at the top of her lungs, 'So which person from here is also getting private lessons from you at home?' she demands.

Yogacharya looks at her, stunned.

'Achcha, show us also the asanas you like doing with your favourite student! We can also learn some sex education that way,' the belligerent wife is saying. Then she looks around and observes that half the class is awkwardly stuck in Adho-Mukha Swanasana. I'm one of them but am dying to release the asana and sit comfortably and watch this mudfest like some of the other shameless students seem to be doing. The thing is, I'm standing right in front and none of us in the front row have relaxed their pose. We are all slyly trying to look at Mrs Yogacharya's face as she hurls these insults at her husband.

'Inverted dog pose? Haan, that must be your favourite one, nahin? Because you are only a dog, a kutta. And then you are finding bitches who are doing all these things with you. Tamē ēka kūtarō chē. Narkamā jāva ne,' she yells in Parsi Gujarati. My arms cannot take it much longer and I decide to sit properly with my legs crossed. Cannot even fold my mat and march out of the class as 1. nobody else is doing it and 2. I don't want to miss the show.

Not knowing where to look I pretend that I'm looking at the tip of my nose as the yogacharya often asks us to do to improve our focus. I watch the angry wife pick up an Iyengar yoga brick lying next to my mat and hurls it towards his crotch before storming out of the class. Yogacharya yelps in pain as the brick strikes his knee instead of his family jewels. We collectively gasp and marvel at his good fortune and his wife's poor aim.

Although the entire class, which consists mostly of women and a handful of men, is aghast at what we have just witnessed, not one of us appears too displeased about it. Smirks are being exchanged, giggles suppressed and some jaws are dropped...but each one of us is thrilled with the show. One girl at the back seems to have recorded everything on the camera of her mobile phone. That is really low! I wouldn't mind looking at it again myself though since I could not get a good look at his face in between.

I'm ashamed to be partaking in the excitement myself, but I must admit that there is nothing as pleasurable as a local juicy scandal involving people one knows.

As the yogacharya slinks out after his wife's high-octane drama, the rest of us huddle in corners to confab.

Ujjwala, a middle-aged woman from the class I haven't even noticed before, suddenly announces with an air of authority, 'I'm not surprised this happened.'

'Why?' we all ask in unison.

Ujjwala does not need much coaxing. Pleased with the attention that she is getting, she gladly spills the beans on the scandal. It seems that the yogacharya was giving personal meditation lessons to a woman named Kiki, who has attended only a handful of classes at our centre over the past few months. Kiki preferred private lessons at home, during which she was no doubt taught some exceptional tandem yoga moves from the Kamasutra.

Then, last month, Art of Joy organised an offsite meditation and yoga camp in Lonavala. It was mandatory to share your room with another person during the camp, and poor Kiki could not exercise the option of inviting the yogacharya to her room for some private tutoring. However, the guru and the disciple put the big meditation hall to good use at the crack of dawn. As luck would have it, Ujjwala was also attending the camp and she and another girl too responded to the rooster's call and deciding to start their day early landed up at the meditation hall. What followed was literally 'coitus interruptus', and the news finally found its way to the yogacharya's wife in Bombay via her sister who is a close friend of the other girl Sheetal who caught the lovebirds in the act. The wife then decided that there was no better way of exacting revenge than the public shaming of the man.

I cannot wrap my head around the fact that a girl like Kiki was sleeping with a man like our yogacharya. They do not even belong to the same social class. But this has given us all some fodder to chew on. Who needs Netflix when one lives in the midst of such luscious scandals?

I'm sitting with Sumer later and helping him finish his math homework when I receive a call from Trisha. She wants to know if I'm doing well, but before I can answer, she starts telling me about just how her love life is blossoming into something more permanent.

'Are you leaving Nakul?' I ask, moving outside Sumer's room.

'I don't know.'

'Then what do you mean by saying that you and Gurpreet are becoming something more permanent?'

'Guneet, not Gurpreet! And what I'm trying to say is that we have decided that what we feel for each other is far too intense to be taken lightly. He is not like other men. He is different, Nats.'

'How different? Does he have telekinetic powers?'

'Please don't get all sarcastic, Natasha. You think you are funny, but your words can scorch, you know? Sometimes, just sometimes, can you just be my friend instead of Varun's wife or this narrow-minded, judgemental woman from the 18th century?' she says irritably.

I'm unable to come up with a riposte to her searing opinion of me, but later, I do wonder if I'm being overly hard on my friend. I wonder if my reactions to her affair stem from envy. Is it possible that I resent her the love and excitement that Guneet brings into her life, something that I don't have with Varun any more? Yes, I do get the odd flowers, the loving apologies and a piece of jewellery now and then, but it's not the same as having him with me.

My ruminations are interrupted by Sofie, who reminds me to order fresh uniforms for her, and I dash off an email to the school. The child is shooting up, and only this morning I realised that she is looking like an urchin child in her PE tracks. It would be wise to order some new ones right away before people begin to wonder what hard times the Singh family has fallen upon.

❀ ❀ ❀

Dinner at Nafisa's is everything that a sit-down dinner ought to be, a gloriously old-fashioned and utterly charming *Downton Abbey*-inspired affair. That girl's eye for detail is awe-inspiring. The table setting is straight out of an *Architectural Digest* party, complete with flower arrangements, the candelabras, the crockery and silverware (her Parsi granny's), which has added just that extra bit of elegance to the evening. She is in a gorgeous green silk wrap dress with exaggerated blouson sleeves and a high necktie. I had to get my own dress approved from Her Highness. A chiffon saree with a sequin halter blouse was shot down by her immediately and I was asked to wear my strapless pinstripe dress instead. So here I'm, dressed exactly as I was asked to and wondering if I will have a good time at a dinner where I know nobody except the hostess.

Nafisa takes me by my hand and introduces me to everybody present. We are all standing around the bar where she has uncorked some exquisite wine that everybody except Parthiv is drinking because 'I'm just a single malt guy,' he is explaining to the people around us in general. As if anybody asked him!

Sukh walks in breezily through the main door in a black formal suit, a bottle of wine in hand. He is on his way to another dinner, but he wanted to 'simply swing by and say hello to his two most favourite girls in the world,' he says, as he plants a kiss each on Nafisa's and my cheek. I'm sure he says this to every girl he meets at every party he goes to.

'And you are still seeing that bore Parthiv?' he asks Nafisa under his breath.

'Stop it Sukh! Not tonight please,' she giggles. Parthiv, I'm sure, can tell that he is being discussed because he is looking slightly self-conscious.

I feel bad and walk up him to make conversation and make him feel included. 'Tell me Natasha, how old are the children?' he asks me as though there is nothing else left in the world to talk to me about. I tell him their respective ages even though all I can think about is just how wonderful it will truly be when Nafisa dumps him. More guests join, more wine is uncorked, cold cuts are passed around for the meat eaters, and a special vegan cold cuts' platter as well for born-again vegetarians like me.

The last one to walk in is novelist Oliver Davies, the Englishman and Indophile who made this country his home and is on every important guest list of India because of being a bestselling writer, and because, well, he is white and has the right connections in the literary world. He says hello to everybody at the table and courteously introduces himself to the ones he doesn't know from before.

Shortly after his arrival, we settle down into our respective places at the table. Sukh has waltzed off to the next party, leaving me behind with this motley crew but it's my best friend's party and I must drink more wine and be my sociable best even if it kills me.

I look at Nafisa who is giggling over something that Samir Parikh, who runs a large cruise company, is telling her. She has thoughtfully placed me at the table in such a manner that I'm right in the centre with Kaizad Dastur, the talented fashion photographer who is known to sleep with all the hot models he works with, to my left and Samir to my right.

It is indeed an eclectic mix of people on the dinner table today. The dishiest of them all though is Kabir Khanna, a dashing son of a movie star and theatre actor who after making his debut on the West End, went on to do work in some indie films out of Hollywood. An erudite man, he is always immaculately dressed and his fan base is divided equally between the heterosexual and homosexual population of the country. The jury is out there though about his own sexual leanings and the women are still hoping that if at all he is gay, he will eventually change his mind. We all just hope for humanity's sake that he isn't asexual after all.

'Oh Antarctica, it was just something else,' says Samir loud enough for everyone on the table to hear. Samir has just returned from an expedition to the South Pole.

There is a chorus of 'Oh wows' from the table at the mention of Antarctica.

'Tell us all about it,' Nafisa says eagerly.

'Oh, you see glaciers melting right in front of your own eyes. It's a sad sight but so dramatic.'

'Let's send Donald Trump to Antartica. Maybe then he will accept that global warming is a real thing,' remarks Nafisa.

Everybody at the table laughs.

Parthiv isn't enjoying any of this I can tell. He is looking at Samir with thinly veiled derision for hogging his share of attention from the guests.

'And what do you do Natasha?' Oliver, who is seated right next to Nafisa, turns towards me and asks.

'I'm raising my children and, well, I'm also a columnist,' I say almost apologetically.

'Natasha, as fabulous as she looks, is a delightful, hands-on mother of three. Would you believe it? She used to be the editor of *Envy* when we became friends,' Nafisa, forever worried that I'm undermining myself, chimes in. I do love her, she is the best friend a girl can have.

'Oh, you were editing *Envy*?' Barkha Lalvani, a Bollywood actor of mid-range fame, who hadn't registered my presence up until now, asks with an eyebrow arching till her hairline.

'And she was bloody good at it,' Nafisa offers helpfully.

'Wow, and you gave that up to be a mom! That's amazing! And please tell me where your column appears – I must read it,' Samir exclaims as if he has just discovered that I'm a marine biologist who also works part-time for NASA.

I may not know most of the folks on the table but that does not discourage me from talking incessantly to the editor-in-chief of *Sassy*, Meenakshi, sitting across from me and Kaizad. I cannot help but notice that he is only a passive participant in our conversation and I find him looking at Nafisa longingly even as I chatter about this, that and the other. There is something developing between the two clearly. No wonder Nafisa is open to the idea of calling it quits with Parthiv.

Kabir is being very charming, witty and well-mannered, doing his best to speak to as many people as he can. Every time he speaks to me, I feel a bird flutter inside my heart. Maybe tonight will be the night he will change is mind and declare himself hetero!

It must be the wine I think, looking at what seems to me a rapt audience, that suddenly produces in me the illusion of being a person whose opinion on everything under the sun was witty, valuable and worth listening to. Hemingway drank wine to make other people more interesting, I drink wine to make myself interesting to other people. If I were single again, I hear myself tell him, I might have liked to be a painter's or a photographer's muse in the manner of Emile Floge, artist Gustav Klimt's muse and that woman in *The Kiss*. He meets my subtle offer to get photographed with little more than a perplexed expression. I then quickly change the conversation to the art market and the Kochi Biennale to let him know that I'm a well-informed and cultured type of a person.

Barkha Lalvani is determined to wangle a free trip from Samir and she will not be embarrassed to ask for it. 'You should send me to Antartica. I will Instagram the hell about it and tag you everywhere. I have 2.2 million followers, Samir.'

Nafisa, who has heard Barkha's sales pitch, exchanges a look with me that says, 'This one was a mistake, never again!'

'So where is your husband today?' dishy Kabir asks me, putting his cutlery away while the snow peas salad is served on his plate by a white-gloved waiter.

Nafisa, sitting right across from Kabir, decides to answer on my behalf because wine is apparently producing the illusion in her that I'm unable to speak for myself. 'Varun is a prince, a real prince FYI. He is working on some exciting architectural projects and also doing heritage hotels, which is why he could not be here today,' she says as she makes a toast, I'm not sure to whom.

'As I have said to you before Natasha, royalty shouldn't have to work so hard. Aren't they supposed to be good at making other people work hard for them?' smirks Parthiv from the other end of the table in an effort to sound clever. I ignore the subtle insult packed neatly within these words. I must see to it that he is dumped before the week is over.

Varun's regal antecedents, however, raise much curiosity at the table, and I'm asked to give a full Wikipedia entry on him and his royal heritage.

'Oh my, you are married to a prince. Show me his photo please,' says Samir excitedly. 'Very, very handsome. You are a lucky girl,' he enunciates with an air of drama as he pokes me with his very gay finger. 'Well done, you!' His eyes by now are not on the photograph but on Kabir.

Even Kaizad, the photographer, who has been obviously unsociable until now, suddenly begins to regard me with new-found admiration and respect. 'No wonder you look like a princess yourself,' he says to me.

It always comes down to this. This is my achievement. I'm the woman who married well while the rest of them go on to write books, film documentaries and edit magazines. And what a marriage it is that I'm always going to these dinners with my McQueen clutch bag instead of my husband. A feeling of dismay rises inside me like a bubble which I quell with a big gulp of wine. Then I look around me to entertain myself and I notice that Parthiv has finally found his audience in Meenakshi who is listening to him with such admiration you would think she was listening to Yuval Noah Harari. Parthiv is no doubt thinking that she is madly in love with him.

'I have promised an interview to Meenakshi, but I have already told her I will only do it if Kaizad shoots my photos and she has agreed,' not satisfied with a one-member audience, Parthiv says to Kaizad from across the table. Kaizad, who by now has probably finished having imaginary sex with Nafisa a few times over, looks a little befuddled at first but then nods politely. 'Oh, of course,' he says. If only pompous Parthiv knew that this is possibly the last time he is attending Nafisa's dinner party as a lover he would perhaps let go of that perpetual sneer from his face.

***

In the morning, Varun is looking exhausted when he comes home from the airport. His face lights up though when, as always, he is given a reception befitting a decorated soldier returning after the Vietnam war at home with the kids, the dogs and me all vying for his attention.

Varun hugs the children, gets them all to kiss him one by one and in exchange for the kisses he hands over a small duty-free bag of chocolates to each child. Even the dogs get dog treats.

He wants to lie down, so I go downstairs to see what the kids are up to and find two drenched dogs and Sumer and

Ria playing with the water hose. When I ask them to stop they ask me in a chorus if I can please take them swimming. It seems a decent alternative to feeling irritated at Varun for being tired and unavailable as ever.

Sitting by the poolside, I ask for some tender coconut water and dial Nafisa. Even more important than a party is doing an after-party analysis, which is precisely what she and I spend the better part of my poolside afternoon doing. I get her to admit that she fancies Kaizad and she goes on to confess that once after a drunken night of partying they ended up kissing. She did not want to date him, she says, because that would make things awkward professionally if it did not work out. Kaizad does shoot for *La Beau Monde* from time to time and so working with him is unavoidable. I didn't even think Kaizad was all that great but he was certainly better than Parthiv. And the idea of Nafisa dumping the odious man for Kaizad was simply too appealing to discourage her from seeing him.

'P was being rather cold with me I felt. He did not tell me why, but I think it was because I was having such a good time with everybody else...anyway, I have decided to call it off nicely,' she chuckles, her voice a little hoarse from too much drinking. 'Enough about my dinner though. The main reason I called you was to help me work on this special supplement on fashionable women entrepreneurs. Will you Natasha?'

'You are discussing work on a Sunday, Nafisa?'

'I will not have the time tomorrow. I am leaving for Moscow remember, and I wanted clarity from you and a commitment. Do you ever intend to work seriously or not?'

'Oh, lucky you. Surprise me with a big present, preferably something with fur on it.'

'You haven't answered my question. Do you want to work, yes or no?'

'We read about these women all the time, Nafisa. What is so new about doing a story on them?'

'I haven't asked for your opinion on the supplement, just tell me – will you do it or not?'

'I have to start putting together Varun's birthday party with Trisha, and she isn't a very responsible person, which means I will have to do it all by myself…'

'So it's a no. Fine, I will ask somebody else.'

'Oh, don't get upset Nafisa. Sometimes I think you and Varun have been speaking behind my back to get me to work so I can just stop demanding time from him. And you.'

'Oh, shut up Natasha. We both love you. And no, I'm not upset. I am just surprised that you keep passing opportunities up. Anyway, I must go now. Mum has asked me over for lunch and it's late already. Speak later?'

'Yes, I guess,' I say. 'And listen, give me a few days to think about your assignment, please.'

'Don't do it if you don't find it inspiring enough,' she says sharply before she hangs up.

Chapter 10

There is no telling about the lengths that some people will go to acquire important social contacts. I have been keenly observing this social climbing routine ever since I became a mother and am dismayed at the realisation that parents are unabashedly using their children to further their connections.

It's interesting to see how some women belonging to the upper strata of our society have perfected social networking via their offspring to an art form. The modus operandi is simple: Identify a person you want to be well acquainted with, unleash your child on theirs somehow and then parlay that into gaining entry into their lives. Friendships in this city are zip code-based for most, people from South Bombay, for instance, won't even show up for chauthas if the poor dead sod lived in the outer suburbs. On the other hand, when they want to befriend A-list families, putting your tots through hour-long car rides becomes worthwhile. It is also a given that the more power or fame you have, the more 'adorable' your children appear to other people. Watching social mountaineers gush over the supposed cuteness of the kids of society divas whom they aspire to befriend isn't at all uncommon.

It's with a heavy-as-lead heart that I'm reproducing an analysis of our family, as seen through the astute eyes of a

six-year-old. I saw Ria typing away on my old iPad over
the weekend and when I tried to pry, she asked me not to
disturb her as she was 'thinking'. This morning however I
went through her private notes on the iPad and here is what
it said:

FamLey

Lola	Notey
Ria	NiSe
Sofia	Meyn
Sumer	IRTATiNG
Mumy	SaM Tims meyn
Dady	Vary Bizy
Chestr	VeRe meyn to Lola

In English, this loosely translates as:
Lola (our nine-month-old Scottish terrier): Naughty

Ria:	Nice
Sofie:	Mean
Sumer:	Irritating
Mummy:	Sometimes mean
Daddy:	Very busy
Chester:	(our ten-year-old Cocker Spaniel): Very mean to Lola

Is this how a child her age should be thinking?

The way she cheerfully goes bouncing about the house
you would never guess at Ria's multifaceted dissatisfaction
with the family. I must let Varun know how she feels about
him, so he realises that I'm not the only one complaining

about him being too busy. Perhaps I can ask Sofia or Sumer as well to express their feelings about their father no longer finding the time to be with his family. That way it might be easier to negotiate a holiday with him in December.

I'm not above using my children to get through to my husband, and I'm not ashamed of it either.

Varun and I have differing notions about parenting because his own mother did not exactly raise him herself. My dear husband was raised by his dai and then packed off to a boarding school for a proper education soon after. I cannot help being a clingy parent. I want to be able to meet all their emotional needs since I'm not doing anything else with my life anyway. When my babies have bad dreams at night, they call out for me and not Shanta or Sunita or Mary. I don't want to outsource their upbringing when I can do it myself.

Of course, some people are more concerned with other peoples' children than their own. I was at the school gate today to fetch the kids and I could not help but notice the obsequious way some mothers were behaving around star wife Surveen Khan, who was there to fetch her youngest son. Interestingly, today I noticed that the blue-eyed socialite Somya Bajaj was at school also to fetch her daughter who I wouldn't say is a particularly adorable looking child. But one school mother, who is all Birkin and blonde highlights, obviously did not think so. She was gushing over Somya's child as though she were the only child in the universe while her own kid kept tugging at her T-shirt saying, 'Mummy, Mummy, I have to tell you something.'

Last year, one school mother, Bhavna Thakur, managed to ingratiate herself to Surveen to the extent that she invited her to fly to Couchreval with her in their Gulf Stream jet. This has stoked the social ambitions of other school mothers and now they are doing their best to use the school to get to know celebrities personally and to have their children call them maasi. Everyone knows that getting a child to call you maasi is the easiest way to hit pay-dirt with the mother.

I put all of this in my column 'Society Swans and their Young' and send it to the editor first thing this morning. I'm delighted when she writes back within minutes to say she loves the piece and that it's exactly the sort of peek into the world of the well-heeled that readers enjoy. That's literally the only time Bhavna Thakur has ever come in handy to another human being without profiting from them directly.

Exhausted after all the typing I'm tempted to lie in bed for the rest of the day but that would mean skipping yoga class which, along with being my body's line of defence against disease, is also the source of the details of the yogacharya's train-wreck affair.

I'm early and amused to see that our desire for gossip is such that everyone else is already there – fifteen minutes early – even the chronic latecomers. This gives me time to learn the truly horrifying news that Kiki's husband, who was apparently having multiple affairs for years, somehow heard about the yoga class episode, confronted Kiki in front of his parents, and wasted no time in showing her the door. No surprises here, it always ends badly for the woman. It's all so wildly depressing.

After the class I drop in at the Nectar Café to cheer myself up with the sweet basil-tapioca pudding for myself and who do you think I find sharing an apple crumble on the tiny white terrace? Trisha and Guneet, that's who. I quickly scan the terrace and find that there are just a few other people there as well, two of whom are obviously tourists and one smitten young couple who is decidedly bunking college. Trisha is in a coral pink strappy top, her flawless skin complimented by the colour and Guneet is wearing a Hackett tee in yellow. I cannot believe that together the two of them are so infinitely dumb that they have chosen colours that would make them stand out at a circus, to say nothing of an all-white café.

Luckily, they cannot see me from where they are sitting – she with her back to the dessert counter and he with his eyeballs in the poetic ravines of her cleavage. I have no intention of saying hello to them, so I place my order as unobtrusively as possible and stand behind the palm tree waiting for it. At my height of 5 ft 3, an indoor plant is good enough to cover me, but Guneet picks just that time to respond to nature's call and sees me standing there on his way to the toilet.

'Wait, Natasha?' he asks, tapping my shoulder with his hand.

'Oh, hey, it's you!' I say feigning surprise.

'Come, say hello to your friend,' he says as he turns back and leads me to their table.

'Na-ta-sha, my darling,' Trisha trills as she gets up to give me a warm hug. She seems genuinely happy to see me. I wish I felt the same.

'Join us for a bit Natty,' she squeezes my hand and says with such affection that it's hard for me to refuse.

'So hanging out, in the open, really?' I ask Trisha.

'Natty, nobody from our circle comes here any longer. Everybody has moved to other newer places. Anyway, now you are here, so it's all good, see?' she says chirpily.

'Well, you know what is safe and what isn't. Anyway, listen Trisha, we are a month away from Varun's birthday, we must get to work tout suite,' I say. A smaller dinner would have been so much easier and probably what Varun would have preferred but of course, a party was never my choice anyway. It was unusual for a surprise party to come as a surprise to the person throwing it but there you have it.

'Oh...ya, of course. Tell me what it is that you need me to do, and I will be more than happy to help,' she says eagerly. 'In fact, let's make a checklist and divide our work – that way we can make sure everything is covered.'

Trisha's words are music to my ears. Planning a big bash is a lot of hard work, and Trisha does know how to put together a good party, I'll give her that.

'Will you take care of the caterers? I will do the rest. I was thinking of hiring Blue Cilantro or Saffron Tables. You are good with food, so you speak with them. Discuss the menu with me first though, and negotiate a good rate. And the cake? Will you take care of that too?'

'I will Natasha – why are you so worried? Give me two days, it will all be done, just get me the number of guests. Oh, and what about the music?'

'I have already shortlisted the DJ and the live band. Varun's secretary is booking the Swinging Brothers. They are asking for 5 lakhs for a performance which I find steep, but Cynthia is negotiating.'

We are still discussing the party when Guneet returns to the table and Trisha, not wanting him to feel left out of the conversation, says, 'Okay, now let us talk about something else, this is of no interest to Guneet.'

'Please carry on with your planning. I'm not getting bored. In fact, I'm just happy to sit here and look at you,' he says to her with such intolerable tenderness that I'm briefly filled with dismay for myself.

When I last saw them together, I had assumed it was just that radiance of things being new and forbidden pleasure and all that, but I wonder now if they do actually – God I can't bear it – connect at a deeper level. It must be said neither Trish nor Guneet are the brightest bulbs and perhaps they've just met their match in each other. I wonder if I'm being bitchy because I can't remember the last time Varun looked at me like this.

'Do you mind if I leave the two of you alone and go to the washroom quickly?' Trish asks me. Wow, even their bladders are synchronised now. Love is amazing.

Just as Trisha leaves for the restroom, I see Varun's name flash on my mobile phone, and I answer the call nervously. 'Where are you Nats?' Varun asks me, his voice sounding serious.

'I'm having coffee with Trisha,' I say in an uneven voice.

'Okay, call me when you're home. We need to talk,' Varun says crisply before hanging up.

***

I'm writing this on the antique table facing the enormous, creaky wooden four-poster in Maa's haveli in Jhalakpur.

That dreaded call from Varun the other day wasn't to confront me about Guneet and Trisha but to coax me into travelling to Jhalakpur over the weekend to attend a party the Maharaja Mamaji was hosting. Since his cousins Devraj and his insufferable wife Bambi were flying down to attend the party too, it was incumbent upon me to show up on Varun's behalf.

I almost collapsed with relief at first. I had left the café that day with my hands shaking with nervousness as if I had Parkinson's disease. Trisha also looked deathly pale after I shared my fears with her. I was so busy celebrating the fact that his call wasn't to confront me about my reluctant involvement in her love affair that I behaved like docile sheep, as the guilty often tend to do, and readily agreed to this trip.

It was later that the relief was replaced by irritation. Spending a weekend in Jhalakpur was only preferable to spending it in a tankful of piranhas. And typical of my mother-in-law to not even call and ask me herself and have her son relay the message like an order. I was about to express some version of this followed by a refusal to go when Varun made matters worse by adding that he had far too much work on to go himself but requested that I take the kids and visit Maa because 'what else are you doing with your time during the weekend anyway honey'.

I protested at first but a few hours later, I yielded because I'm spineless and incapable of holding my ground and also because Varun reminded me that it would be a good change for the kids who apparently 'loved being around Dadisa'.

So here I am, looking out of the window at the kids tripping over themselves in happiness, playing croquet with their cousins in the large lawn, to make myself feel better about my complete inability to put my foot down with Varun.

Cousin Devraj is affable enough but his wife Bambi is so completely intolerable that one longs for an unfortunate incident with a hunter. I responded to her cold and indifferent hello with a forced smile today. I get the feeling that Bambi is jealous of me. It isn't for me to say but I am, without doubt, nicer looking than her and weigh far less. Also, I'm not a completely hateful snob. Anyway, I remind myself to put in some extra effort to speak warmly to Devraj and tell him about the recent popularity of my columns and slip in the news of my Rotary award.

I shall be catching up with the rest of the family over lunch and then of course at the big dinner tonight. I can't believe Varun couldn't make it. He knows how uncomfortable being here without him has always made me.

Incidentally, my 'Society Mom to Society Swan' column appeared this morning in Bombay, and Sheila tells me it has created a bit of a ripple in our extended circle of friends.

I'm just about to call Nafisa to ask her for her feedback when Varun surprises me by walking through the door of our room in the haveli. Hanging up on Nafisa, I run into his arms. Varun laughs loudly when he sees my enthusiasm. 'My fourth child,' he says patting me on my head.

With Varun there, dinner isn't half as bad as I had feared. I look far better than Bambi in my beautiful rose-pink Chantilly lace saree. She is draped in shaded chiffon, and looking like a pouty chameleon in shifting colours. Even Devraj tells me as soon as he sees me that I'm looking, 'Lovely as always, Bhabhisa.' I look around to see if his wife hears his praise for me, but sadly she is at the other end of the room the one time I've wanted her around.

Red wine, compliments and Varun have made the whole evening very enjoyable. I'm even able to overlook the guest clearly flirting with my husband. Noyonika, from the Cooch Behar family, is friend of the family and shows up in the odd gathering. Now I'm not a jealous woman and Varun is nothing if not utterly consistent, but no one needs a beautiful single woman putting their hand on one's husband's knee and letting out a tinkling laugh while reminiscing over holidays that their parents took them on together while they were children. And what is Noyonika remembering about the family vacation to Kashmir? Is it making her first snowball or falling over while skiing? No.

'Of course, I was very young then and absolutely in awe of you,' Noyonika says, batting her eyelids.

'I'm sure you weren't,' Varun says charmingly, but I can see him virtually glow with pride. Wretched woman.

'I'm so happy we've reconnected after so many years. If you are ever in Calcutta, you must get in touch,' she says to me.

'And if you are ever in Bombay, please don't,' I imagine myself saying.

Maa too surprises me by putting on a grand act of being a doting mother-in-law, proudly receiving high praise on my behalf from her friends Stevie and Sash, who are in town from Switzerland and staying in Varun's mama's palace.

'Yes, yes, she is so pretty, isn't she? Of course, my Varun had to find someone like her. He is so handsome himself. People always tell me he should have been in the movies.' Varun is good-looking no doubt, but I have never heard anyone say that.

Earlier this evening too, my mother-in-law was all sugar and honey with me in Varun's presence, fussing over me during tea with, 'Have one more slice of this cake Natasha, you don't eat enough.'

Seeing Noyonika and me by the ornate centre table lit up with candles in all sizes, Maa walks up to us and begins to lavish praise on her friend's daughter. 'Oh, Noyonika, you're a sight for sore eyes,' she says with admiration dripping from every pore in her body. 'I always tell your mother that she hasn't raised just any beauty, she has raised a girl with beauty, grace and style.'

'Aunty, this is such a huge compliment, coming from you,' Noyonika says, stupidly, gushing with gratitude.

'And this dress is soooo wonderful, you look most fetching in it. Turn around, let me see how it fits you,' Maa goes on.

Noyonika giggles and pirouettes in the oversized red number that I think she looks pretty ordinary in. And just for the record, I wouldn't spin on my axis like that even if the Queen of England asked me to.

Then come the veiled insults from my mother-in-law. 'Natasha, you should also get something like this for yourself. Although one has to be tall to pull off this kind of look.'

I watch Noyonika's eyes light up even as I recoil.

'Ah thanks, Maa. I think this gown isn't for me – it isn't my style. Varun prefers a softer look on me, no offense Noyonika,' I say sweetly.

I excuse myself to catch up with some of Varun's more companionable male cousins, and when I turn around to look for Varun, I see Noyonika with him again standing by the centre table with a big vase, giggling a bit too much. I love my Varun but he isn't exactly stand-up comedian material. I try to eavesdrop by walking towards them and leaning against the table, but I can only get close enough to hear her somewhat forced tinkling laughter. I also realise that I am looking slightly foolish standing by myself, tilting my neck to one side to be able to listen in. Thankfully, Devraj joins the two of them and soon Varun gets busy catching up with his relatives across the room, paying the witch no further attention.

'Eat crow, lady in red,' I think. 'He's mine.'

It's with a feeling of rare contentment that I board our return flight to Bombay, feeling especially close to Varun. The old familiar feeling of togetherness has been restored after spending just one day with him and after being reassured that he has eyes only for me. I'm lovingly resting my head against his arm on the plane and trying to take a nap when he suddenly asks me about my meeting with Nirav. 'I completely forgot to ask you about it. How did that go? When do you start working with him?'

'Oh that, well, Varun I met him but I'd rather be writing obituaries than those brochures quite frankly,' I say picking a strand of my hair from his shirt sleeve.

'Really Natasha? For someone who doesn't have a job I must say you are being quite choosy,' he says turning towards me.

'There is no need to talk to me in that tone Varun. Writing about a vacuum cleaner isn't my idea of a career.'

'Then what is? Lunches and dinners and yoga? Are you quite happy living like that? Like a society lady? How are you happy being this unproductive? This wasn't who I married!'

'Well, this wasn't who I married either,' I retort. 'And, it's good to know that you think so little of me,' I say sharply. 'And I know why you want me to work, so you can get me off your back just so I sweetly start putting up with your absentee husbandism,' I add.

'Is this why you think I want you to work?' he asks, his eyes dark with anger.

'Probably,' I say exasperated.

'Good then that you understand me so well!' he says under his breath and turns the other way.

I return the favour by putting on my Beats earphones. I refuse to look in his direction for the rest of the flight. Back home, Sofie and I get into an argument about the shows she is allowed to watch on Netflix and I let her know that Thirteen Ways to Die and *Pretty Little Liars* aren't suitable for her. She accuses me of not allowing her to grow up and goes bawling to her father to complain about me. Wanting to move away from it all I go in for a shower and by the time Varun comes looking for me, ostensibly to talk about Sofie, I'm sitting in bed with my nose ostentatiously buried in a Milan Kundera book.

After his long, wearing days, Stalin liked to linger awhile with his associates and relax by telling them little stories about his life. For example, this one:

One day he decides to go hunting. He puts on an old parka, clamps on skis, he takes a long shotgun and treks out thirteen kilometres.

'Natasha, Sofie is very upset. We must find a new way to tackle her. She is at a delicate age right now,' he says to me evenly. 'Can we talk about this?'

I continue to read my book without looking up.

Of course, I'm reading the same five lines over and over again while he is waiting for me to respond at the edge of the bed, hand on hips.

When I turn the page without looking up, to let it be known that I'm indeed very involved in the book, he silently goes out into the living room.

I go over to tuck in Sumer and Ria and on my way back to my room Sofie and I pass each other by in the passage. She looks at me guiltily, her anger dissipated. 'Sorry Mamma for shouting at you,' she says. I kiss her on her forehead, tell her it's alright and ask her to go to bed. 'Now? So quickly? I'm not Sumer's age,' she says sounding agitated again.

'It's fine. Sleep when you cannot keep your eyelids open any longer,' I say wearily.

***

I wake up the next morning and drag myself to my kick-boxing class. I have plans to ignore Varun but he has slipped out early for a game of polo.

At the class, I pull my sciatic nerve – sciatica being the most definitive reminder of advancing age. Wanting to get the column out of the way and to distract myself from the pain, I open my laptop, but my mind is a blank and arid land.

I'm still staring at an empty word document when Varun returns from his game. 'I'm leaving for Delhi today. I thought you should know, and then from there I might have to go to Kashmir,' he says distantly.

I smile at him politely and nod before returning to my laptop to let him know that I am not interested in conversation either. But did he just say Kashmir? Oh, how desperately I have been wanting to go to Srinagar. The timing of our cold war could not have been worse! I wish I could overcome my pride and ask him to take me along with him. I assume that he is going there to convince the erstwhile maharaja of Kashmir to lease his summer palace to our company. I hope his trip doesn't work out this time and the maharaja calls him in February after a good snowfall instead.

I'm especially upset because he knows I'd have liked to have been asked to join him on this trip and yet he isn't apologising to me. Maharaja Shiven is a family friend, a charming and agreeable man. Though his wife is a crushing bore, I'd have liked very much to enjoy their hospitality. I feel worst of all for my poor mink coat, which is longing for a chance to be on Instagram.

I'm just beginning to wonder if I might have overreacted with Varun. Is it possible that he meant well? This isn't to say that he wasn't wrong in saying those unkind things to me, but maybe I do need to change a few things about my life.

My meaningful introspection is interrupted by a call from Nafisa who has just returned from Moscow and wants me to meet her for a drink at Sake House this evening. I say yes, of course. It's always fun to spend time with her after she has returned from a fancy trip.

Varun wheels out his suitcase and says a polite goodbye to me. I'm unable to say anything nice to thaw the situation between us and so I just wave at him and coldly wish him best for his meetings. I know I said I was trying to overcome my pride and ego after my Art of Joy classes, but I have failed and I'm sorry to see myself lapse into my lesser self.

Later in the evening, I'm getting ready to leave for Sake House to see Nafisa and Sofie, who is sitting on a stool inside my closet, is watching me get ready.

'You look like Shakespeare's mother in that blouse,' she says, pointing at the lace detailing in the front of my silk top.

I pull out a pair of white high-waisted pants with a lovely yellow blouse next.

She rolls her eyes and says, 'You look like you are desperate to look young and cool.'

A crushing realisation strikes me once again that I'm no longer my older child's hero and have long been yanked down from the pedestal of perfection that she had once placed me on.

The desperate mamma fashion faux pas show is mercifully interrupted by a call from my father to his beloved eldest grandchild and I'm spared her scrutiny when I finally step out in distressed denim and a red shoulder top.

Nafisa is already at the bar by the time I get there. She is in a chic navy shirt-dress worn with Mary Jane styled heels and is presently engaged in a conversation with an attractive man in a suit. He gives her a peck on her cheek and takes her leave even before I have reached the bar smiling. 'No, he wasn't trying to pick me up. He is my friend Sheena's brother before that twisted mind of yours imagines things,' she tells me with a wicked grin.

'I said nothing. Why are you even clarifying?' I say.

'And I have carried this back for you from Moscow,' Nafisa says, as she hands over a duty-free bag containing Beluga caviar and vodka for me. Caviar isn't meat, and I eat all eggs without discrimination.

'Oh! Thanks, babe! One must always invest in friendships with people who come bearing fancy things,' I say, bending over to hug her.

'And here is your belated birthday present darling,' I hand her a lovely silk DVF dress I had bought for her in the US.

Nafisa loves the dress and hugs me tightly to thank me. 'I thought of you all the time in Moscow. It was such an amazing trip Nats,' she gushes. 'I'll tell you everything but first, let's order.' We pore over the menu and order skewered tofu for me and chicken teriyaki sliders for Nafisa.

The bartender places a small carafe of sake in front of us and we help ourselves to the ice-cold liquor.

Nafisa's tells me her trip was made fabulous not only by the beauty of the rich city of Moscow but also because of a flirtation with a celebrity chef from Australia who was all out to woo her. 'After my split with Parthiv I needed this,' she coos.

She goes on to rhapsodise about fashionable Muscovites as she pours more sake into my cup. Free of any responsibility and so fulfilled by her career, Nafisa is truly living the life. And how often she has tried to get me to work and yet...

Seeing that I'm somewhere else mentally, she asks me softly, 'Natasha, are you even listening to me?'

'Umm, yes I am. I was thinking about how badly I behaved the last time you spoke to me about work and that I don't understand why I do this. Varun is disappointed in me too.'

Nafisa hugged me again. 'I'm sure he isn't disappointed, Natasha, frustrated maybe. Look, if you are sincere about this, I'm willing to look for some meaningful work for you Natty. But you cannot flake out on me.'

'You will see a new Natasha, just try me.'

'And isn't the Rotary thing coming Sunday?' she asks. That is Nafisa for you, never one to forget things. 'So is an entourage coming with you to cheer for you?'

'It's just you and the kids,' I tell her, downing the last sip of my drink. I then tell her that I have no intention of asking Varun to the award ceremony. 'He doesn't think I'm doing too much with my life anyway. I don't want him sitting in the front row and sniggering at my trophy.'

'He means well Natasha, and like me, he thinks you are wasting your talents,' she says. 'Please be sensible about this.'

Not wanting to discuss my life any more, I ask her what she liked best about Russia. Nafisa tells me that it wasn't the caviar and vodka that she derived a high from, but a peek into the haute couture world of the Russian upper classes, the kind that stored their priceless furs in the walk-in fur refrigerators of their nine-bedroom, sixteen-car garage mansions.

'Really? Is that how fur should be stored?' I ask her picking up the last bit of tofu from my plate.

'Of course! It prolongs the life of the fur.'

'How did I not know this before? My only mink coat has been hanging inside the non-refrigerated wardrobe of our Bombay home for over four years!!' I say, panicking. My mother-in-law ordinarily wouldn't have given me a stray cat's pelt but she no longer fit into her mink and didn't want to look at something that reminded her of her expanding figure.

'You've been hanging mink?' Nafisa says, palpably shocked. 'Why would you be so cruel? You have to keep it on a flat surface in a cold room. The same way that you would keep an Alaskan Husky or a polar bear in a temperature-controlled room when you to take them away from their habitat.'

I'm certain that PETA representatives would get apoplectic if they were to hear this conversation and don't get me wrong, I don't at all believe in animals dying for our pleasure, but I try to tell myself that it's not like I bought it – the sacrifice was made decades ago for my mother-in-law.

Straight after dinner, I dash home from the restaurant to rescue my poor wilting fur from the unremitting moisture of my non-refrigerated wardrobe. Extracting it from the depths of the wardrobe, I lay it down on Varun's side of the bed. That night I reach out and stroke the plushy depths of my coat, lying in his place, only just stopping myself from telling it that we should stop fighting and go to Gulmarg together.

Chapter 11

When and how does one talk about homosexuality to children? It's important to make it a part of normal conversation and talk about it in such a manner that children receive a tolerant message from their parents and do not develop gender-variant bigotry as they grow older. I recently overheard an older child teasing her younger brother and calling him gay, thereby reducing the word to a semi-abusive adjective. Like religious tolerance, gender tolerance too should be inculcated in children from a very young age.

With most of our schools still waiting for children to glean sex education from the birds, bees and YouTube, it's up to us parents to sit our children down at an appropriate age and address everything that falls under the umbrella of sex education.

'Mamma, is Sumer gay?'

I'm having breakfast with my youngest child, Ria who is resting at home today after waking up with a stuffy nose.

'Where did you hear that word, Riu?' I ask her.

'Mamma, Sofie was teasing Sumer and he started crying, so she said, "Boys that cry are gay, boys that cry are gay",' she says, imitating Sofie. 'Then Sumer cried more and more.'

Ria is too little to be spoken to about homosexuality, but I don't want her picking up wrong ideas from her elder sister, like using 'gay' as a term to ridicule someone.

'When a boy wants to marry another boy, that is called gay,' I tell her.

She seemed a little confused, but thankfully her curiosity is quelled for the time being. 'Does Sumer want to marry a boy Mummy?' she asks innocently. 'I don't think so Ria. He is young like you. It's too early to think of marriage,' I say casually.

Fortunately, my mother calls me just as I'm looking for a chance to end this conversation. With curious children, there is no telling how long the whys can go on for. I answer her call, and with Ria jabbering away in the backdrop, my mother and I chit chat about her shopping at the Dastakar Mela and my Manali trip.

'Why is Ria at home? And what is my chatterbox saying in the backdrop?' Mummy wants to know.

I tell her about Ria's cold and also fill her in on her conversation with me minutes before her call.

'You cannot be talking to your children about gay and all,' she says disconcerted.

'Mummy, gay isn't a bad word. What is wrong with you? Homosexuality is normal.'

'Please, it may be normal for your generation but by talking about these things to children you are planting ideas into their heads,' says my mother, her voice becoming shrill.

'Gay doesn't happen as an idea that is planted Mummy. don't talk like Baba Ramdev!'

'Anyway, you don't try to teach me. I'm also modern, but there have to be limits,' Mummy barrels on. 'Mummy,' I say exasperated. 'Even our Supreme Court approves of it now, but you don't. At least don't say these things out loud.'

My mother is silent for a few seconds but not necessarily convinced. 'What does Varun have to say about talking about all this to the children?' she asks sternly.

'Varun is in Kashmir. What will he say?' I say in a voice that makes my dismay immediately apparent to my mother.

'And you did not go? You were saying to me just a few months ago that you want to go to Kashmir,' mother has sniffed trouble.

'No, I did not because he did not ask me to,' I blurt out.

Well, the truth is that two days have passed since Varun and I had a proper conversation. He did go away to Kashmir finally and he sent me a message to tell me that. But he hasn't called me since.

'I'm sure you are fighting with him Natasha,' I hear Mummy say to me from the other end of the line. 'Women who fight too much with their husbands push them into the arms of other women, I can tell you that.'

Great! Now all I need to add to my present troubles is to start worrying about another woman! I'm tempted to interrupt my mother's homily about men and marriage and ask whose arms my beloved father is seeking comfort in after all her quibbling about his post-retirement hobbies, but I let it slide.

For the rest of the day, I let my mother's words play havoc with my imagination. I wonder if Varun feels any romantic love for me. I am his family yes but what if he doesn't feel the same way as he did before? I dismiss the thought as ridiculous. He only sent me those flowers a few days ago, he would not do that if he still didn't love me. But people can put on an act, can't they, like Nakul and Trisha have been doing all these years?

Not to mention the industrialist Vikram and his wife Alka Sethia. Vikram is supposedly gay, and even though the couple does some religious and spiritual things together, they lead separate lives in Mumbai.

There is also the megastar Dilsher and his stunning wife Surveen Khan who put up a great act of being in love but everyone knows that Dilsher keeps a very young and very luscious mistress Simran Singh, in a swanky flat two buildings away from mine.

Disturbing thoughts about men, infidelity and the fate of women play on my mind in bed that night.

In the morning, I receive news from my yoga gang that that Lothario of a yogacharya has been relieved of his duties at the Art of Joy. The salacious murmurs have died a natural death and normalcy has unfortunately been resumed. Kiki now lives with her mother and yogacharya has gone back to his wife with his tail, and a crucial body part tucked neatly between his legs. She will ensure he is stuck in the corpse pose for the rest of his life if he so much as looks at a woman, to say nothing of imparting yoga classes for them.

In a hyperbolic display of machismo, Kiki's vile husband has bought the most expensive sea-facing penthouse in Bandstand and hired a publicist to leak the news to the media. It has been reported in several papers that his purchase has rocked the real estate market in Mumbai because never has a flat been sold at such an exorbitant price. Perhaps this is a sophisticated matrimonial ad to the world, for we do know that in a city like Bombay, the size of a man's apartment matters more than any other attribute (physical or otherwise) when it comes to attracting a worthy mate.

With all this happening around me, sometimes I wonder if Varun too has this secret other life that I know nothing about, a family hidden somewhere, for instance, or sex on exotic beaches with unknown women? Scary visuals of him lying on the sand with voluptuous, sun-kissed Nordic beauties flood my mind and send shivers up my spine. Maybe there is a kernel of truth in what my mother said today, and I should strive to make Varun's life pleasant unless I want him to go to those exotic beaches with exotic women.

After doing some asanas on the terrace by myself, I send Varun a message to prevent him from running into some Kashmiri beauty's arms. 'All well? When are you back?'

He replies three hours later. Three full hours later! I should not have bothered writing to him at all. He can find another woman for all I care!

'Shiven has agreed to give us the hotel. Back on Sunday.'

Brevity may well be the soul of wit but it can be the Waterloo of a relationship.

If Varun wants to have be aloof and have a measured conversation with me, so be it. I may be heartbroken, but I am fully capable of giving him a taste of his own coldness once he returns. He can sleep with the dogs in our room, I am going to move in with the kids after Sunday.

❖ ❖ ❖

It's Sunday morning and also the day of the Rotary event. Nafisa is more excited about my award than I am. She pulls me up for dressing too simply for the occasion - I'm wearing a yellow silk top with white chikan embroidery and white linen pants with wedges. She's herself dressed in a beautiful pink cotton wrap dress with cut-work. 'What is wrong with you? I will not allow you to go on stage like this. Let's please go to the washroom and swap dresses,' she says the minute she sees me in the hotel lobby. 'Writers are always simply dressed, I want to be taken seriously. So no, thank you,' I tell her. Sofie and she both roll their eyes at me jointly and we all walk towards the banquet room downstairs.

Next, a saree-clad Rotarian leads me up onto the stage to place me next to the other three awardees at the Trident Hotel, all of whom are famous, well-accomplished people, which brings me to wonder how I made it to the list. The hall is packed with people. My heart sinks as I hear one awardee after another give impressive speeches, for I have come absolutely unprepared for this eventuality. I finish the entire bottle of water kept on the table in front of me out of nervousness by the time my name is announced, my anxiety only compounded by a full bladder.

'I wasn't aware that I was supposed to take up the audience's air time today and so I shall keep this brief, because mostly I'm insufferable behind the mic. Thank you for honouring me with this award and for all the good work that you as Rotarians are doing for society when most of us are merely bothered about earning more money and going to the gym.'

I watch Nafisa and my three stooges beam at me from the audience.

'I haven't been doing much with my life except raising my three children, and we know that this is something even cats and pigeons do. So it doesn't exactly count as a laudable personal contribution to the world.

'Of course, my husband, who is always encouraging me to go back to working full-time, thinks that I'm dividing my day between receiving shiatsu massages and shopping online…Sometimes I feel my dogs too would show me more respect if I disappeared from 9 am to 5 pm every day. Then to be standing here in such good company and receiving this award from the honourable governor feels reassuring.'

Everyone in the audience claps louder than I had expected and then I spot him. I see Varun, standing, right at the back, and clapping.

I can hardly believe my eyes. Did I have to make all those jokes about him? When did he get here? I return to my chair at the centre of the stage with mixed feelings as I process everything.

When I step down from the stage there is a lot of commotion with people shuffling about. Varun walks towards me, a big dimpled grin on his handsome face, and offers me his hand. I place my hand in his and he squeezes it before pulling me in his embrace. 'I love you baby,' he whispers in my ear. 'You came,' I say choking. 'How could I not be there?' he says softly.

Over lunch at Frangipani, the coffee shop at the hotel, I learn that Sofie and Varun had been in touch all along about the date and time of the event. Arriving at the venue before us, he sat unobtrusively at the back, biding his time to spring the surprise at me. Varun runs his fingers through his thick hair, looks sideways and grins when I tell him I love him in front of everybody. I haven't felt this happy in a long, long while.

Early next morning Sofie wakes me up with stomach cramps. We realise a little later that she has got her first period! My baby got a period! This is a biological landmark in a woman's life no doubt, but it's a cause of much distress to a mother like me who cannot accept that her children are growing up so quickly. Sofie is writhing with abdominal cramps and just as he is leaving for school, I find that Sumer too is burning up with fever. On days like these, I'm especially happy not to be working. How else would I take care of my children?

Seeing her in pain, Varun is feeling sorry for Sofie. He sits by her bed, stroking her forehead lovingly before getting ready for work while I attend to Sumer.

When Trisha rings me at noon asking me to lunch I tell her I'm nursing two sickly kids.

'I'm coming to see you right away then,' she hangs up without waiting for me to say anything else.

It takes her about an hour to show up, but when she does walk in through my door, she has more than a few shopping bags. There is one from Desiree containing Sofie's favourite chocolate cake, and a large box of steamed momos from The Dim Sum Place for all of us. She has also found the time to pick up a Lego for Sumer and a small box of Lego friends for Ria, even though she isn't home from school yet. The bag that stands out the most though is not for us. It's a tangerine Hermès shopping bag. It has to be a gift from Guneet and she has brought it along to show-off to me about.

Trisha's splurging on my children is nothing unusual – she has always been the adoring Aunt Santa to them.

Much hugging, kissing and thanking takes place when Sofie meets Trisha Maasi and then we both go inside my room for a chit chat.

'Are you okay? I mean about Sofie getting her period,' she asks me, looking genuinely concerned. I can hardly focus on her words any more, distracted as I'm by the bright orange bag still dangling from her arm. I'm dying to find out what's in it but I can't possibly ask. And so, I sit her down and relive my trauma of finding out that my little girl has come of age.

'It was a little unsettling, Trish. She has grown up so fast. I felt a huge pang when she told me.'

'I know what you mean. Sofia is like my baby too. I'm feeling the pang myself,' Trisha says, placing her hand over her solar plexus to indicate the location of her pang. I'm moved by the consistency of her love for Sofie. I feel sorry for all the times I've been harsh with her.

'What's in that bag, Trish?' I have to know, it's beyond my control now.

'This is the reason I rang you in the first place. This is from Guneet.'

'Of course, it is,' I mutter under my breath.

'For you,' she says, handing it over.

'Me? Wha…? But why me?' I say, surprised.

'Guneet adores you Nats,' she says.

'Really? But why?' I ask nervously. You know you're doing something wrong if the person sleeping with your friend's wife on the sly is *this* fond of you.

'Read the note in the bag,' Trisha says.

I open the bag and find an envelope with a monogrammed card inside, monogrammed with the name Guneet Sodhi.

Dear Natasha,

You have been wonderful. I did not know how else to thank you for being there for us. Here is a small token for you for being such an amazing person.

Love,

G.

Inside the bag are two boxes. I untie the ribbon on the bigger, flatter one to find a gorgeous silk crimson coloured scarf with four cheetahs printed in the centre. The card accompanying the scarf, among other things, states that it's a limited-edition scarf. The other box has a beautiful, brick red Hermès wallet in it.

I admit I'm overwhelmed by the warmth with which these gifts have been lavished on me. I can't accept such expensive gifts from the illicit lover of my friend even if it's a limited edition.

'I cannot accept this Trisha, it's too much.'

'Don't hurt his feelings, just keep it. He is very moved by the fact that you don't judge him. He understands that it cannot be easy for you, Natasha. And yet you have covered up for me so many times without being difficult about it. He wanted to take you out to dinner, but we know you wouldn't do that. He had no other way...' she trails off.

'Well' I say, running a finger over the butter-soft leather of the wallet, 'I don't want to hurt anyone's feelings.'

God, I'm awful.

After Trisha leaves, I quickly hide the Hermès bag under my bed. I don't need Varun finding it in our walk-in closet anytime soon.

Chapter 12

Do we live to satisfy ourselves or are we living to impress other people? This is a question that I have often asked myself. I think it is a little bit of both. One does seek validation from others, be it in the way one dresses, travels or entertains. But sometimes it has the opposite effect. A well-known industrialist, known for the 'good times' he lavished upon his many friends is now being lampooned for his extravagant lifestyle and over-the-top parties. Today, he lives the life of a fugitive on an island far away, forgotten all too quickly by the people who were at the very top of his guest list. This makes one wonder if one should spend any time or money impressing people at all...

It's finally December, and I feel like I'm in a Frank Sinatra movie. I want to sing all the time. Winter is my favourite time of year when the air seems rife with possibilities, and everybody is in good cheer. Christmas, frosty winter mornings (in other parts of the world), Varun's birthday... there is much to celebrate this month.

I'm dashing off to meet the florist to work out the party decor and then Trisha and I have a meeting with the caterer to sample the menu. What was going to be a modest get-together has burgeoned into a big bash, and I hope I will be able to put it all together in time. This is typical of my husband, who will not share a fixed guest list with me when I ask for one and will keep adding new names to the invitee list with abandon with each passing day. I don't even know some of the people we are inviting and at this rate, our party will resemble a wedding.

'Nobody is doing regular orchids or carnations these days. We are only doing hybrid orchids, anthuriums, hydrangeas and other exotic flowers,' Saba, my florist, tells me while taking me through her portfolio of various party arrangements on an iPad.

Surrounding me inside her store is a forest of peonies, roses, chrysanthemums blooms and I want to suddenly make this evening unforgettable for everybody.

'My suggestion is that you go with the trend and do a white and blush or coral pink theme,' Saba says. 'Something like what Gauri Khan did for her party last year.'

I see on the iPad before me photos of staggeringly high arrangements in white orchids and peach roses towering over the tables lit with candlelight within the high-walled precincts of the star wife's house.

'Look Saba, I want the décor to look stunning but this isn't the Chelsea flower show. So let's get a little more creative with the décor and not rely only on the flowers. And I like the ashes of roses colour. Can you find me those? Or peonies in icy pink and massive white orchids?'

'We could try – December is a good time to source flowers,' she says. 'I will give you other things too, like lanterns and lamps, but everyone really does prefer over-the-top flower arrangements and it looks very good. Look here, this is the Poonawala's anniversary bash. We created this entire canopy with white roses right from the entrance of the house till their gardens.'

I picture my own guests walking under a canopy of roses and carnations and I can already sense just how utterly magical and exciting it's all going to be.

'Alright. I'm in. So what amount should I budget for this?'

'Hydrangeas are Rs 550 a stem, exotic orchids Rs 1450 a stalk, roses, anthuriums will be used too. They are local flowers. So they are all within Rs 100 a stem, but that ash pink colour, that will cost more…so I think if you budget for about Rs 12-14 lakhs for a space like yours, you'll be able to get the look you want.'

'154 lakhs? For party flowers?' I gasp, nearly falling off my chair. This is crazy. If I spend so much on the flowers alone, what will I feed my guests, grass?

'We could do it with cheaper flowers too,' Saba suggests. 'But then you won't get the look and feel you want,' she says as she fiddles with her mobile phone.

I mull over this as I sip my coffee inside her freezing office and against my better judgement, I find myself confirming the décor. After going through her slide show of the most atmospheric parties of the city, I cannot throw an ordinary carnations and roses affair, can I?

Moreover, I'm saving all that money by not having the party at a hotel. We have not had a big bash in years, so I must do this well or not do it at all.

'But keep it under seven, eight lakhs, please. If you overshoot, you pay,' I warn Saba.

Her enthusiasm suddenly disappears and the expression on her face turns somewhat cold.

'So no table décor then either?' she asks as I get up to leave.

'Oh, I hadn't thought about that. What do you suggest?'

'I was going to suggest a lot of crystal candle stands of varying heights with white candles and a low arrangement of flowers along with that. I could work out a cost for you depending on the number of tables,' she says in a patronising voice.

When my mother rings me for chit-chat, I tell her that I'm busy planning the party and that naturally Dad and she are expected to fly down for it because Varun has already asked his mother to do so. Mummy says she will confirm after discussing with Dad.

When I speak to Trisha about the cost of flowers later, she says I must go all out with the décor because that is what can make or break a party. 'Just give a blanket budget to Varun and tell him prices of things have gone up and a good party cannot be had on the cheap.'

I will have to find my husband in a good mood later this evening, perhaps when we are driving to Worli for a boring venture capitalist's dinner party that we are to attend at the Four Seasons. I'll just find a way to slip it in casually. 'Varun, the party is going a bit over budget.' Or maybe, 'Oh, it's going to be an amazing party. The flowers and the table décor are costing a lot but Varun you'll just love the look.'

In the evening, my hair is tied up in rollers, and I'm lounging on my bed in my jammies chatting with Varun who is sipping his protein shake on the couch near the window.

Ria comes barging into our room just as Varun is telling me that the Kashmir project might be delayed. 'I'm hiding under your bed, don't tell Sumer,' Ria cautions us in a loud whisper before disappearing under the bed.

Seconds later, Sumer pushes the door open and walks into our room. 'Is she here?'

'Who? Sofie?' Varun asks.

'No, papa, Ria.'

'No, she isn't here at all.'

Unconvinced, Sumer looks under the bed, and we hear Ria giggle. 'Ha, found you. You are so stupid, you cannot think of new places to hide,' he says as Ria emerges from under the bed dragging along my orange Hermès shopping bag along with her.

'Look, what I found, look!' she says to her father and me as if she has harpooned some lost treasure out of the bottom of the ocean.

'Riu, put that away,' I say, reaching for the bag.

'No, no, no I want to see,' she says, moving towards her father.

Before I can react further, the wilful brat reaches for the flat box inside the bag and is about to open it when I roar, 'You will not open the box, Ria.' Ria looks at me stunned and then flings the bag on the floor angrily. 'Why you shouted at me,' she says, curling her lower lip and leaving my room in faux tears.

'You need not have scolded her like that,' Varun says, getting up from his chair to follow Ria to the other room.

'Varun, she does drama whenever you are around. I'm only teaching her manners,' I offer. I want to slap myself for overreacting. Why can I never be calm, composed and collected like some other women I don't know?

'What is in this bag anyway?' Varun asks, picking up the bag from the floor. 'May I look at it, or will you shout at me too?'

'Oh, it's just a gift from someone I had helped,' I say, doing my best to sound casual even though I have butterflies in my stomach. Even with the AC on, I feel I'm going to break into a sweat.

Varun looks inside the boxes with vague interest and he shuts them and puts them back into the bag carefully while I hold my breath and cast my mind through the various options of what Varun could ask.

He then carefully pulls out the card, the damned card with Guneet's name embossed on it.

'Who is this Guneet? And why is he thanking you?' he asks.

'Oh, just someone who funds an NGO, a friend's husband actually, and he had asked me to write the brochures for the NGO for free,' I say. 'So this is their way of thanking me.'

'Oh, so you don't mind writing brochures after all!' he says a little sarcastically. 'Surely the cost of Hermès is more than the fees he would have paid you for writing them,' he adds arching an eyebrow at me like his mother.

'I felt the same,' I say. 'And that is why I had shoved it under the bed, so nobody opens it before I send it back to him. I don't want to accept gifts for doing social work. I'm not that low, Varun! And I'm a socially responsible person. I will never say no to NGO work, but it's different from writing brochures for a career, right?'

Satisfied with my answer, he gives a half smile as he drops the envelope back in the bag and places it on the bed. 'Anyway, let me go and check on Ria. Can you get ready in the meanwhile?

I feel a sense of relief explode through my body when I see him leave the room.

* * *

The preparations for Varun's birthday are in full swing as is my diet. I'm trying out intermittent fasting that all celebrities are swearing by these days. I'm to drink lemon water all day, have a minuscule meal in the day and one meal at night. Too much fluid and too little solid is making me feel drained, but it will all be worth it when I drop a size and look fabulous on the day of the party. On another slightly depressing note, however, I have spotted some stark grey hairs today that has left me deeply disturbed. I'm not prepared to grow old just yet. Why have these strands turned grey overnight? Trisha has a secret lover and still has a head full of beautiful black hair. I'm leading an uninspired, hermit-like existence and mine has begun to turn grey. The unfairness of life has thus been demonstrated.

As with everything else, Varun finds my obsession with my hair amusing. 'Face it, we all have to grow older,' he says.

He has a few greys too, this man. But those streaks make him appear only more regal and handsome in a George Clooney sort of a way. If I go grey I will most likely look like Lalu Prasad Yadav with long hair, and that isn't something that I look forward to.

Later, as I'm lying in bed and flipping through TV channels, I realise that the universe is waiting for a chance to confirm the theory about men ageing better than women. Sitting on a couch across from the anchor Priya Thapar in a powder blue shirt and denim is Riyad Siddiqui. I'm suddenly reminded of that mortifying episode with him from the party, and I flinch at the memory of it. But I tell myself that he doesn't know me and so it does not matter. The camera zooms into Riyad's face, and I notice his distinct cheekbones, angular jaw, pale skin, the spikes of silver in his hair and I realise, not for the first time, that he is a disturbingly handsome man.

'Should we all be feminists?' the super at the bottom of the screen states. 'It's a much-misunderstood word. There are generations of brainwashing that have gone on in India, which is why my last films were women-oriented. My protagonists don't just react to men, they have opinions of their own,' he is saying.

Watching him like that, I feel myself swoon, although this may well be the result of my liquid diet.

'Don't get carried away. He is just making the right noises. It's posturing, that's all.' Nafisa, the killjoy, texts me when I send her a gushy message asking her to watch the show.

Varun rings me just when I'm mooning over another man to give me some more names for our ever-expanding guest list, which is looking like the Mumbai yellow pages now.

Short of calling our dry cleaner and the milkmen from Pride of Cows dairy, we have invited almost everybody we know. We already have about 250 people on our constantly expanding list. When throwing a bash this size, though, there is much joy in inviting people you like; there is, even more, joy in leaving some people out, particularly the ones who have been less than kind to you.

'You are just being petty,' Varun tells me when I struck off some names from the proposed list two weeks ago. I can live with being called petty, but I'm too old to be polite and invite people who we have never exchanged more than a passing hello with.

However, I have decided to surprise Varun by asking his Doon School friends to our party – some of whom are flying in from Delhi, especially for the big do. I know that nothing will make him happier than having his childhood friends around on his special day.

Realising that the next three days will be spent making RSVP calls in between my facial, hair and acupuncture appointments, I make a dash for my kick-boxing class. Doing vigorous exercise on an empty stomach isn't for the faint-hearted, but like Arjuna from the Mahabharata, I'm only focusing on the end goal, which is to look good for my party. Every time I feel a little dizzy in between all the punching, I drink some lemonade with activated carbon and jaggery that I have bought an entire pack of from Food Hall. Varun will just fall madly in love with me when he sees me looking so fit and toned in my gorgeous blue dress.

'None of the musicians you had wanted are available on our dates, but I've found another fantastic band for the party,' Trisha calls me just as I'm returning from the class. 'They're called The One Empire. I heard them play in Goa when I had gone for Alka's anniversary. I just spoke to their manager, and they're free on the 18th.'

'Thank you, Trish, that's awfully sweet of you,' I say. She's been a huge help and God knows I already have enough on my plate.

I tell her how horrifyingly long the guest list has got and how I had planned something so much smaller but now that we're inviting everyone, there's no point doing it by halves. I say it hoping for a little sympathy but what she says instead leaves me incredulous. 'You are calling so many people. Can you not extend an invitation to Guneet for your party as well?'

'Don't be ridiculous, Trisha!' I say, writing it off, unable to believe she ever suggested such a thing.

'Nats, no one will know – you've called the whole world. Guneet could be anybody,' she says insouciantly.

'You know I can't even consider this. Anyway, I have just reached home, and the florist is sitting here waiting for me. I will ring you after I have done the food tasting. Send me the band manager's number please,' I say before disconnecting the call, flustered. Invite Guneet indeed! I'm pleased that I managed to be uncharacteristically firm. There will be no talk of this in the future.

One look at Saba's new cost estimate and I can feel an angina pain coming on but it is what it is and I'll deal with Varun later. 'What's coming will come and we will meet it when it does,' to quote JK Rowling.

I then take her downstairs to inspect our lawn with me to help her visualise the set-up. To my horror, I find that the gardener hasn't even trimmed my palms, a patch of our grass needs mowing and the ficus trees also need pruning. I summon the slothful man and am just about to have a word with him when Trisha rings again. 'Please Nats, there are going to be too many people. Nobody will even realise that he is there. Let Guneet come, he will be in town anyway on work on the weekend of the party.'

'Trisha, stop harassing me. He can't come and that's that! And exactly what am I supposed to tell Varun when he asks who this friend is whom he's never clapped eyes on before?'

'There will be 300 people there – it's like a wedding. Even if Varun does run into him, you can always say he tagged along with someone else.'

'Look, I have twenty things to attend to right now. I'm sorry I just can't deal with this…I haven't the bandwidth to go on arguing with you.'.

'Sorry Nats. Is there anything I can help you with? Do you want me to negotiate with the band manager?' she asks weakly.

'That would be nice, could you please do that for me?'

When I come back inside the house, I find out that Chester has been throwing up all over my room. Sylvia tells me he hasn't eaten a thing since morning. I call up the vet and ask him to have the dog checked right away.

Finally, with my poor sick dog out of the house, I'm just settling into my couch with a cup of coffee when Trisha rings again.

You can fault Trisha for many things, but you have to give her credit for her perseverance.

'I spoke to the manager. He will do the gig for you at 1.75 lakhs. His usual rate is three. Now can I please invite Guneet?'

I'm tired down to the bone, and I have lost my will to argue. 'Alright Trisha,' I snap. 'Have your way. But I don't want you to be seen with him nor can you expect more from me. I will pretend I don't know him at all.'

***

My voice is hoarse from making personal calls to people about the party. This morning I discover that I'm croaking while wishing Varun a happy birthday in my lacy nightie that I wore specially for him last night. 'Oh look, I found my frog princess,' he teases me as he pulls me closer.

After a short nap post lunch, I head to the lawns to ensure things are moving as per plan. My parents have just arrived, which is lovely. Varun's mother will be following shortly, which is not so lovely.

The decorator has been at work since yesterday, and the florist's truck full of hydrangeas, lilies and other assorted blooms has just arrived. I'm slightly concerned that my choice of flowers is more suitable to Barbara Cartland's ninety-ninth than Varun's fortieth. After all the trouble that I have taken I just hope all my guests do turn up.

Sumer has been walking around the house inspecting all the arrangements and is now sitting on his little cycle watching the florists at work.

All the people in this world who matter to us are going to be present in our house. I'm so ecstatic that I might not even need champagne tonight.

I can hardly wait to get into my dress but the make-up lady is taking forever to finish doing up my face. My hair is tied up in a messy do, leaving enough space to show off my new, adequately bony shoulders. When I finally look at my reflection in my stunning gold heels, I cannot believe how good I'm looking.

'Happy birthday to me,' Varun says when he sees me come down the stairs into the drawing room. Varun is looking dashing in a fitted white shirt with rolled-up sleeves, a deep blue velvet bundi jacket with a yellow pocket scarf that he is wearing over white breeches and longwing brogues. 'Nice?' I ask him. 'Spectacular,' he says. 'You're not looking too bad yourself,' I tell him.

I'm hoping to have a warm-up drink with him before the guests start trickling in but Varun, who hasn't so much as looked at the party plans up until now, starts asking me about housekeeping matters. 'I hope there is enough champagne? And what vodka are you serving?'

'Do you have Belvedere or Grey Goose?'

'Can I speak to the man in charge of the bar?'

'Are there enough air conditioners under the marquee? It can get stuffy very quickly even though it's cool outside.'

'Wine glasses? Natasha, I hope they are not using those cheap glasses to serve wine. Please use decent wine. Don't serve Yellowtail.'

Men can be so annoying! I feel like strangling Varun, but I answer all his questions one by one, controlling my urge to snap at him only because it's his birthday.

'Varun, can we both have a drink now, please? It's too late anyway to look into the party arrangements,' I suggest, picking up a glass of champagne and handing it over to him.

As promised, Nafisa is the first one to arrive in a beautiful red low-cut cocktail dress that flatters her curvy figure. She has brought along Kaizad, the photographer, as a date for the evening. She introduces him to Varun and hands over his birthday gift to him that he feels awkward accepting. 'Come on now, just take it Varun. You can give me a better present for my birthday if you are feeling awkward,' she chuckles.

'The setting is looking bee-u-ti-ful,' Nafisa trills, 'especially the flowers and that canopy…I could be in Florence right now. The colours are so summer-in-Italy,' Nafisa says, looking around.

The four of us sit around on the bar stools and sip our drinks. My parents, mother-in-law and Bela Aunty, Nakul's mother, are sitting upstairs, discussing politics in all probability over their first drinks.

The drawing room opens into the garden and is lit up and fragrant with Jo Malone candles. From where I'm sitting, I can see the DJ setting up his console inside near the corner where we usually have guests dancing, the saxophonist from the band has started playing Stairway to the Stars in the meanwhile.

I'm expecting the crowd to float in and out between the marquee in the lawn and the drawing room, except when the band is playing. On the bar, outside, white-gloved waiters are wiping champagne flutes that are being laid out on silver trays, and in the far corner, the extra hands from the band are plugging in the instruments for the performance.

Flowers in shades of burnt pink, coral and green adorn the tables, the diaphanous white drapes of the marquee, the moonlight night outside – this is going to be an evening to remember.

Trisha and Nakul finally arrive, a Tom Ford shopping bag in hand. Trisha is doing her usual mutton dressed as lamb routine in a short, one-shoulder Halston Heritage dress in gold with Rene' Caovilla rhinestone heels. Only she would wear something that short to a party!

Not that she does not look gorgeous, she always does, even if inappropriately dressed. I notice her flat stomach with a stab of envy. Ever since she embarked on her love affair with the chest expander Guneet, she has rediscovered a passion for fitness. She works out every day now and it's showing.

We all pay compliments to each other and then the ladies pose for pictures for the party photographer who insists we allow him to click some photos of just Varun and me before all the other guests start arriving.

Minutes later, the marquee is full of people, there is champagne flowing, music filling the air along with sounds of conversations and laughter. I have managed to put together an incredibly charming evening, even if I have to say so myself.

***

After all that champagne from last night, my head feels like the Gaza strip this morning, and for some time I'm not even sure if I'm in my present life or the afterlife. All doubts about my dimensional crisis are clarified when Sumer comes bouncing into my bed with his toy truck, and Ria comes chasing after him seconds later to inform me that her nani has asked her to check on me. 'Daddy is not helping me with my Lego. He came to my room and said he would play with me, but he is sleeping on my bed now,' Sumer complains as I lie there, struggling to open my eyes. And then like a bolt of lightning, a surge of memories from last night strikes me. I feel a hollow in the pit of my stomach suddenly, like a whirlpool sucking in the rest of my body with it. Varun's angry face, the satisfaction on Maa's face and the horror on Bela Aunty's, Trisha swaying...one by one, the images swirl in my head.

I should not have given in and allowed her to invite Guneet. Trisha is not in her senses any longer, but when did I lose my mind?

It was a delightful evening, and we were all having a perfectly wonderful time when I noticed Guneet's face in the crowd. I remember seeing him speak to one of Varun's banker friends and feeling relieved that he knew someone other than Trisha in the crowd. Later, I was dancing on the floor inside with Varun's friend Anil Kapoor from Delhi when Varun excused himself and taking me by my hand led me up the stairs. I was giggling away, certain that he was taking me away to give me a surprise, a present perhaps. I did notice that he was squeezing my arm tight and practically dragging me, but I was so happy with the bubbly working through my veins that I didn't pay much attention to it.

When we reached upstairs, he walked me to the den where Bela Aunty and my mother-in-law were already engaged in an animated conversation. Seeing us enter, they stopped discussing whatever it was that they were talking about and looked in my direction with cold hostility. Varun had let go of my arm by then, and my flesh was still stinging from where he had held it fiercely seconds ago.

As it is, my stilettos were killing me, and when I saw the scary ladies look at me murderously, I had to grab the study table to steady myself.

'Maa, show her what you saw,' Varun demanded.

My mother-in-law walked up to me and handed me her phone coldly.

I nearly had a heart attack and had to steady myself when I looked at the screen, for there was in front of my eyes a shaky video of Trisha and Guneet kissing each other passionately inside our dimly lit study, playing right in front of my eyes.

The kiss went on for nearly a minute with Guneet running his hands hungrily over Trisha's breasts as he went about exploring her mouth. Undoubtedly the video had been filmed by my devious mother-in-law who seemed to have had shot it carefully from the corner of the room.

'May I know who this man is?' Varun demanded fiercely.

'I don't know Varun. I have never seen him before,' I said, unable to meet his eyes.

Bela Aunty and my mother-in-law in the meanwhile were putting their peepers to good use by boring imaginary holes through my body with them.

'Are you quite sure you don't know who he is? What is he doing at our party if neither you nor I know him?'

'Varun, there are plenty of people downstairs I haven't seen before – I assumed they were your work associates or friends. Maybe he has tagged along with one of them?' I said in an exasperated voice.

'Anyway, Natasha, we don't know what the truth is, and poor Bela has to live to see this day. We have to tell Nakul about it, but we wanted clarity from you before we speak to him,' Maa said icily.

One day, when she is old, and her bones are creaking, and her memory is playing truant, I will leave her outside the gate of St Catherine's Home for the aged in Nasik, and no one will ever find out what happened to her.

'When did this happen though?' I asked Varun, presenting my most innocent and wide-eyed expression even as my throat felt parched and my legs weak. He stared at me with a clenched jaw, his arms folded against his chest. He took a deep breath and closed his eyes and then said, 'Maa will tell you the rest. I need to go downstairs and look after the guests.'

'But why the hell are you all mad at me? What have I done? I mean, that's not me in the video. Why am I being made answerable for what Trisha is doing?' I screamed, addressing everyone in the room.

Varun was somehow convinced I had a role in Trisha's story and stormed out of the study.

'When did this happen though and how did you get the video?' I looked at Maa and asked.

'I shot this video from the side of the sofa, crouching on my knees as you can probably tell. The band was playing some lovely old Abba songs, and I wanted to shoot a video. I could not find my phone in my purse, so I came inside and told your staff to find it, but they couldn't. Then I remembered I might have left it in the study because this is where we were sitting and having our drinks with your parents before the party started. Now your servants are honest I'm sure, but my phone is new, and these days you cannot trust anybody, so I came upstairs quickly to look for it myself.'

My throat was feeling like emery paper by now, and I needed a quick drink of water but there was none around and parched as I was, I did not have the strength to walk to the kitchen for it.

For a minute, I thought I might just pass out. Unable to stand in my heels much longer, I took my shoes off and sat down on the sofa. It wasn't easy to sit there and listen to my mother-in-law's theatrical and somewhat boastful account of her espionage with my heart racing and my head pounding like it was.

'I found it on the side of the sofa finally, and what do you think I saw when I bent down to pick it up? I saw your shameless friend walking inside the room and grab that man. It was disgusting. I had to film it, or she would have called me a liar later.'

Even imagining a scene like that was sending chills up my spine. Of all the ways to get found out, this one had to be the worst. 'That is terrible! I can't believe this has happened. Poor Nakul,' I said with tears in my eyes. I wasn't acting, I was terrified – for Nakul, for Trisha and for myself.

And then, I panicked that Varun might find out that I know Guneet and that my lie would come to light. Leaving the two women in the study, I jumped up from the sofa and forced my feet into my stilettoes. 'People will notice I'm missing. I should go back,' I said as I rushed downstairs. I had to find Trisha and drop the bomb on her.

Once in the garden, I saw that dinner had already been served, but the revelry was continuing inside where people were dancing away to the DJ's beats. Outside too, there were people sitting around in groups, chatting, drinking, laughing. Kaizad and Nafisa walked hurriedly towards me and asked me if I was feeling well. 'We were looking for you

everywhere. Is anything the matter? You look pale Nats,'
Nafisa said.

Not wanting to go over the details of the soup I had
landed myself in, I assured Nafisa that I was well but
overwrought because of some confusion. 'I will tell you
everything later. Right now, I need to find Trisha.'

Nafisa looked perturbed. 'Listen, let me get you some
water,' she offered.

'Not now, later please,' I said and leaving Nafisa and
Kaizad behind, I made my way through the guests to find
the wretched Trisha.

I had barely walked a few steps when I was interrupted
by the last person I wanted to meet at that point, Ananya.

'Natasha, I was looking for you. Where did you
disappear?' she put an arm around me and asked.

'Oh, I was just around,' I said trying to seem as unruffled
as I could.

'Come, have a drink with me,' offered Ananya.

'No, no, I think I have had quite enough for the night.'

'No darling, I think the one who has had quite enough
tonight is our Trisha. Just look at her,' she said, pointing in
Trisha's direction at the far end of the marquee. And there
she was swaying her perky butt to the strains of Arianna
Grande's latest track all by herself, blissfully unaware of
what her folly was about to cost us.

'I must go and ask her to slow down,' I said, removing
myself from Ananya's arm and moving quickly towards
Trisha. I could feel Varun's eyes on me. He was at the bar
and speaking to Ananya's husband and another gentleman I
had never seen before in my life.

I was feeling nervous and dizzy as was, but now seeing that I was 'under observation' by Varun I felt like death. I had to stop and lean against the unoccupied barstool placed along the way to steady myself before approaching Trisha and to make it all appear casual, I asked the bartender for a drink of water.

I stood there for a few seconds, taking in a few deep breaths when I got intercepted by an exceptionally jolly Guneet, who had evidently forgotten that he wasn't supposed to acknowledge me. 'Natasha, what a rocking party,' he said hugging me warmly while I froze in horror. The music had slowed down, and I was certain Varun could hear us from where he was standing. Was Guneet blind? Had alcohol deprived him of his senses and rendered him absolutely stupid? I wanted to murder the man.

I did not say or do anything to acknowledge him. I just stood there staring hard at Guneet, imploring him with my eyes to retreat. But no, he was in no mood to read non-verbal clues and went on to praise my dress. I quietly raised my finger to my lips and made a gesture of shushing but even that was lost on the dimwit.

'Oh, don't stop me from praising you. You always look good, but today is exceptional – this turquoise blue, it's so lovely on you,' the idiot said, giving me a wide, uncontained grin that only alcohol induces in people. The whole scene was taking on a poorly scripted comic sketch-like quality. I walked away from him in a daze while he was still talking. It was too late though. I knew Varun had heard everything.

There were fireworks going off in my brain with anxiety, and everything was feeling a little woozy. Trisha, the shameless harlot, had stopped swishing her derriere and was throwing her head back and laughing at something that Sheila was saying to her. I stood there, not knowing what to do next when I felt Varun's hand on my shoulder. I turned back slowly, beads of perspiration forming on my brow, my hands feeling clammy against my chiffon dress and I looked at him. 'I think we both know what I'm about to say, Natasha,' he said coldly, his eyes dark with anger. 'I saw that warm interaction with that boyfriend of Trisha's,' he hissed at me. 'It turns out that it isn't only Nakul who is being deceived here.'

Unable to meet his eyes, I looked away. 'We need to wind up this party quickly. I'm asking the DJ to stop. I cannot put up with this nonsense a second longer,' he said through clenched teeth.

There was a beautiful birthday cake that was waiting to be wheeled out on a trolley for Varun, but there was no way we were about to cut any cake. I remember wanting to cry. Maybe I did. I have no memory of what happened after because I think I might have collapsed into a heap right there on the lawns in front of all our guests.

***

As I'm lying in my bed, recalling all the unsavoury scenes from last night with my stomach in knots, my mother walks in to check on me. You are never too old to receive a dressing down from your mother about the state of your health and life as I'm just about to find out. She sits at the foot of my bed and delivers a hearty lecture to me without any hesitation.

'Why do you drink so much if you are going to be like this the next morning?' Mummy asks, looking at me swaying as I walk. 'Tum logo sey control hi nahin hota hai. Do you know that the number one reason for ageing before your time is alcohol? I was so worried about you last night.'

I beg her to spare me the lecture and let her know that I'm only a social drinker, not a dipsomaniac. 'Well, it always starts like that. You have three children to take care of, and you cannot be lying wasted like this. Bachchey hain tumharey, kya sochengey? Did you ever see me drunk and fall at parties?' And the inquisition continues.

'Mummy, can we please do this another day?' I snap. 'And can you please ask for some coffee for me?' I say before collapsing into my pillow again.

Mummy sends me a concoction of lemon and honey to help me with my hangover instead of the coffee I need so badly. I drink it greedily in the hope that it will help me resurrect myself and revive my addled mind. Who will tell me what happened last night after I blacked out? I can sense that something terrible happened after Varun confronted me at the bar. I reach for my dying phone desperately to call Nafisa but I find several missed calls from her instead.

I ring her immediately. My voice is quivering already when I ask her for the details. Nafisa brings me to the watershed moment of the evening. 'Before you start, quickly tell me, does Dad know, does Mummy know?' I interrupt her.

'I'm not sure,' she says. 'They might have retired for the night by then, it was late.'

According to Nafisa, the party wound up immediately after I passed out. Varun blamed my fainting on my low BP and being overworked and apologised to our guests. (I don't know if I will ever be able to overcome this shameful moment of my life.)

Trisha came running to my side when she saw me collapse and unaware of what lay ahead for her, helped Varun and Nafisa move me into my room. Shortly after, she was summoned by Bela Aunty in Nakul's presence and then Varun and Maa joined them inside the room also.

'I know something happened last night, but I don't know exactly what. Do you want to tell me?' Nafisa demands.

I fill her in on everything, including my role in it. 'Natasha, how could you be so stupid?' she says incredulously. 'The least you could have done was to not invite him to the party. I don't blame Varun at all,' she says sounding exasperated.

'I don't know what to do now Nafisa. Except apologise to Varun and Nakul and Bela Aunty,' I say, unable to hold my tears back.

'Sorry isn't good enough. I don't see how you can do anything to make this better, quite frankly,' Nafisa says. 'Anyway, pull yourself together and live out your penance. I'm sorry to say but you get no sympathy from me on this one Nats. You know that saying – If you fly with the crows you get shot with the crows. You were destined to go down with Trisha.'

If I lived in an ice hotel in Sweden minus any of the reindeer fur upholstery, I might be in a warmer place than the living hell that is my home.

My mother-in-law seems to have shown no restraint whatsoever in telling my parents about Trisha and Nakul. My poor parents were horrified when they heard about it although these things are not unheard of in diplomatic circles. I suppose they never expected this to happen in their own daughter's home and possibly with her help. I think Maa did have the decency to not highlight my role in it, possibly to spare my parents some humiliation. Mummy asked me if I had invited Guneet but I obviously denied it. I don't think she was entirely convinced though. 'Natasha, but Varun looks upset with you. Why is that unless you knew about this Guneet boy.' Mummy sounded unconvinced of my innocence. I told her that I was only guilty by association because of being close to the culprit. No lie is too big to assuage her anxieties though.

After seeing my parents off at the door the next evening of the party, I follow Varun into the study, hoping to catch him in a less ruffled state. He has kept a perfectly calm demeanour with my parents that evening and this has given me hope.

'Varun, I cannot tell you how genuinely sorry I'm. But it's not what you think. I never…' I say with Monarch butterflies in my stomach. But Varun does not even turn up to look in my direction. It is almost as if I am invisible and inaudible. However, I decide to finish saying what I have got to say in my defence, whether he looks at me or not. 'Varun,' I say again with emotion, 'at least look at me. Give me a chance to tell you how and why I got involved in Trisha's life.'

The cold, unfeeling man walks out of the room even before I can start my speech of contrition, leaving me standing alone, feeling sorry and stupid at the same time.

Messages to thank us for the 'fabulous party' and enquiring after my health continue to pour in and among them is one from the insatiably curious Ananya, who, after checking on my BP, wants to know the reason for Varun's and my disappearance from our own party. I choose not to reply.

Within a few hours of her message, the florist arrives with a bunch of flowers from her with a note saying, 'Hope you are feeling better. Much love, Ananya, and Deepak.' She clearly wants to entice me into writing to her so she can probe deeper, but I am not about to give her the satisfaction by doing so.

The rest of my day is spent swinging between remorse and anger.

Last night sleeping next to Varun was the hardest. His anger had formed an electric fence around him, and I spent the interminably long night in the desperate state between sleeping and waking.

My mother-in-law was booked to leave yesterday afternoon but has stayed on ostensibly to lend moral support to Aunty Bela. I, however, know it's actually to witness my ruination. Maybe I'm imagining it, but I did spot a flicker of glee on her face this morning when she noticed that Varun's coldness towards me had become permafrost.

She has been lingering around our house, spending the better part of her day on phone calls with Aunty Bela, her loud commiserations to her overflowing with melodramatic sighs every time I happen to pass by. 'Oh, Bela...I have no words, no words.'

'Bela, my poor Nakul. I wish I could help...tch tch.'

'There is a God above – he is watching.'

I feel like a guilty dog walking around the house with his tail between his legs after destroying a precious Persian carpet. At least dogs can conveniently hide under the bed for hours when they are sorry, but there is no such privilege available to me.

I'm sure even the kids can tell their mother is not being spoken to by anybody in the family. It's that apparent.

With Varun and Maa being in a funereal mood at home, I'm unable to turn to my column. In my present state, even scribbling a nursery rhyme about eggs would prove challenging, to say nothing of writing 800 words that do not read like bull's excrement. So I send an email to *City Reflections* requesting them to allow me to miss my column this once, citing my low blood pressure as a reason.

You would think that by now Trisha would have found a million ways to grovel and apologise to Varun and me but there is radio silence from her end. I wonder what she is going through herself. I hope whatever it is that she is feeling includes some literal self-flagellation for doing this to me, her only ally. I don't know what Nakul is going to do with her.

I can't even imagine how Nakul must feel – cheated and let down by both Trisha and me. He is the one I need to seek forgiveness from most.

Three days have passed, and Varun hasn't even looked in my direction. His anger feels like an entity that lives between us now. This morning, I try again to break the ice with him when I find him packing clothes in his small cabin bag. 'Going out of town?' I ask him casually. Silence follows. 'Varun do you need anything ironed?'

'No thanks,' he says curtly and continues folding his clothes and laying them inside the case.

'Will you be gone long?' I ask him, knowing well that with a luggage case that size he could not possibly be going away on a long trip. This question too merits no answer, and he shuts the suitcase with an exemplary force and goes into the bathroom.

The kids and his mother are recipients of warm farewells from Varun, although he leaves without saying goodbye to me. Shortly after he has left, Maa decides that I must be hauled over the coals in her son's absence and marches straight into the study where I'm staring vacantly at wikiHow's suggestions on how to get a person to forgive on my laptop screen. You would be surprised at what splendid advice is available online for these kinds of things.

'Natasha, do you have a minute?' she asks me in a tone full of condemnation which makes her words sounds more like, 'Natasha, you better have a minute.'

I nod – there is no escaping her this time.

'So your friend is heartless all the way. Gone off without her children,' she says, finding herself a comfortable corner next to the armrest on the leather sofa.

'She is a friend of the family's and not just mine,' I say without emotion. But gone off? Where has she gone off, I wonder.

'But she was close to you. So she is your friend, and you have made her have this affair.'

'I did not "make" her have an affair! She was having an affair already when I got looped in,' I reply tartly.

'But you let her bring him to the party. And then you lied about it. Trisha is a…well, we all know what she is now. But surely you could have thought about what my poor

Bela or Nakul and even Varun would go through? How could you be so thoughtless?'

I remain silent. She is right for once.

'Poor Bela, at this age for her to see her son's home break…It can kill anybody. She is so depressed, poor thing. I could tell from the start that Trisha was a cheap type of a girl with not a bit of class. Even yesterday she left their home screaming, shouting and yelling. The twins must be so disturbed, but does she care?'

So this is what Maa meant when she said 'gone off'. I had no idea that Trisha had moved out.

'So tell me, Natasha, why did you do this?' she demands, settling into the sofa to make this inquisition comfortable for herself.

The words I need have suddenly gone missing under my mother-in-law's unforgiving gaze.

'I'm sure you have something to say?'

'I…I have nothing to offer, except that I got carried away after expressing my reservations initially. I thought she would bring him to the party anyway, with or without my consent, and so when she pestered me, I gave in. I do owe an apology to Nakul, Varun and Bela Aunty, but it's ridiculous to say that I made her have this affair,' I say looking directly at her face to let her know that she wasn't the one to whom I owed an explanation or apology.

I then ask my mother-in-law politely to excuse me so I can focus on the column I know I'm not about to write.

I wonder if Trisha has gone back to her father. It does not seem likely though, he being the sort of man who will not let his daughter walk out on her marriage after walking out on her engagement once. What a stupid woman she is for throwing away her life over this.

I always knew subconsciously that this would not end happily-ever-after for her. Strangely, even though I'm in so much trouble because of Trisha, I find myself feeling validated. The disturbing realisation crosses my mind that schadenfreude is inherent to human nature and that, sadly, I'm no exception.

When everything is so bleak around me, my only hope and solace come from being around my babies. Over the past few days, the significance of birthing three children has been revealed to me amply.

The most convincing justification for having progeny in our dark and unpredictable times is that there will be days when you will battle storms of various kinds; you and your spouse may not see eye to eye or people around you may let you down. Your children, at such times, will envelop you with their love and consume you with their pocket-sized concerns and worries and you will benefit greatly from both for there isn't a better way to restore your sanity. But tomorrow morning the kids too will be gone for a few days to Delhi because my parents feel they do not get to spend enough time with them during their short visits to Bombay. Just a few days ago Varun and I were talking about going away to Hong Kong for a week or so for the winter break, but now that there is winter in our own house, we don't need to go away anywhere else.

Just before I retire for the night, I finally gather my thoughts and pour all my contrition into two emails, one addressed to Varun and the other to Nakul.

Dear Varun,

I understand how upset you are with me and I do feel sorry for hurting you and letting you down. I cannot go back in time and undo the damage that this has caused to Nakul's life, but I can tell you that I disapproved of it all, along even warning Trisha that her little adventure would cost her one day.

She told me she had been unhappy for a while, that things weren't quite right between her and Nakul for the past few years. She sounded very clear, and there seemed little I could do to influence her.

I was torn between being Trisha's confidant and Nakul's friend. I could do no more than reason with her and point her in the right direction. I could not tell you because it was her secret, not mine.

I did put my foot down when she asked me if she could invite Guneet to our party but she harrowed me with phone calls through the day. I was too frazzled with all the party preparations to realise that Trisha had extracted a 'yes' out of me for inviting Guneet.

Your mother thinks I made her have an affair. Nobody has that kind of influence over anybody, and you know it. I will apologise profusely to Nakul as well, although I'm not expecting to be forgiven by him anytime soon. But you know me, and you know that I have no malice towards anyone, least of all Nakul.

I understand that I have not only disappointed and hurt you but have also embarrassed you and I can do no more than apologise for that. Please give me another chance.

Yours,
Natasha.

Dear Nakul,

Shame is a terrible thing to live with and the shame of letting you down will be mine for life.

Words fail me, and I don't know where and how to start apologising to you for everything that has happened. I can only assure you of one thing and that is that I have had no role to play in whatever has transpired in yours and Trisha's life. I did try and dissuade her, yes, but she had her own ideas about how she wanted to go about things. After a while, I had to just accept her choices and in doing so I concede that I have wronged you. I knew what she was doing could ruin many lives and I felt helplessly torn over this. I did not willingly invite that man to our party.

You have been family to us, and a dear, dear friend to me. If you choose never to speak to me again, I will understand but I do hope that someday in the future, we will be able to put this behind us.

Warmly,
Natasha.

I send the emails on the wings of a prayer and collapse on my bed. By this time fatigue is beginning to have a crippling effect on my body and soon I drift off into a dreamless state, the mental exhaustion now claiming my entire body. When I wake up in the morning, I have a message from Trisha.

I know what you must be going through because of me. I never meant to get you into trouble. You have been a friend and a sister to me. Please forgive me for getting carried away. I can lose others, but I cannot lose you.

For a fleeting moment, I'm about to go soft on her but I quickly remind myself of her selfishness and, in no time, I catapult back into the Trisha-is-a-wench state of mind.

After breakfast Maa makes her long-awaited departure for Jhalakpur with a cold goodbye to me, giving me hope that today might be a better day.

Seeing that I have not responded to her previous message, Trisha sends me another.

I was stupid and selfish, and now everyone is suffering because of me. I know what you must be thinking of me, and you are right in doing so. I'm a terrible person.

I'm too angry to have a conversation with her but my curiosity is getting the better of me. I finally write back.

Quite frankly, your saying that does not alter things for me. I'm in the dog house and I owe it all to you, Trisha. Anyway, I hear you have moved out. Where are you now?'

Trisha tells me that she is staying with her (fat) cousin Harsimran in her tiny flat in Khar at present. Guneet has gallantly offered to put her up at the Taj Lands End in a suite, but for once she has allowed good sense to prevail and declined his offer.

I let Trisha know that Varun and I are not speaking with each other because of his assumption that I have had an active role to play in the collapse of his best friend's marriage.

I will tell Varun and Nakul that this is all my fault and that you have discouraged me all along. Natasha, I will set wrongs right.

❋ ❋

It's an overcast day outside. The air is cooler, and the roses and the chrysanthemums in our garden are blooming.

It's eerie at home without the children, and I have decided to end my self-imposed exile by going to my kick-boxing class followed by a detour to Nature's Basket to buy quinoa bread on my way back. Staying indoors isn't exonerating me in any manner, so then why go on punishing myself?

It's early evening and I'm walking barefoot on the grass in our garden – it's meant to be therapeutic, and I could do with all the therapy in the world right now. Neither Varun nor Nakul have acknowledged my email so far, not that I was expecting it so soon, but I have been checking my mailbox all day. I ring Varun's secretary and then indirectly ask her about Varun. He's gone straight to the site from the airport, she tells me. Perhaps he will speak to me once he is home today, although I feel breathless just thinking of being alone with him at home.

I'm still in the garden when Ananya rings me. 'Natasha, I have been worried about you. No response, no acknowledgement of the flowers. Are you quite alright?'

'Oh sorry, I had low blood pressure and was the worse for wear after the night of the party. This month has been very hectic, and I think all the running around took its toll on me,' I say in a voice so convincing that I'm ashamed and proud of myself all at once.

'Oh, I knew you were unwell, but I also thought you were avoiding me because of Trisha. You know everything, of course.'

'I don't know what you mean.' I say weakly.

'Come on, Nats, don't pretend,' she says. 'I'm only repeating what you know already. I heard that Trisha has packed her bags and moved out of the house. Do you think she has left Nakul?'

'Who has told you all this Ananya?'

'I have my sources. Don't forget that our drivers know each other. They have their network of news,' she laughs, completely unabashed about the fact that her source of gossip is her driver.

One has to be truly vile, not to mention desperate, to go sniffing for gossip around their staff.

'Ananya, I thought you could do better than that!' I say without confirming the news.

'My driver told my mother-in-law, and she is the one who told me. I don't gossip with my driver,' she says self-righteously.

Varun's car arrives on the porch just as I'm wondering how to get rid of Ananya's call without sounding rude. 'Varun has just driven in. I'm seeing him after two days. Let's talk later, Ananya,' I tell her politely and hang up.

Spirals of fear rise inside my stomach as I see him get out of the car and walk towards me. As he approaches me in his khaki cargos and a soft pink shirt, I notice his gaunt face and the dark circles under his eyes. It almost looks like he is on his way to attending a funeral. Surely he cannot be so troubled over Nakul's marriage that he is suffering physically himself. 'It's Nakul who has been cuckolded, not you,' I want to tell him.

'Natasha, can we talk?' he asks me sternly.

'Would you like some tea first?' I ask.

'No, thank you.'

He walks towards the rattan chairs and signals for me to sit on the cushioned chair across from him.

'How long had you known this for?' Varun fires the opening salvo in a manner that gives me little room to frame my thoughts.

'I want you to know that I did not approve of it and Trisha will tell you that as well.'

'This isn't what I asked Natasha. I repeat, how long have you known?'

'Uh, I stumbled upon it three months ago.'

'And you did not think of telling me this?' he asks, squeezing his brow into a deep furrow. 'How could you just watch Trisha wreck his life and say nothing about it?'

'I owed it to her to keep her secret Varun. She had confided in me. Wouldn't you do the same in my place had Nakul told you his marriage wasn't working and he had found someone else?'

'Not if it was going to break up a family,' he says indignantly.

'That is what you say now. And I did let Trisha know I disapproved. I tried to talk sense into her, but she was too far gone into the relationship to be rational by the time I discovered it by accident. And not only was her affair morally wrong, I could not believe that she was cheating on a man like Nakul with this two-bit, nouveau riche man…' I can't believe I just said that. I want to shoot myself immediately.

'Is that the only thing that is bothering you about this affair, Natasha?' There are certain looks on certain faces that I never wish to see again, and this look of disbelief intermingled with derision on Varun's face is one of them.

'That's not what I meant. I was just trying to tell you that I disapproved of him in every possible manner,' I say in an even voice trying to redeem myself from the profoundly foolish words I have just uttered. 'You don't understand. I was not able to dissuade her from seeing this man…She was helplessly in love with Guneet. I realised that marriage is a complicated business and that I'm nobody to judge. I cannot help it, I'm just empathetic,' I say.

'What you did isn't empathy. It's foolish, deceitful, gullible and idiotic,' he says sharply. 'And don't tell me you disapproved of him. Wasn't that Hermès bag a gift from him? It did not take me long to figure that one out. Oh, to think of the lies you told me to cover it up,' he shouts. 'You know what? You are no less than Trisha yourself. I'd not be surprised if...' he says in a raised voice and then stops. I cannot believe he remembered the Hermès gifts. I should not have gotten tempted and kept it with me. But I'm not going to confess that to Varun.

'Finish saying what you were about to Varun. Let's hear how little you think of me. Go for it,' I say angrily.

'Oh well, let's finish saying what I came here to say first. What were you even thinking when you invite that cheapskate to my big birthday dinner?' he says, slamming his fist on the marble top table so hard that I am startled.

'How dare you say I'm like Trisha? She tricked me and brought him to the party. I mentioned that to you in the email, didn't I? Varun, I have made a mistake, I'm sorry. But you seem to be in no mood to forgive me. I'm human too, you know. I'm Trisha's friend, not her moral guardian. And it isn't like I was the one having an affair. You need to give me a chance.' Angry tears are streaming down my cheeks, and if I let them go unchecked there is a whole dam inside me waiting to burst, but I suddenly become aware that the driver has come back from his tea and can probably see me weeping from a distance.

'I don't see why you are crying when you are the one at fault,' Varun says without a trace of softness in his voice. 'Did it ever occur to you that Nakul isn't only my friend but also my business partner? And did you even pause to think that while you might be getting your jollies out of being Trisha's confidant, your being involved may change things for us at work forever?'

To be honest, the thought had never crossed my mind. If Varun's business is affected, our marriage could go too. Another wave of hot terror sweeps through me.

'Varun, I hadn't thought of all this. I'm truly sorry. I hope you can see it,' I say with as much sincerity as is possible of a human being.

'You can apologise all you want, but I'm unable to put this behind us,' he says coldly as he gets up to leave. 'Let's be mature about it and keep it functional for now. Alright?'

He abruptly gets up and leaves. 'I will not be having dinner at home today. I have to sit with my team with some stuff,' he turns around and tells me without directly looking at me.

As I watch Varun drive out of our gate in his car a few minutes later, I wonder if we will ever be able to get past this.

When Nafisa rings to check on me I insist that she meets me for dinner. 'I'm too tired to go out tonight. You come to my place now if you want to see me – we'll have a pajama party,' she says.

'Guilty people have no choice but to live out their sentence, Natasha,' she tells me as she places a glass of wine in my hand, later when I meet her. 'Just give it time, he will come around. And Nats, he is right about his work. This could jeopardise his business. Don't be offensive, it will just upset him further,' Nafisa says, sprawled on a sofa in her elegant apartment.

'But I apologised and apologised. What else does he want me to do? And you should have heard the tone in which he said, "Let's keep this functional." I'd gone from remorseful to furious after Varun was done. Why is he painting me with the same brush as Trisha? Do you know today he was on the verge of accusing me of cheating to? But thankfully for him, he did not say the words. For once I'd have slapped his condescending face before turning over the soil from my newly potted plants over his big head if he had finished saying what he was about to say,' I smart as I think of his eyes dark with that unspoken accusation.

Nafisa starts laughing, the wine working its way through her veins and even mine by now. 'Don't laugh, Nafisa. Anybody would relent after seeing how truly repentant I was. Varun could never bear to see me cry and now, he has turned so hard-hearted. This isn't the Varun I know!'

'Men! They expect to be forgiven and pardoned for all of their sins, Nats, but let them down once, and they cannot take it. How many women do we know who have taken their men right back after they were caught cheating? And then show me one man who has been able to put his wife's deception behind him and forgive her.'

'True. The patriarchal construct has served men well for far too long, and I don't mind them being cuckolded if it can teach them to not take women for granted. But I still feel bad that I allowed it to happen to a man like Nakul.'

'Drink some wine and you'll feel better,' says Nafisa, pouring some more wine from the carafe into her glass and raising it in the air. 'Here's to men learning their lessons,' she says as she tops up my glass with one hand and toasts with the other.

'Nothing works like getting drunk with your best friend. Thank God for you, Nafisa! Being loveless and jobless isn't easy.'

'Well then, listen to me. It's about time you started working. With Trisha out of your life, and Varun giving you the silent treatment, you will have a lot of time to spare, I guess,' Nafisa teases.

'I will now. My sabbatical is over. Get me work. I promise I will deliver,' I say.

I wake up with a heavy head again in the morning. Serves me right for drinking so much wine last night. Forget the rest of the ageist world, even alcohol turns its back on you when you hit middle age.

I somehow manage to get myself to the terrace while I wait for my coffee, reading and responding to text messages. I have a message from Trisha asking me to please meet her.

I'm appalled that after getting me into so much trouble, she still has the nerve to ask me to see her.

I, for once, exercise discretionary thinking and reply in the negative. In keeping with the tenets of the new marital peace-keeping agreement between my husband and me I have no choice but to maintain a long-distance relationship with her, if at all.

Trisha texts me once again, requesting me to speak to her even if it is for a few seconds. *It is about Aarna and*

Aaditya, I do not know whom else to discuss this with.' I give in to her entreaties, I am a soft-hearted fool after all.

As much as I feel that Trisha deserves to suffer, as a mother I do understand that without her around, her children too are going to be miserable and I feel terrible for them. Aaditya and Aarna are too young and too innocent to even comprehend the collapse of their family unit and its aftermath on their lives.

I ring her an hour later and come to the point straight away without making small talk with her. 'So you wanted to talk about Aaditya and Aarna,' I say coldly.

No sooner have I mentioned the kids than the floodgates open and she begins to sob so loudly that I have to withdraw my ear from the phone briefly. 'My poor babies. They have done nothing to deserve this,' she says through her sobs.

'But you lie in the bed you make for yourself, and as a mother, you should have considered the future of your children before getting carried away,' I tell her frostily.

'Say what you feel like Natasha, I'm in no position to defend myself,' she says in a voice muffled with tears and I realise that I might have been unnecessarily cruel.

Guneet calls Trisha on her spare mobile just as we are speaking, and I hear her modulate her voice to make it sound even more depressed than she is. My friend Trisha, I realise at that moment, will use all her guile to stay afloat and I needn't be too worried about her.

❈ ❈ ❈

At home, Varun has been behaving deranged. One minute he seems cheerful and normal and then so cold in the next that it almost feels like our planet has entered the glacial age. If I did not know any better, I might have worried that my husband had become mentally ill.

Thankfully the children have returned from Delhi with wide smiles on their faces after the pampering and many Christmas gifts they have received from their grandparents. 'I missed you, Mumsie,' Ria throws her arms around me and tells me as soon as the kids come out of the airport.

'And Sumer and Sofie, what about you?' I ask the other two.

'I missed your nagging, Mamma,' cheeky Sofie says.

'I also missed you,' Sumer adds.

'He is lying Mamma. Sumer never missed you,' says Ria with a devilish glint in her eyes.

'I did, I did,' he says pushing her.

And life starts to look normal once again. I'm happy to have them back. I couldn't imagine having to start the new year without them.

Nakul, Trisha, Varun and I have practically ushered in ever New Year together in Bombay, Jhalakpur or at Varun's villa in Goa. If not in Hong Kong we would have at least been in Goa this year but now, with our New Year's Eve plans asunder because of marital discord, deception and whatnot, it's going to be an uneventful evening spent in front of the television like people at a retirement home. But at least I will have my babies around me.

There are a few things more depressing than the prospect of having to ring in the New Year from your couch while everybody else you know has plans. I'm sure even the homeless around the world get together and wish each other on New Year's Eve. Everyone I know is doing exciting things tonight, even my parents who have driven down to Chandigarh from Delhi to Mehra Uncle's farm house for the next two days. Nafisa is with her cousins in Hong Kong, Ananya and Sheila are in Bangkok with their families, Sukh is in the Maldives, and since no adult in my family is on talking terms with me, I'm punishing myself by going to bed along with Ria and Sumer at 10 pm tonight.

'I'm ashamed of you, Mamma,' Sofie says as she sees me in my pajamas, snuggling with her siblings in bed. 'Please don't let any of my friends' parents know that you had nowhere to go on the 31st night or I will be considered a freak at school.'

'Social popularity isn't everything in life,' I tell her.

'Of course, it's everything! Please dress up quickly and go somewhere,' she says.

'Your dad just wants to chill at home, and frankly, I don't mind it,' I lie.

At midnight, I'm still awake and against my better judgement, I look at my Instagram feed where everyone is partying in their glamorous clothes and wishing their followers a Happy New Year. There must be a statistic somewhere about a maximum number of people committing suicide on New Year's Eve. I want to slit my wrists right now as well.

❈ ❈ ❈

Trying to put the disappointments of the previous night behind me, I start the new day of the new year by tenderly asking Varun if we can start our relationship over. Seeing that our communication has reached an impasse, I have to ask him, irrespective of whether I mean it or not. He runs his fingers through his hair, regards me briefly as if making up his mind and then offers me a reluctant one-quarter of a smile, which could easily have been confused for slight indigestion. But it makes hope rise in my suffering heart. My offer is accepted by my self-righteous husband with a nod.

There is no need for conversation after that. I feel a cloud has lifted and the sun has shone through. I'm going to do everything that I need to do to be a better me from this day on.

The whole purpose of being born a human being, after all, is to evolve as a person. I draft my resolutions for the year soon after.

1.　Learn to say 'no' to all unethical, immoral and criminal proposals.
2.　Discourage adultery vociferously.
3.　Become a better mother than I am already.
4.　Be patient around children and allow them to make mistakes without reacting.
5.　Spend less time on social media. Be present and give my full attention to the person in front of me, especially my children.
6.　Obsess less about ageing or weight gain. Accept ageing and fat as facts of life and be graceful about it. Example: Maharani Gayatri Devi.
7.　Apply face pack daily. Moisturise twice a day.
9.　Buy no more shoes. Okay, fewer, buy fewer shoes this year.

10. Attend all PTMs without grudging Varun for not being able to attend even one of them.

11. Cook occasionally (?)

12. Accept MIL from my heart and start ignoring her vile comments (to be reviewed monthly).

13. Find an occupation/career (speak to Nafisa about it).

14. Consider Brazilian wax (to be revisited when marital conditions become sanguine).

When Varun does actually speak to me, I realise with much irritation that it's only to lecture me. 'I have been thinking about this,' he says, just as I walk back into my room after committing my New Year's resolutions to paper, 'You're so bored that you wanted to create excitement in your life by getting involved in Trisha's!'

I'm appalled at his insinuation and for mistaking my compassion for boredom. This passive-aggressive attitude is typical of him. He could have told me what he thought about it all when I apologised to him ten days ago, but no, for Varun, there is no joy in berating me in one go. Which husband would not stretch this out as far as he could? I shall have to suffer his verbal onslaughts in instalments in the hereafter.

Tears sting my eyes, and I retreat into my room immediately. I expect him to follow me, but he stays glued to the sofa in the living room. I weep for a while, letting all my agonies out into my pillow and then after splashing my face with water a few times, I go over to Sumer and Ria's room.

My children have gauged that there is something not quite right between their parents. With Varun's tetchiness with me apparent, it's almost like we have been living under a mushroom cloud of misunderstandings and unpleasantness.

How long is the period of forbearance and contrition supposed to officially last? I text Nafisa when she sends me a message to wish me Happy New Year.

Still sulking, is he? She writes back.

I write back: *No, it's worse than sulking. Varun is behaving like a lunatic. Cannot make up his mind whether to let it go or to go on punishing me. What is the point? Hadn't we decided to start afresh? Frankly, this is getting boring. Remorse too comes with an expiry date, you know? And mine – its sell-by life is almost over.*

Ananya rings to wish me Happy New Year. Surprisingly, she does not bring up Trisha at all and asks me to see her for lunch soon instead. 'And don't worry, I won't bring up Trisha with you. I do want to see you though and make sure you are doing alright,' she tells me sincerely. What does that mean? Why would I not be okay? Are people talking about Varun and me too?

'I'm fine Ananya. Why would I not be okay?' I say in an even voice.

'Oh, I just assumed that things being the way they are with Trisha, you might be upset too about their marriage and all that. That's all.'

I breathe a sigh of relief.

Varun approaches me just before dinner and offers his hand to me in the manner of President Putin offering his hand to the foreign affairs minister of Ukraine.

'I'm willing to put this behind us and start over, Natasha,' he says to me in a conciliatory tone. 'I don't think this is a healthy atmosphere for our children. I'm willing to let this go for their sake as well as ours.'

I breathe a sigh of relief and accept his outstretched hand in mine. This is the most physical we had gotten in weeks.

❊ ❊ ❊

A listless, uneventful month has passed. Varun has been travelling a great deal but even when he's around, there's a chill in the air. He isn't angry with me any longer, but we don't talk or laugh like we used to. One of the main problems is that we cannot talk about Nakul any longer.

We have had a proper conversation only once in this duration, which was on my fortieth birthday on 26 January, and he also reacted to a joke I made with a suppressed laugh on two or so occasions.

Not only has Nakul not replied to my letter of apology, but he also did not wish me on my birthday either. It's unfair to expect any communication from him, I know, but I was secretly hoping he might decide to forgive me by now.

On the bright side, it's a good thing that my fortieth birthday fell during my period of exile from love and life because apart from my few close friends nobody even realised that I had turned forty. Just as well, I'm not even looking good these days. I have been seeking comfort in food this past month and that seems to have taken its toll on me and now I look like someone who has been on a stringent diet of instant noodles and beer.

I wonder how Princess Diana continued to look resplendent and skinny through her sad marriage while I'm looking like a close cousin of Zia-ul-Haq. I curse myself for being the person who turns to food for comfort instead of turning away from it altogether, like glamorous women do.

It isn't all doom and gloom though. A small frisson of excitement is ignited in me via two emails that have found their way into my inbox. One is an email from Nafisa, introducing me to Priyanka Talwar, bureau chief of *Vanity International* magazine which is in the process of setting up a bureau in Mumbai. The other is from Priyanka herself telling me she enjoys my columns and then asking if I'd be interested in contributing to the magazine.

I write back to her right away, letting her know what a privilege it would be to do stories for *Vanity*. I appraise my response again before hitting send, and realise that I'm sounding too desperate for the assignment and need to tone it down. I replace 'privilege' with 'pleasure' and send off the email.

I hear back from Priyanka within minutes. She wants me to do a piece on Riyad Siddiqui. Riyad Siddiqui! I can barely look at him on screen without blushing, he's so handsome.

'Riyad is media shy and getting him to agree isn't going to be easy, but you have been around long enough to find a way to convince him, I'm sure,' Priyanka writes to me.

I immediately feel nervous excitement at the prospect of writing about a man whose work I have admired for as long as I have admired his taut derriere.

Now remains the question of getting in touch with him and I decide that the best way to reach out to him would be to approach him on Twitter, which I do promptly. *@RiyadSiddiqui-I'm doing a story for Vanity International and they want to feature you in it. Do let me know how to take this forward.*

I check Twitter every five minutes after that for a reply, but seven hours later, there is still no response.

Next morning, even before I have managed to fully prise open my eyelids that have been glued together with under-eye cream, I reach for the phone. There is a reply in the form of Riyad Siddiqui now 'follows you'. I am so thrilled that I nearly faint with happiness. I then take a screenshot of the window and send it to Nafisa.

As expected Nafisa pings back the same minute. *'Good, now you can have an affair with him and get him out of your system.'*

'Yes and then join Trisha in purgatory.'

'But seriously, doesn't he have a life? Why is he following a mother of three?'

'He is only following me on Twitter, not in life, alas. Maybe he is following a mother of three because she looks like a twenty-something virgin in her profile picture – I airbrushed it,' I write back.

'Don't get greedy. You already have Varun who, I might remind you, is as perfect as a man can get.'

'You mean he used to be perfect.'

'Don't talk rubbish. How many women must envy you for waking up next to him each morning. Have you ever wondered about that?'

'Nafisa, you have that beautiful ivory white gown with a trail that you bought from the Florence outlets, yes?'

'What has that got to do with this?'

'So have you stopped buying more dresses because you have this one gorgeous dress and women envy you for it?'

'You are crazy, Nats. This is such a stupid metaphor. Did you just compare your husband to a gown?'

'Haha, I think I did.'

'*Okay, is there anything important that you wanted to tell me? As you can see, I have a job.*'

I thank her for introducing me to Priyanka Talwar and let her know that they are keen to assign me a story right away. A story about Riyad Siddiqui, no less. '*Jokes aside, I'm terribly excited Nafisa. This could truly be the start of the new career that I have so desperately been in need of. I hope I can deliver though.*'

'*Self-doubt is the hallmark of every great artist. You, my dear, have all that it takes, if you focus a bit and stop being frivolous,*' she writes.

I decide that I will do exactly as she says. No more frivolity for Natasha.

Chapter 13

Why are adolescent girls unrelentingly mean to each other? Children treating other kids badly isn't something new but what is it about their teenage years that makes them unconscionable and nasty? As the parent of a teen, I can see it now – girls are truly at the most complicated and hard to navigate phase during this stage of their lives. They are sensitive, unsure of themselves and have the communication skills of Manmohan Singh. Belonging to a clique means everything to girls in middle school. It helps them to carve out a sense of identity for themselves at school, and this isn't necessarily a bad thing. But girls also operate on the principle of inclusion by exclusion, and when you lose your place in the group, you lose your identity.

As a parent, the greatest challenge that I'm facing is raising a child with a strong sense of self who does not feel the need to attach herself to a clique. But when you are that young, heartbreak and disappointment come in various shapes and sizes – your best friend may withdraw from you without reason, the group you play with during recess may inexplicably replace you...

The worst calamity that could strike a home has struck mine. My dear husband has returned from Puducherry with the ordinary flu, but he is behaving like he is about to die. The whole house is in a tizzy. Steam lao, garam pani lao, honey lao, doctor ko andar lekar aao, garam soup banao, soup ka taste bland hai, wapas lekar jao, Natasha I have a headache give me something, call the doctor again...so much drama. Nobody has ever kicked up such a fuss when I have been unwell. In fact, Varun moves out of our room when I'm sick and am expected to remain in quarantine till the germs pass. But with Varun, if he so much as sneezes, I'm supposed to hover around him like Florence Nightingale.

Arrested development, that's what most men suffer from. And it's all their mothers' fault. News of her son's illness has travelled to my mother-in-law in Rajasthan, and she has been calling me every few hours to inquire about his health. The two of us have maintained a convenient silence with each other ever since the 'December fiasco'.

I haven't missed her at all in the past month and would gladly carry on with our status quo, but Varun's trifling illness has forced us to keep in touch. We are keeping it strictly cordial between us, though.

I'm tempted to tell Maa that no man ever died of the common cold and that her son is in no imminent danger of succumbing to one, but she is far too distant with me for me to inject our conversations with humour.

Amid all this, Sofia has just returned from school in an utterly foul mood. Her best friend Shreya has stopped speaking to her and allied with Kavya, her worst enemy in class. 'Now I have no best friend,' she tells me in tears.

'Why don't you call Shreya and ask her if something is the matter? She might tell you why she is upset with you.'

'No way, I can never do that. It's so desperate.'

'Clearing up misunderstandings isn't desperate. It's the only thing that can save friendships,' I say.

'How embarrassing to have to ask someone to please be with you when they don't wish to anymore.'

A lengthy discussion between mother and daughter follows on the subject and it ends in Sofie running out of my room in tears. I hear a loud bang. Her bedroom door is to be the undeserving casualty of our exchange, apparently.

Taking a break from playing wife, mother and nursemaid, I decide to check Twitter for further communication from Riyad and am disappointed to not find any.

I then send a direct message to his inbox sharing my email address with him and asking for his in return.

Six hours and many Twitter checks later, I have an email from him. Be still, my beating heart, I tell myself, this must be from his PR person. I open the email nervously. It's HIM. It's from Riyad Siddiqui.

Hey Natasha,

This is Riyad. You can email me on this id.

Thanks,

Riyad.

Oh joy, oh happiness, he said my name. He said my name. I can picture him saying my name. This is most unbecoming of a forty-year-old mother of three.

Realising that it's too late at night to write back, I flip my laptop shut and go to bed with a smile on my lips.

❈ ❈ ❈

The hardest part about being a mother is having to wake up for school in the morning and trying to evoke feelings of maternal love within yourself when all you want is for the kids to leave so you can go back to bed.

I suddenly remember that I haven't yet emailed Riyad about the interview, and I immediately abandon all thoughts of sleeping.

When Varun emerges from the room, looking well rested, albeit with Rudolf's nose, he is surprised to find that not only am I awake but I'm also working away on my laptop.

'Are we having a midlife crisis? Are you all right? Should I call the GP?' he remarks.

'Funny you said that. I was thinking my new column should be about midlife and its troubles. And no, I'm just trying to take my work seriously. A little encouragement instead of these jibes would be nice for a change though.'

'I am very happy to see you work is all that I'm saying actually.'

I ask Varun to leave me alone and then compose an email to Riyad.

Dear Riyad,

Vanity International has just set up their outpost in India in Mumbai and is keen to feature you. This isn't surprising, given that your movies have been lauded not only amongst Indian audience abroad but have also gained traction in festival circuits outside of India.

As a freelancer for the magazine, I'd be delighted if I could write this feature on you in the form of an interview. As you are probably aware, we do not feature gossip or focus much on people's personal lives in the magazine. We will be broadly discussing your work and cinema at large. I'm really hoping you do this interview with us.

Do let me know when it would be convenient for you to meet.

Best regards,

Natasha Singh.

9820302025

Not sure sending him my regards sounds appropriate. He is in his mid-thirties after all and not a school principal or an ageing singer who needs to be regarded so. But, 'Cheers' sounds like I don't have an education and 'So long' sounds overfamiliar. Wish I could write 'Yours truly' and mean it.

I spend the rest of the morning checking my inbox.

I reflect on my life. Am I this bored? Are all women my age as bored as I am? Nafisa is right. I want to be so busy professionally that I never have to spend the day waiting for piecemeal excitement from a celebrity as I'm doing today.

Riyad has written back.

Dear Ms Singh,

Happy to speak to Vanity International about my work. Unfortunately, I'm shooting all of this month. Will it suit you to travel outside of Bombay to interview me in two weeks when we are at a slightly more hospitable location in Manali?

My office, of course, will be more than happy to assist you with any travel arrangement if required.

Yours truly,

Riyad.

I forward his email to Nafisa.

Dear N,
What do you think? ;)
  xx
  Nats.

She takes a minute to write back.

First, he follows you, then he takes you on an outdoor shoot.
Please use protection, unless, of course, you want to have four
children. *wink *wink
  xx
  N.

Dear Nafisa,
You have a one-track mind. Sex is so overrated. In any case, I'm only
going to spend a day or two on the set. Have no intention of shagging
him, not during this interview at any rate!
  xx
  Nats.

Dear Nats,
Spoken like a woman who has been married too long. Anyhoo, I'm
only kidding. You know that.
  So excited for you though.
  xx
  N.

Riyad and I exchange a few more emails to work out a suitable date for me to fly to Manali and I finally decide on two weeks from now.

Varun is resuming work today after three days of upsetting the natural rhythm of our household and I can say with certainty that the staff of the house will be happy to see the back of him.

One man in my life has recovered, but the other, my driver, has come down with the flu now and asks if he can please be allowed to leave work early. Seeing that he is indeed looking indisposed, I send the poor man to the doctor and drive to school to fetch the kids.

For the first time in many years, Ria's face does not light up on seeing me at the school gate. 'I want to tell you something, Mummy,' she whispers in my ear. 'Tell me also, tell me also,' pipes in Sumer. 'No, I will only tell Mummy,' she tells her brother angrily.

Sumer starts to get rambunctious in the car so that I cannot hear what Ria is trying to tell me. Frustrated at not being heard, she begins to cry. This pleases Sumer no end. I decide it's time to use a little hand action and I pull over my car on the side of the road and turn back to slap him across his face. Now there are two bawling kids in the car! Inner peace, don't elude me, I need you now.

I calm Ria down with great difficulty and ask her what is bothering her. 'Paree and Vir Arjun have become friends, and I don't like it. I feel like telling her that he is not her honey, he is my honey.' Dear God, my little one who sucks her thumb to sleep every night, is in love! I do my best not to laugh but am unable to control myself. 'I don't like you. You are laughing at me,' Ria says when she sees me laugh in the rearview mirror. More tears are shed over this matter.

I wish I could tell Varun that our Ria is in love and feeling all those fuzzy emotions that are integral to love – insecurity and possessiveness – but I'm scared to bring up the topic of love with him for it might get him thinking of Trisha and Guneet.

I have been meaning to have Aaditya and Aarna over, but I have altogether avoided broaching this topic with Varun. I finally made up my mind to ring Trisha today to explain this to her.

As is expected, Trisha, until yesterday, was in the place that the Tibetan Buddhists call the Bardo – that intermediate state of consciousness between death and rebirth where having finished one lifetime on earth, one waits for the next.

'In many ways, a part of my life is over Natasha,' she says grimly. 'And I have no idea what to expect from the next part. It's all very scary.'

It can't be easy to be lodged in this nightmarish limbo, where you wake up in your cousin's cramped flat near the gurdwara instead of your sea-facing Bandra penthouse. Not that I'm about to commiserate with her.

'But what is Guneet doing in all this?' I ask.

'He's been very concerned and says he needs a few days to decide what he wants to do next,' says Trisha.

I warn Trisha that these things take time; life would be unrealistically fair if one could climb their way out of one's marriage at the snap of a finger and be received into the loving arms of their lover in their plush boudoir.

'Well, anyway,' I say, 'The reason I rang you was to explain that it has been difficult for me at home the past several weeks and I was unable to talk to Varun about Aarna and Aaditya, but I do plan to have them over tomorrow anyhow, provided Nakul does not have a problem with it.'

She sounds happy with the suggestion and thanks me for being so thoughtful.

When I see Varun in the evening, I ask him to convince Nakul to send the twins over. Even if Nakul hates me right now, he knows my children at least are innocent, and his kids feel happy around them.

The twins come over straight from their piano lessons this morning. Aarna looks like a doll in her yellow polka dress with matching ribbons in her hair. I hug and kiss her and ask Sofie to take charge. Aaditya, a spitting image of his father, refuses to let me cuddle him and goes straight to Sumer's room to play with his toys and spend his afternoon in the tree house in his room.

'They are missing Ma'am,' their nanny Rosa tells me, bringing tears to my eyes.

'Sir is also not telling them anything about Ma'am, so my Aarna was crying last night in her sleep saying "Mummy, Mummy",' Rosa says.

I have to speak to Varun and ask him to negotiate a better deal for Trisha where she can at least see her children, but he may get upset with my suggestion, and I may be forced to shack up with some aunty ji near some gurdwara and sing kirtans for the rest of my life as well.

❋ ❋ ❋

Trisha sounds ecstatic on the phone this morning. Guneet has told his wife that he wants to leave her. Trisha sounds relieved to learn that her lover is truly committed to her. I feel relieved for her myself. She says he is going to fly to Bombay to discuss matters with her in person.

By the afternoon however, calamity strikes. I receive a newsflash from Trisha informing me that Guneet's wife has tried to end her life by overdosing on sleeping pills after hearing first hand from her husband the news that he is going to leave her for good. Guneet is by her side at the Max Hospital somewhere in Delhi getting her stomach pumped. I can hardly commiserate with Trisha over her lover's wife's failed suicide attempt. She fears that it has scared Guneet witless and that he may not want it on his conscience.

Given the pressing circumstances, Guneet is likely to do a volte-face on Trish and go running back to his wife for certain. His wife though must be a smart woman to have attempted suicide with the intention of getting saved, knowing very well that he would change his mind about leaving her as an act of contrition.

In the meanwhile, Nakul has spoken to his lawyers and wants to file for divorce right away. Reconcilement with Trisha is out of the question, Varun tells me, with a sense of triumph. Hell hath no fury like that of a cuckolded man's best friend!

Bela Aunty and my mother-in-law are no doubt too busy commiserating with each other about their respective misfortunes of having awful bahus like Trisha and me. Maa hasn't spoken much to me since Varun's flu. She calls now and then to speak with the children, but when she speaks to me, she keeps it short and to the point. This is the only positive outcome of Trisha's love affair as far as I know.

In the evening I'm lying on the bed and staring at the ceiling when I notice Varun frothing at the mouth. Quite literally. He is peeping out of the bathroom and calling my name, but that is the most I can make of it.

'Rinse your mouth and come into the room and then talk to me Varun,' I say.

Two minutes later, he walks over to his side of the bed and tells me with irritation that the toothpaste in the stand next to the basin has gotten spoilt. 'Varun, the toothpaste cannot get spoilt. You don't need to start making up reasons to find fault with me now.'

'But this is your department, and the paste is spoilt. Go try it for yourself if you don't believe me,' he says.

I walk over to the bathroom determined to prove this man wrong, and I discover that somehow the dogs' new tube of toothpaste has ended up in the glass. Pet dental – chicken flavour, it says clearly.

The universe has avenged me for all of Varun's sins against me. Holding my belly with laughter, I take the toothpaste tube and hand it over to Varun.

'How can you keep a dog's toothpaste next to my toothbrush?' he says with disgust. 'No wonder my mouth tastes like liver, eww.' He lunges over the bathroom to rinse his mouth again.

'Look at the colour of the packaging. It looks exactly like Dentyne. How is a man to know Natasha?' he says, a bottle of Listerine mouthwash in hand.

'You're just getting too old Varun, your eyesight is failing you,' I say through paroxysms of laughter.

Watching me laugh like that Varun starts laughing hysterically too and before we know it we are both laughing uncontrollably at this silly incident.

'You're completely crazy. I hope you know that,' Varun says finally recovering from his laughing fit. 'And, you need to figure out how to fix things with Nakul. One email from you isn't enough after that gift of loyalty that you gave him, my dear.' I had mentioned to Varun a few days ago that Nakul had ignored my apology and to tell him on my behalf how sorry I truly was.

'But I have been so busy pacifying you that I haven't had the mental bandwidth to approach Nakul,' I explain, my belly still hurting from all the laughter.

'Send him another email, or go meet him perhaps?' suggests Varun.

I take Varun's advice and go across to the study to write Nakul another long email asking for his forgiveness.

My mother rings me to tell me about a family friend's wedding she wants me to fly down to Delhi for.

Dad's golfer friend Khurana Uncle's daughter is getting married, and it has been mandated that all of us are to attend. Social exigencies aside, Mummy is particularly keen that I help my cousin Sonia shortlist a groom for herself at the wedding. Marriage ceremonies as we know are an ideal hunting grounds for potential suitors and nothing gives my mother more happiness than matchmaking.

Sonia's mother is my maternal aunt and the two live by themselves, having lost Sonia's father in a road accident many years ago. It has fallen upon my mother to find her a match as Sonia hasn't been able to help herself much in this department.

Varun is at work, and I ring him to tell him about the wedding on the phone. 'Do not expect me to accompany you to the wedding. It will be full of loud, overdressed and overbearing Punjabis anyway.'

'But Varun this sends out the wrong signal to people. They may think I'm single and start sending me rishtas, and then?'

'Don't worry, I will take that chance,' Varun chuckles, very pleased with his own wit.

In the evening, on his way back from work Varun informs me that he has orchestrated a meeting between Nakul and Trisha at our place to discuss the divorce amicably.

I have been warned to stay out of it and to just make arrangements for them to be served coffee etc. at home. I disappear after receiving a gaunt Nakul, who is cold as expected and Trisha doing her best to appear demure and repentant in a conservative salwar kameez.

Once I bring Sumer home after his squash lessons, I call Trisha to get an update on the meeting between the estranged couple. Trisha tells me she is packing her bags to go visit her parents. 'I'm ready to talk to them about the official termination of my marriage,' she says, sounding unusually calm.

The calm, I realise, stems from what she tells me next. 'Guneet says he is not going to give up on us. And since his wife is mentally fragile, he will stay by her side, but he wants us to rent a place here in Bombay for ourselves soon.'

This Guneet keeps pleasantly surprising me with his resolute commitment to be with Trisha.

'Irreconcilable differences' is the term they intend to go with instead of 'adultery' while explaining to friends and family about their divorce. They have decided to go in for joint custody of the children.

'Yes, he was decent about it. But we did not end up discussing money at all. I was too embarrassed to broach the topic.'

'That's not like you at all Trisha. You have no money of your own, you should have discussed it with him,' I say.

'Nats, at this point, all I want is to be with Guneet and my children. When I'm with him, I feel complete. I don't care for money too much any longer. I must find a way to eke out a living for myself, but that will come later.'

This isn't the fiery, unapologetic, money-minded Trisha one used to know. This is a sentimental woman willing to give up the good life for love.

I think about her for a long time. All those clichés about love that one reads and sniggers at must have a kernel of truth to them. Maybe there is that one person who is your ideal other half, and if you are lucky, you will find that person.

By now everybody in our circle of friends knows about Trisha and Nakul's separation and because I'm perhaps the only one who has insight into their lives my popularity has surged. I have never had so many invitations for coffee from Bombay society as I have had in the past few weeks.

❊ ❊ ❊

Delhi is a refreshing change from Bombay for me as always. Being around my family, meeting new people at the wedding, shopping at Malcha Marg and Santushti and sitting up late chatting with my parents and my cousin…three days in the city pass in no time at all. Udit, the boy my cousin Sonia has been slated to meet for an 'arranged match', himself seems charming enough for her to not write him off immediately.

I make the requisite calls to check on Sofia, Sumer, and Ria and realise belatedly that Varun's accompanying me on this trip was going to be impossible anyway since there would have been no one to take care of the kids.

Spending time with Mummy, Daddy and cousins, I forget I'm a mother or a wife and I become, once again, just their daughter.

Sonia and I are speculating about the possibility of Clara, Udit's American friend, being his love interest at the wedding when I notice five missed calls from Varun on my phone. There are also two messages from him asking me to call him back. I panic, my mind running unbridled in all directions. Hoping the kids are all right I curse myself for not checking my phone sooner. I ring him back in a state of panic, and he informs me that Sumer has a fever and since he couldn't get through to the doctor or me, Sylvia suggested he speak to Trisha who obliges him right away with exactly what is to be administered.

The fever is now under control. 'But Varun, I have printed prescriptions and stuck them on the soft board of Ria's and Sumer's room – didn't the maids tell you that?'

'They did, but the medicine names were different from what was lying in the medicine box, and I got confused… Anyway, Trisha was a big help.'

'I think if the fever rises again, you'll just have to come back Natasha,' he says seriously.

'I'm at a family get-together after ages Varun. You have the doctor and the medicines all available. It's unfair to ask me to come back when you are around,' I tell him.

'But I'm not good at these things. I have never done all this before. You are the mother, Natasha,' says Varun, panic getting the better of him.

'And you are their father,' I say coolly.

There is a pause. 'Well anyway, please don't keep your phone on the silent mode at night. I may need to call you Natasha,' he says before hanging up.

How is it that children manage to fall sick at precisely the same time as when you are enjoying yourself?

I send Trisha a message to say thank you, and she writes back to reassure me that there is nothing to worry about as Sumer's fever came under control with Ibugesic right away. She asks me not to rush back, promising me that she is going over to see him first thing in the morning tomorrow.

When I speak to Sylvia in the morning, Sumer still has a fever and Varun is still utterly hapless. I go over to my parents' room to tell them I have to return to Bombay. 'But this is how kids grow up. He will be fine soon,' Mummy says reassuringly. I'm not sure if she means Sumer or Varun.

Chapter 14

The past decade has seen a fair amount of progress towards achieving gender equality but despite all the positive changes one has witnessed at the workplace and society at large, complete equality between women and men still remains a distant dream. Even if women today are given the same opportunities as men while growing up, the demands of managing a house after marriage and motherhood leave them at a comparative disadvantage compared to men not only because often a mother's life isn't her own to lead but also because of the woman's lack of financial freedom.

This ends up limiting a woman's choices to live her life in a manner that is suitable to her needs and desires. Not only does it deprive us of our identities but, in many cases, educated women are suffering abusive marriages because they are not financially independent.

We can only have gender equality when men and women share all responsibility equally, be it parenting or financial.

Sumer's fever disappears the moment I land in Bombay. I'm nevertheless happy to be home to read him stories and ensure that he stays in bed.

'Trisha was here to see him this morning at 7 am,' Varun informs me. 'Nice of her to do that,' he adds.

Later, I ring Trisha to thank her for all her help. 'How can you thank me for this, Nats? After all that you have done for me this is nothing,' she says earnestly.

When I ask her about her own situation, she tells me that last week she met her father in Delhi and told him about her divorce personally. The news did not go down too well with him as expected. Guneet at least is feeling more settled. While he can't leave his wife while she's so unstable, he's decided to get a place for himself and Trisha in Bombay where Guneet will spend at least some of his time. I respect the man, his LV belt and shoes notwithstanding. The fact that Guneet's marriage has produced no children makes matters less complicated overall.

I have sent out my column to *City Reflections* and have already explained to Trisha that my article is sending out a message to empower women to work to be able to retain their freedom and that she must not think I'm in anyway talking about her specifically.

Trisha cheekily asks me if I intend to practise what I'm preaching.

'After seeing your situation Trish, I really am trying to,' I tell her. 'I'm just afraid that if I start working, I may not be able to do justice to my children. I will always be torn between work and home and that I will eventually make a mess of it. I don't want to bite off more than I can chew just so that Varun starts taking me seriously.'

'You are very talented Natasha and be fair to yourself first, then think about others. And even though I know you will never do what I have done, I think you will be a happier person if you start working more,' she says to me in a serious voice that I haven't heard before. The past few months have only ever been about her in any case. I'm pleasantly surprised by the interest she's showing in my life.

I think about her words after we say our goodbyes and hang up. The truth is that we do not understand the subconscious workings of our own minds. I realised today that it isn't a lack of ambition but deep-rooted fear that is preventing me from living the life that working women like Nafisa live. I used to be an ambitious girl, I loved my work. I wasn't just Mrs Singh when I walked into a room full of people. I was my own person, with my own job and my own connections that came with it.

My stream of consciousness is broken by a call from Priyanka Talwar who now wants me to do an in-depth piece with Riyad instead of a short feature. 'His work has been receiving a lot of critical acclaim outside of India, and he is the only Indian film director of our times that the magazine has shown interest in doing a full-length feature on,' Priyanka tells me. 'Since you have managed to get an appointment from him just go the whole hog, and we will see how to use the information.'

I inform Varun over breakfast that *Vanity* has approached me to write for them. He says he is pleased with the prospect of me reviving my dwindling writing career.

'Writing for *Vanity International* is prestigious, Natasha. Congratulations,' he says sounding genuinely pleased.

'It is and guess who they want me to do a profile on?'

'Amitabh Bachchan? Shah Rukh Khan?'

'They want me to write about Riyad Siddiqui,' I say, trying not to look too ecstatic.

'Oh, that must thrill you no end. You find him hot, don't you?' he asks teasingly.

'He is attractive. And single. All girls find him hot,' I smile and say.

'He is good-looking, I agree. Although, and sorry to rain on your parade, he is also much younger than you,' he says with sadistic pleasure.

'Not much, only by a few years,' I say, before adding, 'Anyway, I have to go to Manali for two days to interview him. He is on location there.' I feel extremely important as I say this.

'Good. You must go. And try not to obsess over the kids while you are there.'

'Will you manage them?'

'I should be able to, provided no last-minute site visits come up.'

I'm too ambushed by delight at the prospect of travelling on an assignment – a feeling that I haven't felt in years – to remind Varun of how his panic over Sumer's fever had marred the joy of my trip.

'And I will leave a list of medicines, and their quantities for each child should the need arise,' I tell Varun.

'Ya ya, we will manage. We did well without you the last time also,' he says.

'Ah yes, of course, we all remember that well, Varun,' I say with heavy irony that is completely lost on him.

Still, I feel grateful for his support although why I should be so grateful is beyond my comprehension.

Even before I have completely researched the subject of my assignment, I'm plagued with practical concerns such as what to wear to the interview to make myself appear both alluring and professional.

As expected, Nafisa is helpful when I ring her to discuss my sartorial options.

'Blue jeans and a nice white shirt should work. Please remember you are not the one being interviewed. So keep it basic,' she says dryly.

'So my Anne Fontaine shirt? Works?'

'The one that shows off your cleavage beautifully? Yes, it will look good. Might be slightly distracting to Riyad, but all the better for you,' she laughs.

'Shut up. I just think it looks like I haven't taken too much trouble to dress up and yet it's flattering, that's why I suggested,' I say.

'But we know you have taken too much trouble. And you ARE definitely troubling me over it on a working day Nats,' Nafisa chuckles before saying goodbye to me and hanging up.

Chapter 15

Women are constantly being told that they can have it all – great careers, emotionally secure children, toned butts and strong and passionate marriages. This is a big lie, and it's setting impossible standards for our girls. And while we are working towards being aces at everything, nobody is telling the boys that they can have great careers and children too because it's understood that women raise children and men only 'babysit'.

As a mother, I see nothing wrong with this. It has been my privilege to raise three (mostly) tolerable children while forsaking my career. I do have a problem, however, with women buying into the idea that they can have it all. We cannot even begin to have it all until all responsibilities, parenting and otherwise, between men and women are split down in the middle.

Educated men continue to buy into gender stereotyping probably because it works to their advantage. By continually reminding themselves about the alleged maternal instinct that women are born with, men naturally assume that raising children is a woman's job and feel satisfied with token tasks like playing soccer with their child on the weekends.

It feels strange to leave my children in my husband's care and travel on work. I'm feeling excited and nervous all at once. Going away from home for even just a few days means that as always, I must instruct the staff on how to run the house in my absence.

'And please don't call me every few minutes to tell me something has run out, or you cannot decide what is to be cooked for dinner,' I look in the cook's direction and say. Shambhu looks hurt. 'Vaisey bhi hum kahan phone lagatey hain aap ko. Urgent hota hai tabhi lagatein hain na,' he tells me in his thick Bihari accent.

I then plan the children's schedules with Sylvia, set their lunch-box menus for two days and leave firm instructions about not allowing them more than thirty minutes of television time, no matter what. Even though my dear husband is 'babysitting' our kids, there will be mayhem in the house if I don't lay down rules.

If going away for two days needs so much planning, I hate to imagine just how challenging life would be if I were working full-time or worse still, dead.

It is with a sense of exhilaration that I board my flight to Manali. On the plane when an elderly lady sitting next to me asks me if I'm traveling to Manali on a vacation by myself, I proudly tell her that I'm on an assignment.

We arrive at the quaint hill town two hours later than schedule because of a late take-off from Chandigarh. Even so, Riyad's assistant Jacob has been tracking the flight and has made arrangements for a car to fetch me from the airport. 'Sir wants you to come to the set directly and requests that you should have lunch with him,' Jacob tells me as soon as

I have sat inside the car. I feel so important today that if I had traded places with the prime minister of India for a day, I could not have felt more important.

My drive to the hotel takes me past apple orchards in full bloom and thriving cherry blossom trees which I thought only grew in Japan and parts of Europe. After a speedy check-in at the Carlton Hotel, my car pulls up outside a beautiful Kangda-style bungalow where Riyad's new movie, presently untitled, is being filmed.

I'm offered a chair not far from the set from where I watch Riyad at work from a distance. Tall and lean in his snug black T-shirt and light blue denim, he is so compellingly handsome that I have to force myself to look away from him.

Riyad explains something to the cameraman on the crane and beckons his lead actor Rishab Arora to look towards the horizon. An older man, a well-known character actor by the name of Shyam Prakash, comes from behind and puts a hand on Rishab's shoulder. The latter turns around and looks at him with a start while mouthing something.

'And cut....' Riyad shouts.

After reviewing the scene on the monitor, he walks towards me in long strides.

'Hey Natasha, hope you didn't mind I made you come to the set directly,' he smiles a slightly lopsided, George Clooney smile at me with his hand outstretched.

I offer my hand to Riyad and apologise for not being able to keep time. He shrugs his shoulders and laughs, 'We work in Bollywood and have no expectations of anybody showing up on time ever. Shall we eat lunch and then we can do the interview as I'm only going to shoot after 3 pm now?'

There is a cold breeze whipping around the corner even as the sun gets masked by a dark cloud. Rows of bulrushes flanking the driveway of the isolated bungalow are making an eerie sound as they rustle in the wind. We walk towards the van quietly. 'Haven't we met before? I get the feeling I have seen you somewhere,' Riyad turns towards me while he holds the door of the van for me.

'Really? I don't think we have met before at all,' I tell him as I enter his van. Surely, he cannot remember me from that embarrassing night of that magazine awards party!

'Hmm, you do not look like a journalist, however,' he says matter-of-factly as I step inside. The van itself is like a shrunken hotel suite – every amenity at hand – including a tiny velvet couch, a bedroom with a berth to sleep on, a pull-out dining table, a television set and a bathroom.

'Sorry, this basic meal is all I can offer you,' says Riyad pointing at the food laid out by a unit hand on the pull-out table. 'Thank God I will be returning to Bombay soon. I want to eat ghar ka khana,' he mumbles to himself. I help myself to some salad and noodles from the boxes laid out in front of me. It's difficult to be seated in front of a good-looking man and allow him to watch you tuck into a hearty meal because hunger is so un-classy.

As it is, sharing a meal with another person is a somewhat intimate experience which is made harder if you are not only virtual strangers but also crushing on that person.

We discuss the general flow of the story over lunch. I tell him that between today and tomorrow I intend to get him to talk about his childhood, his love for cinema, the movies that influenced him, his days at the film school in New York...the changing face of Indian cinema, his creative process, and his favourite books.

'Are you writing my biography?' he jokes. 'If you are, please let me know because I think I should achieve a little more before I become biograph-able.'

'You are elusive, and this is our only chance to talk to you. So we are making the most of it,' I say.

After lunch, I start recording the interview on my phone. We begin by talking about the influence that old Guru Dutt's films have had on his work. 'I was obsessed with watching Guru Dutt's movies when most of my friends wanted to watch the usual Amitabh Bachchan starrers with all that exciting action,' he says. 'I got teased a lot for liking movies that mostly only our mothers liked,' he tells me before going on to talk about the richness of regional cinema in India and Italian cinema.

Before we know it nearly an hour has passed and the AD comes in to call Riyad for the next shot.

The man is utterly charming, very courteous and really bright. While he readies to take the next shot, I check my phone for messages and emails – there are none from home. This has never happened before. I get missed a call from Ria and Sumer even when I go to the washroom in my own house. How is it that nothing that demands my immediate attention has occurred in my absence? Then it strikes me, the kids are still at school. The day is young. Those calls will come.

There is, however, an email from Nafisa.

Hey Nats,
Give me the dirt. Is he hot? How is it going? How is Manali?
 xx
 Nafisa.

Dear Nafisa,
What dirt? I just got here. We had lunch in his van. Oh, he is hot.
Mind was flooded with impure thoughts. I have no morals, I think.
Manali is stunning even though a little worn out in places.
 xx
 Natasha.

Natasha,
Go for it. You will be peri-menopausal soon. Such urges are common
to women your age.
 Am dying of work and so bored.
 xx
 N.

My darling Nafisa,
Is this what La Beau Monde has hired you for? To encourage happily
married women to lose their way? And I'm not peri-menopausal for
another fifteen years at least. I took that test remember, when my
cycle went haywire. They told me my bio cycle is that of someone in
the mid-thirties. So there!
 xx
 Natasha.

Nats,
So much for encouraging you to live a little! I'm so bored, maybe I
want to live out my dreams via you vicariously. Hey, wait a minute,

why don't you do a travel or a fashion story with him for us? I leave the angle to you. His dress sense is very edgy, is it not? We could do a nice fashion feature on him if he agrees. If you do a longish piece, we can even schedule him on our June cover, which is four months from now.

xx

N.

Therefore, God has made friends. So that they can put together assignments that help you in keeping the society of desirable men.

Nafisa,

Yasssssssssssssss!! You are the best. But wait, it's too soon to bring this up. Maybe later after this interview is done, I can discuss your story with him. Doubt he will agree to do a fashion story.

Mwah mwah

Natasha.

Back on the sets, as I take notes while observing Riyad in action, I catch him looking in my direction a few times as well. And then when he smiles warmly at me, I'm certain my beating heart can be heard in the valley below. For a fleeting moment, I feel guilty about crushing on another man, but I tell myself that liking a celebrity is allowed.

I'm finally served coffee by the unit hand and around the same time, Riyad joins me, pulling up a chair, and sits next to me.

'Sorry, this is how it usually goes.'

'Please don't apologise. It's a regular working day for you.'

'Listen, if you want to head back and freshen up at the hotel, we can do this later after I wrap up.'

I assure him my freshening up can wait and that I'd rather ask him a few more questions. 'Okay, good. Then I will keep popping by in between the shots,' he says as he gets up to give a brief to his cinematographer.

When he returns to the chair, a mug of coffee in hand, I'm on the phone with Sumer who is crying bitterly, and the only words I can hear are 'Ria' and 'project'.

I ask for Sylvia, but he will not let go of the phone, and I'm torn between attending to his emotional outburst and giving attention to Riyad, who is, by now, seated on the chair next to me and looking amused with what he can make of the conversation.

By the time I'm done playing referee and therapist to my son and calming him down, a good five minutes have passed. I apologise to Riyad about my long phone call. 'Oh, please don't. My sister has kids. I have seen how her life is. I completely understand.'

'I know about your sister's kids. Our children go to the same school,' I tell him.

'Really? To Chiltern High? Then that's where I must have seen you. I attend my niece and nephew's sports day and annual day at Chiltern High every year.'

Riyad has just started telling me about his dancer mother being his biggest inspiration and the reason why he writes women-centric stories, when a messenger from the leading lady of his film, the dusky beauty Alisha Sharma, tells him that she wishes to meet him about her dialogue. He excuses himself promising to be back shortly, but thirty minutes later, I'm still sitting by myself on that chair feeling the cold wind play havoc with my body's thermostat. 'Alisha Ma'am is getting her make-up done in her van while discussing the dialogues with Riyad Sir; that is why it's taking long. He has sent a message to tell you that he may take a little more time,' the assistant director walks up to me and says.

I feel a stab of envy when I think of Riyad and the young actress together inside that van, but I quickly dismiss this disturbing thought and remind myself of Varun.

This interminable wait for him to return and the long drive have left me feeling exhausted, and when pendulous drops begin to fall from the sky suddenly, I take it as a sign to head to the hotel.

I hurriedly scribble a note for Riyad after escaping to my car and send it into the van with my driver requesting him to please excuse me briefly and to get in touch with me once he is at the hotel. Riyad rings me right away and apologises for keeping me waiting and asks if I mind having dinner with him. And if I enjoy Tibetan momos. I tell him I do. I love Tibetan food even though it has very few vegetarian options. 'Perfect then, I'm taking you to this tiny restaurant downtown. I hope you will be able to take it though. It's quite simple really,' he asks.

I tell him I love hole-in-the-wall joints so long as they maintain hygiene and have character. This isn't entirely true, but I don't want him to think I am fussy and unprofessional.

Riyad tells me I won't be disappointed and promises that I'm about to taste the best Tibetan meal on the planet. We decide to meet at the hotel lobby at 7.30 pm.

I'm certainly impressed with his impeccable manners of probably interrupting a shag with his leading lady to call me about momos and obviously, I don't mind having dinner with him.

You would think that Varun would manage the children for just this one evening by himself but no, my phone begins to ring the moment I have stepped inside my room. 'Natasha, please tell me what to do with these children. I have had enough,' he says, sounding exasperated.

'Calm down Varun. What happened?'

'What calm down? Sumer pushed Ria, she fell off the mini scooter and got a cut on her foot. It's a small cut, but it's bleeding. Thankfully I was around, I came back early from work to be with the kids.'

'But Varun…why are you angry? This is what I do every day when you are at work by the way. And then you keep telling me to go to work. Is this how it's going to be?'

'There is no time for all this Natasha,' he snaps. 'What is to be done now? We have put a dressing, but the edge of that damned scooter was sharp. So I think the bleeding is still not stopping.'

I FaceTime with Ria and inspect her makeshift dressing over the wound. It really is just a scrape and doesn't require this much drama around it.

Ria cries a little more for effect while an agitated Varun stands in the backdrop, his arms folded across his chest.

'Take her to the hospital and just carry her medical record. I'm not sure her tetanus booster is covered, it should be though,' I tell him calmly.

'Noooo, I don't want to go to the hospital,' Ria shrieks.

'You hang up the phone. I will manage her,' he tells me abruptly.

You often wonder what I do with my time, well, now you know sweetie, I hear myself thinking.

A little while later he sends me a photo of Ria holding an ice lolly, looking terribly pleased with herself. By the time I have dealt with this long-distance medical crisis I am ready for dinner – it's 7.30 pm.

Over a broth-like soup and steamed momos eaten with a fiery garlic sauce, as Riyad and I chat with each other, I begin to feel an instant connection with him. Interestingly, we both love Hitchcock, Francois Truffaut and Woody Allen, even though I only watched them because Daddy forced me to. *Three Men in a Boat* is the book that has made us laugh the most, and we both find Rushdie impossible to read. Soon we are so lost in conversation that the interview is temporarily forgotten. 'This is fun. Don't worry, you are here tomorrow as well, aren't you? We can do the questions then,' Riyad says when I remind him that I'm not even halfway through my interview yet.

Varun interrupts my enchanting evening with another call in which I'm required to ask an obstinate Sofie to go to bed on time. When I resume my conversation with Riyad, I begin to notice every feature on his face – the manner in which he holds his chopsticks, the glimmer in his eyes as he laughs, fine laugh lines that form around his mouth and, most importantly, the attention with which he listens to what I have to say.

It must be the cheap wine being served at the restaurant I reckon that is making me so conscious of this man's presence. I decide to stop at my second glass to control my admiration of Riyad and ask for a coffee instead.

'I never knew journalists were this much fun or I might have been willing to do interviews sooner,' Riyad tells me in a deep voice, flashing his dimpled smile as he sees me off to the elevator.

I smile back at him hoping to God that he cannot see my dilated pupils.

Later, as I lie in bed at night, I still cannot believe that Riyad and I are so alike. Who would have thought? Being in his presence I felt gloriously alive, profoundly excited and indefinably young tonight.

It felt wonderful to make the acquaintance of someone who has the same taste as you and who is not a class mother. What if he is in bed with Alisha Sharma at this moment, even as I'm lying in this squeaky bed stupidly thinking about our similarities.

As I drift off into sleep, I worry that I am giving this man unhealthy amounts of headspace.

Perhaps I should have carried a picture of Varun and kept it by my bedside as a constant reminder of what I have at home.

I speak with Ria first thing in the morning. She seems keen to go to school and show off her small wound to her friends. It's raining heavily outside, and the shoot has to be held off for a few hours. This works perfectly well for me because I can now hope for an exclusive one-on-one time with Riyad to finish my interview and then head back to Bombay after lunch. This time, I decide, I will keep it strictly professional, and each time my mind plays tricks with me I will say to myself, 'I love Varun, I love Varun.'

We sit in the lobby with rain lashing against its glassy exterior for over an hour at a stretch and by lunchtime, I'm ready to leave.

'Princess Natasha, it was an honour to be interviewed by you. This has been the most humbling experience of my life so far. I never thought royalty would interview me,' Riyad says to me with exaggerated seriousness.

'The pleasure was all mine, Riyad. Thank you for agreeing to do the interview in the first place. In fact, I was surprised you spoke so easily because this isn't the impression the editor of the magazine gave me of you,' I tell him as I wait for my car on the porch.

'Only with a privileged few,' he says as he gets the door of the car for me.

'I love Varun, I love Varun,' I say to myself as my car drives off towards the lower ghats.

I'm now at Manali airport, waiting to board the flight to Bombay, and an extraordinary realisation dawns upon me – that I'm happy to be travelling anywhere, for any purpose, without either the children or Varun. I also feel a heaviness in my chest, a sense of loss, that my exciting encounter, that one I was anticipating with such joy since so many days, is now behind me. I wonder if this is what they call a midlife crisis. If not, then it must be agreed that I'm simply losing my mind. I decide to check my email to distract myself and what I find in my inbox is a sobering reminder of my life choices.

Email from Pride of Cows informing me that they are excited about their new range of dairy products. (As if I care!)

Email from Spring Foods letting me know that they have dropped the price of their gluten-free bread.

Email from Amazon offering me deals on a book titled *Being Ageless*. (How dare they?)

Email from Ferragamo announcing their new collection. (Thereby confirming that I'm an auntie.)

Email from Nafisa (Thank God!)

So, are you going to tell me about last night or not? How did it go?

xx

Nafisa.

Nafisa,

Why are we doing this on email? Anyway, so last night was wonderful. We connected well over dinner. Like friends, don't let your imagination run unharnessed.

Am surprised by how much we have in common. Will tell more about our conversation when we meet.

xx

N.

Natasha,

You cannot serve me an appetiser and not follow it up with the main course. Easier to email than call. I enjoy our piecemeal exchanges in the middle of work.

Did you bring up Varun at all?

I bet you did not, you vixen!

xx

Nafisa.

My dear Nafisa,

I did tell Riyad about Varun. How could I not? While talking about his work Varun's connection to palaces came up, after which Riyad started to refer to me as Princess. Not that it means anything. Now going back to my 'same old same old' life. You are single and lucky for it. You are free to date anyone you like.

I don't feel like going back home. This feeling is unheralded. Loved the fact that I travelled, if only to Manali, for a professional assignment. I have this sudden realisation that I miss my old single, working girl's life. Why am I feeling so emotional today? Feel like crying. Hope it's PMS.

xx

Nat.

My dear PMSing Princess,

Freedom to date isn't always the best thing. Flirting is healthy. That's all that you can do anyway. You got your hands full, just in case you had forgotten.

Get back to working full-time if it makes you so happy. And look at it this way. You got three kids from being married and no career and I have a job, but I live alone with a goldfish.

What next?

xx

Nafis(h)a

It's cruel of Nafisa to throw earth into the grave of my middle-aged dreams.

I must seriously consider her suggestion of working full-time though. This one assignment has revealed a lot about my suppressed impulse. I'm ready to shed my domestic goddess skin. It's time.

I'm too tired to transcribe my notes today and want to spend time with the kids anyway. Sumer and Ria are thrilled to find me at home after school. Ria wastes no time in showing me the gauze dressing on her ankle even as she tries to simulate the pain from yesterday. Sumer wants to know if I bought him anything and looks very disappointed when I tell him that I got him apples and strawberry jam.

I reach for my phone to call Varun and ask him why he isn't home from work yet but I forget all about him on finding a message waiting on my phone from Riyad. My heart almost skips a dozen beats as I open it to read it.

Was a pleasure meeting you. Hope you reached safely. Let me know if you need any other information from my end, Riyad.

All my exhaustion dissipates after reading his message, and I suddenly feel revived, my heart threatening to leap out of my ribcage and do a jig on the carpet. I read the message a few more times before I forward it to Nafisa. I must not feel exhilarated over this one polite message from him, I tell myself. He is only making sure I have all the angles covered.

I write back. *Reached an hour ago, thanks. Was a pleasure. Will work on the story and if anything left out shall get in touch.*

Five minutes later, there is no message from him. Ten minutes later, still nothing. I decide to put the phone away and look at it in an hour, but I return to it in less than ten minutes and feel the weight of unrequited love. Maybe I should have asked him a question to keep the conversation going.

I feel guilty about allowing unhallowed impulses, but then I know this is only just banter, no more. Besides is it not considered healthy to repress one's desires? Peril awaits however one looks at it. Why am I feeling guilty at all? I just have a minuscule crush on Riyad. It's not like am eloping with him. Varun must meet interesting women at work all the time, but to me an encounter like this is not par for the course, although I do hope that very soon my life will be all about meeting interesting people all the time.

The phone beeps. Delight. Much delight. Had forgotten just how much joy small things like a text message from someone you admire can bring to your life. I rush to look at the phone but the message is just from Varun. I'm not this person; my mind is playing tricks with me. It reads: *This meeting is taking forever, should leave for home soon. Don't wait up for dinner, I have eaten heavy snacks.*

When Varun is finally home, I'm sitting in my bed in my pajamas, and I tell him excitedly about how wonderful it was to get an exclusive interview from a sought after, elusive filmmaker. 'So, a good interview?'

'Oh, it was fun. Riyad makes an interesting copy. Polished man. Very bright,' I tell him even as I feel a little self-conscious while speaking about Riyad, which I find inexplicably odd.

'Yes, I read his interview in *GQ* on some flight. He was talking about the kind of briefs he likes to wear, jocks over boxers it seems. Very intellectual,' mocks Varun.

'Don't be mean. He would not be invited to Cannes and Sundance if he wasn't cerebral,' I say.

'Mallika Sherawat gets invited to Cannes, so clearly they don't have a very high standard being observed on the red carpet there,' Varun laughs.

'Good Lord, did you just compare Riyad to an attention seeker who can barely even be called a starlet?'

'Oh, you're really taking up for him. All you women seem to like this guy, what gives?'

'Oh, that is easy. Riyad is different from other scruffy-looking Indian film directors. He is respectful to women and articulate too.'

'You have come back very impressed, I can tell,' Varun says warmly.

I can almost picture Varun, Riyad and me becoming friends and shooting the breeze together. Feeling silly with my ridiculous fantasy, I change the topic and ask my husband about the children.

'Hope you and the kids bonded in my absence, by the way.'

Varun rolls his eyes as he gets into his pajamas.

'They need to be disciplined, especially Sofie. She instigates the other two to disobey when you are not around. I got really fed up last evening. This morning too, she got everyone late for school,' Varun complains. 'And Sumer bosses over Ria all the time when you are not around. I was constantly trying to play peacemaker.'

'That is all it takes for you Varun? Two evenings with the children by yourself and you are at your wits end?' I say, massaging age-defying youth-activating serum onto my skin.

'You have practice, and I don't. That is the difference, Natasha.'

'And who stopped you from getting practice?' I say, feeling irritated with his litany of complaints.

'Er, my work. Okay, don't fight now. Put your night cream and come to bed.'

***

As I key in his answers on my laptop, I realise that I have not asked Riyad about his top ten favourite films. Priyanka had wanted something like that for the blurb. I quickly send him an email about this, doing my best to keep a strictly professional tone.

He replies.

Dear Natasha,
Delighted to hear from you.

Here is the list of films that I have enjoyed watching immensely. Not sure if they have influenced my work but nevertheless, here is the list.

West Side Story
Psycho
Casablanca
A Clockwork Orange
Smokey and the Bandit
The Bicycle Thief

Thanks,
Riyad.

Dear Riyad,
Thank you for your prompt reply. Er, don't you like any Hindi films at all?
Natasha.

Natasha,

My bad. How could I forget? I loved Masoom, Arth, Charulata, Aakrosh and Do Bigha Zameen. Oh, and also all of Karishma Kapoor-David Dhawan movies.

    ;)

    Riyad.

Dear Riyad,

Impressed by your choice of films, especially the Karishma Kapoor-David Dhawan ones. This must go in a special blurb.

    Will impact your admirers at many levels.

    Cheers

    Natasha.

Dear Natasha,

It was a joke. Please don't ruin me by publishing it. I'll buy you coffee in return once I'm back. Does later next week work for you? Say noonish or then even 4/5 pm?

    My deepest regards and respect,

    Riyad.

Oh, this man is so cheeky. Now he wants to meet me for coffee, but he is keeping his stone strictly friendly and casual, so there is no scope for misunderstanding. I'm tempted to meet him too. It's just a harmless cup of coffee, nothing else, but he may think I'm too forward or may assume I like him. At any rate, I must not reply right away.

On second thought, if I don't reply now he will know that I'm thinking this over and perhaps reading too much into it. Must not agree to meet on Thursday as I may look too eager. Can't believe that I'm giving this so much thought. Must forward his email to Nafisa for advice. She is more experienced in this area. My idea and understanding of men is somewhat antediluvian.

Natasha,
What are you thinking? Go meet him. Carry protection. Ha ha ha.
  xx
  N.

Dear Nafisa,
I'm only wondering if I should agree to meet him for coffee. FYI I'm not interested in ANYTHING more. I just find his company refreshing because he does not think me to be silly. I'm a respectable and happily married woman and mother of three, remember?
  You are no help.
  Natasha.

Nats,
Meet him. What is there to wonder then? It's only just a coffee with someone whose company you enjoy. Calm down. I trust you.
  I know you are all those things you mentioned, which is precisely why you should meet him because he makes you feel alive. This is the last decade of your life. I mean at forty you cannot expect Ranbir Kapoor to ask you for coffee. This is your only chance to feel good about yourself. You should be flattered Riyad 'enjoyed your company' as you insist on calling it. Ten years from now, you will probably be recovering from a knee replacement surgery, and you will regret not having this coffee. I know you.
  xx
  N.

Nafisa,
You just nailed it for me. Yes, I enjoy interacting with Riyad because he makes me feel alive. And we have a mental connect. He does not diss me for being a lethargic, freelancing mother of three.

You do remember you are only four years younger than I'm. When I'm having my knees replaced, you will be convalescing on the bed next to me from a hip replacement.

Shall I agree to have coffee on Thursday itself? Will I look too eager? Which I'm, but he need not know that.

Love you,
Natasha.

Nats,
Playing hard to get is good when you are in your twenties. If you are not keen on having an affair with him what do you care if you look too keen? Keen on what? If Riyad were a woman would you have pondered so much about this matter? I think not.

About our surgeries, I will be pregnant when you are having your knees replaced.

Love,
N.

Nafisa,
You are so right. God, I love you.

About the pregnancy, I did not know you could have children after menopause. You can lie about your age, but your ovaries will know.

Shall you and I meet on Friday?
xo
Natasha.

I am so busy thinking about Riyad that I have forgotten about Varun altogether. I wonder if he will mind if I meet Riyad for coffee. Not that he needs to know. I don't have a minute-by-minute account of his day anyway. A struggle ensues between my conscience and me and I manage to snuff out the former. Am I not overthinking this coffee? Don't people who work together meet for coffee in a kosher way? It's exactly like that.

Dear Riyad,
Coffee sounds good. Maybe you can also give me a pen drive with your pictures when we meet. If my editor likes them, we can spare you a photo shoot.
        PS: These should be previously unpublished photos of you.
        Cheers,
        Natasha.

I hate signing off with 'cheers' but 'warmly' sounds too intimate suddenly.

Dear Natasha,
Would you like to pop by at my office for coffee? We have a good Nespresso machine, and I can order you some dessert from the deli next door.
        You do know my office is in Bandra. You mentioned you live somewhere close by so should be easy.
        Looking forward,
        Riyad.

Dear Riyad,

Your office works. Nespresso good idea, dessert bad idea. How dare you assume that I'm the kind of woman who likes her dessert?

See you on Thursday. Send me your office address.

Natasha.

Dear Natasha,

You look nothing like a woman who likes her dessert. My sincere apologies about insinuating otherwise. It was unfortunate and unintended.

See you on Thursday then. 4 pm.

Ciao,

Riyad.

I'm relieved that I'm to meet Riyad at his office. Now it all seems respectable and appropriate. I'm also surprised how quickly an entire day has passed between anticipating emails, reading and responding to them and intermittently smiling to myself like an absolute idiot.

And now I'm already thinking of the clothes I'm going to wear when I meet HIM. Cannot believe myself. Am I a sixteen-year-old trapped in a forty-year-old's body?

While I'm dealing with the imminent perplexities of my life, I catch Sofie obsessing over what she is going to wear to her school fete on Saturday. Never have clothes mattered to her to this extent that their absence or presence has made her weep. 'Nothing looks good. Nothing fits. What will I wear?' she says to me through her tears. The irony of this situation isn't lost on me.

I pull out a bright T-shirt from her closet and offer it to her. 'How can I wear this? I'm not a baby!'

I offer her a nice summery dress with dandelions printed across the pistachio-coloured chiffon.

'I'm not acting in the *Sound of Music* for God's sake Mom.'

I offer her the Burberry shirt dress that is hanging in her closet with its tags still dangling from it.

'Yuck, no one dresses in Burberry. It's disgusting. Please give it away to someone.'

I can feel my own liver secrete extra bile by now, but I remind myself to inhale deeply and contain my exasperation.

Next, she turns her angst at me. 'You never buy me any nice clothes. You just want me to dress like a baby. I'm not a baby.' Waterworks follow, and I'm torn between consoling Sofie and placing the white of my hand firmly against her cheek. Varun walks in just in time to take his inconsolable daughter into his arms and strokes her head lovingly. 'Tell Daddy what happened,' he coos.

I leave the two to sort out Sofie's problems. I have enough of my own to deal with.

***

I have a spring in my step as I get out of my bed in the morning the following day. It's finally Thursday, the day of my meeting with Riyad and I haven't yet decided what I'm wearing. Sofie is looking deeply disturbed about her clothes crisis over breakfast. 'My school fete is tomorrow, and I still have nothing to wear,' she says despairingly.

'Sorry, Sofie, I have things to do today. I don't have the time to take you shopping. You will have to dig into your closet and manage with what you have already,' I tell her firmly.

Varun who has just returned from one of his riding sessions in the morning in a cheerfully charitable mood and feels sorry for his daughter. He offers to take her shopping the same evening.

'Just come to my office straight from school. We will go and get you some clothes,' he tells her. There is something about Varun's expression as he makes this helpful offer that is almost self-congratulatory – an I-am-such-an-amazing-dad look on his face. I should not look a gift horse in the mouth though, this is the first time ever that Varun has offered to take over a parenting-related chore from me. I should be rejoicing.

By half noon, after I'm through with my kick-boxing as well as meditation, where all I could think about was what to wear today, I'm standing inside my closet and looking around me. I cannot do jeans and shirt, I wore that the last time. A casual summer dress would look good, but I have no casual summer dresses. I don't want to look like I made too much effort.

Maybe I could try my cool Gap khakis and a white tee. I hold the combination against me and consider my reflection in the mirror. This look would work if I were going to lunch with my plumber, but since Riyad is not my plumber, I must find something better.

An hour later, I'm standing next to a pile of clothes that I have resolved never to wear again, and I'm still undecided about what to wear today. I have no clothes. I either have clothes fit for red-carpet galas, clothes that I hope to wear to

Benedict Cumberbatch's next wedding in a Scottish Castle, or I have clothes that make me look like a homeless person who lives out of a box. I have nothing in between.

I finally settle for a blue linen top and my white linen Massimo Dutti pants which I can wear with wedges. I could do better than this if I was a cooler, calmer, more collected person who wasn't easily excitable, but I'm none of those things. I'm also too exhausted to think.

I arrive at Riyad's office, fifteen minutes late on purpose. I'm escorted to a sofa inside the tastefully done reception area by the receptionist where I spend the next few minutes feeling impressed with the clutch of awards received displayed on a rack near the seating area. When Riyad comes out to receive me himself in a crisp white shirt and light blue jeans, I have to do all I can to control myself from drooling. 'Hello Natasha,' he says to me formally, 'Good to see you.' I smile at him cheerfully and say hello back. 'Come on in,' he says, leading me to his cabin. 'I love Varun, I love Varun,' I chant inside my head as we walk towards the corridor that leads to his cabin. Riyad leans over and tells his receptionist something inaudible as we pass her by and she, in turn, looks at me sheepishly.

Once inside he laughs and tells me, 'My receptionist was feeling stupid because she rang me inside and told me a model was here for a screen test.'

'Oh?' I mutter.

'I told her every good-looking woman who walks into my office isn't coming here only for a screen test,' he flashes his Colgate model smile as he laughs.

'Well, in any case, I'm too short to be confused for a model,' I say dismissively.

'We just paid you a compliment, don't be modest now. And we always have solutions for height. We make our short actors stand on an elevation,' he says. 'Anyway, I told her that you are a princess, and not a model,' Riyad chuckles, his eyes twinkling.

This conversation is making me uneasy and I wish he would change the subject.

'Anyway, jokes apart Natasha, how do you like your coffee?' he says as if reading my mind.

'Black.'

He intercoms his secretary Martha and tells her to send in two cups of the Vivalto black.

Riyad has many things to ask me – it's almost like I'm the one being interviewed this time. He wants to know about my life as a full-time editor, my column which he has strangely never read before, how I occupy myself when kids are at school and if I ever intend to get back to working full-time.

Finally, at my insistence, we go through his pictures on the laptop together, and by the end of the slide show, my crush has left me breathless. I feel unfamiliar sensations that I should not be as a happily committed woman.

Alright, I'm guilty of a little too much hyperbole, but my crush has intensified based purely on the physical attributes of this man. I remind myself that flirting with women is probably an occupation hazard for Riyad and he probably beds them all as well. This is a sobering thought, and I snap out of my altered state of consciousness.

As I'm about to get up to leave he tells me that he has written a story for his next film that he thinks he would like me to read. 'You are a very bright woman Natasha, and a writer yourself. So I'd like to hear your perspective on my story, especially since my protagonist is a woman.'

'I'm flattered that you would want me to read something that you have written Riyad, although I'm not sure I will be able to add value to it.'

'Don't worry about that. My sister has read it. She gave me her inputs on the story as will you I'm sure. My protagonist is a strong, individualistic woman, and I need similar women to read my story and see if it resonates with them,' he says, smiling at me generously, revealing a set of beautiful teeth along with dimples.

He called me strong and individualistic. Could he be right about that? I have never thought of myself in this vein. We sit there in silence for a few seconds after that, with Riyad looking at me, his wide smile now reduced to a kosher grin, and me feeling a little silly as I sense a blush spread over my cheeks. All those clichés one reads and derides are beginning to apply to me evidently.

'Okay, so mail me the story whenever you are ready. Oh, and I shall let you know if we will be using these photographs,' I tell Riyad as I finally get up to leave.

'You are leaving already?' Riyad says. He sounds disappointed.

'I need to get back to…some stuff Riyad. I'm sure you have tons to do yourself,' I tell him.

'But I'd much rather talk to you. I like talking to you. We are on the same wavelength,' he says earnestly although I'm sure these well-rehearsed lines are part of his practised charm. But why would he use it on me? There must be no dearth of women vying for his attention.

'When do you think your story will appear?' he asks to fill in the awkward silence.

'Next month,' I say as I get up to leave. 'I shall keep you posted, Riyad. And thank you for the coffee.'

'Thank you, Natasha, for your time,' he says with a grin as he sees me off to the elevator.

I ring Nafisa as soon as I'm out of the elevator.

'Yes Natty, this better be important. I'm to go into my CEO's cabin any minute now to ask him for a raise,' says Nafisa as she answers the phone.

'It's about Riyad. I met him.'

'OMG. Tell me all. The raise can wait.' Something tells me Nafisa is going through a dry spell lately and is living vicariously off my crush.

'Nafisa I really like him. I don't want to. But just the way he speaks to me and looks at me…I'd have to be a dead mummy to not feel anything back for him.'

'But you are a mummy, darling.'

'Oh, not that mummy, stop it! I meant Egyptian mummy. Like Nefertiti's mummy.'

'Hmmm…it's okay to like somebody even if you are married, my darling. You are limiting it to liking and not acting on those impulses, so chill,' she says. 'Look, I'd not indulge you if I thought it was any more than a fan-girl thing. You have been a devoted wife to Varun and I have so much faith in you, and I know that that is never going to change.'

'I'm not going to act on any impulses. You can be sure of that. But you do not know how guilty and conflicted I feel Nafisa. I find myself thinking of Riyad a lot more than I should. Sometimes even when Varun is around. Then what is the difference between Trisha and me?'

'You are not Trisha. Even if you tried you would not be. Maybe if you met interesting people like him often enough, you would get over him. Anyway, he is just being charming, and it's new for you since you have been squatting at home for far too long,' she laughs.

'Ha, yes. I suppose he does this all the time. Regardless, it's a slippery slope for me.'

'I'm glad you said that yourself. Now that you have access to him do a piece for me with him, please. Two thousand words. I promise not to use it until long after your *Vanity* interview is out. Our October issue is on famous people and their role models. Maybe he could write a piece for us.'

'Shouldn't you be asking me to never see him again instead of assigning me a story?' I ask.

'Natasha, you are giving this too much importance. Finish this assignment with him and be done with it. Either way, the enigma will wear off as will the novelty in due course. In a few days, you will do another interview for *Vanity International* with another man, and we will be having this conversation all over again, I'm sure.'

Nafisa always simplifies my dilemmas for me. She is right. I'm taking things far too seriously. I shall try and do the story with him on email. This way he will not think that I'm trying to see him again.

Priyanka rings me later to ask me if I can go to Jaipur to do an interview with Chinese actress Michelle Yung in four weeks. 'She is acting in the next movie in *The Mummy* series. The studios have gotten in touch with our US office. We can do a longish feature on her.'

'Oh, I'd love to do an interview with Michelle Yung, Priyanka. Thank you. I'm also sending you the Riyad Siddiqui piece by tomorrow latest,' I say.

'Actually, Natasha,' says Priyanka. 'I need to hire a deputy editor. Someone who can come on board full-time. I was talking to Nafisa about this today, and it occurred to me that you might be the right person. Do you think you would be interested in something like that?'

This is most unexpected – from freelancer and columnist to a full-time employee. It could be a good opportunity, no doubt. I tell her that I will think it over and get back to her at the earliest.

Chapter 16

Prince Harry and Meghan Markle will be in Bombay soon, and the news of their visit has sent ripples of joy among all sorts of people across the city. Those who can afford to be present at the dinners being planned in the honour of the royal couple are busy pairing their Mikimoto pearls with their evening gowns that will be pulled out especially for this occasion.

What is it about the British royalty that causes such excitement among our people, I wonder? Are we still under some obligatory debt to our captors that we feel beholden to them? Does it need reminding that the Crown looted us dry for over two centuries and all the sincere apologies from their young, evolved, intellectually aware descendants will not make up for our collective suffering as a nation? I admit that Harry and Meghan, with their vastly different backgrounds, is an exciting and unconventional marriage and they are a couple who I'd not mind meeting at a dinner party at all.

But would I elbow out other people to be in the same photo as them? Maybe not.

My mother-in-law rings me this morning after a long gap. She sounds quite unnaturally cheerful as she goes about asking after the children, Varun and, believe it or not, even me. 'I hope you are taking care of your health,' she says with mock concern.

'My health? What is there to take care of Maa?' I ask her.

'Oh! You know, I feel you have started to neglect yourself. I saw your WhatsApp picture today and realised that you are looking pale and fatigued.'

My mother-in-law lives by the dictum that if you have nothing nice to say, then you must say it. Even her concern for me is spiked with slights. Is this her idea of smoothening things over with me? As surprised as I'm with this revived familiarity between us, I reassure her that I'm doing well and have accepted ageing as part of life.

'Why don't you go and get a good facial done now? I think if you need it, Botox isn't a bad idea either, by the way.'

Point taken. Next, she will tell me face-lifts are a good idea too.

Then she cuts to the chase. 'I'm coming to town next week. This time it's going to be a terribly hectic trip. You know it's the polo semi-finals, and Dadabhai Sahab's team has made it.'

There is no asking the lady of the house if it is going to be convenient for her to receive guests, as usual.

'That's wonderful. Congratulations,' I manage to say.

'I cannot tell you how excited I'm my Varun is playing,' she exclaims, her voice suddenly taking on a higher pitch. 'But you know about the fundraiser for Harry and Meghan, don't you?' she asks.

My mother-in-law makes the British royals sound like they grew up playing with earthworms in her backyard.

'Harry and Meghan, the prince and his wife you mean?' I ask with feigned innocence.

'Natasha, how many Harry-Meghans are there?' She almost sounds irritated but keeps it in check.

'Oh right!' I say. 'So are you going to the fundraiser in their honour? Where is it?'

'You know Dadabhaisa has bought a table at the fundraiser. It's at the Taj. Ab banta hai na hamara, old family association after all. If monarchs won't support monarchs who will?'

That's right – the old family association between monarchs! The height of her delusions, I say! I'm holding my belly and stifling my laughter on the phone.

The Windsors are coming to town, and obviously, they do not know my mother-in-law, but her father and grandfather have allegedly played polo with the senior Windsors during their glory days. Maa has waited her entire life to acquaint herself with the British royals, and now that they are coming to India, it seems like my mother-in-law has every intention of hovering around them like a drone.

'Quite frankly, this Meghan is a divorcee and she's not just a commoner but also has black blood in her. Did you look at her mother sitting there in the church? I was feeling sorry for the Queen. God knows what pressures she was under. This girl has done nude photos, chee. I'm so disappointed with the way bloodlines are being diluted,' she sighs. I knew this was coming. Her colour and class prejudices don't take long to show up and the import of what she's trying to convey isn't lost on me.

'I think she is just right for the stiff Windsors. And you know, monarchy is dead around the world. All that's left is a name. People need to get over their royal antecedents and accept that times have changed,' I say this to drive home the point that she can stop living in the past. 'In England, they have kept it going because of tourism,' I turn the knife in further.

'What rubbish are you saying Natasha? Monarchy is thriving in England because it has the greatest line of monarchs in the world and not because of tourism. That was absolute nonsense!'

I can almost imagine my mother-in-law going red in the face, it's wonderful!

Realising that I'm enjoying this, she winds up our conversation.

'But anyway, Harry is a real prince and I'm so happy he is coming to India. I told Varun about this dinner last week, and he said both of you would not like to attend it. Typical Varun! But I got you both invited anyway because I knew you will be very upset otherwise. Now you convince him, he is your husband.'

'I'll try, Maa,' I tell her wearily. 'But why would I be upset? It hasn't been my dream to dine with the British royals.'

'Fine. Don't come. It's a family table, that is why I asked you,' she snaps.

Realising that this can get bitter I change my tone. 'If it means something to you, I will be happy to be there,' I say.

'And you know it's black tie for men and Western or Indian formals for women. The invites will reach before this week is over. You know how it is. For security reasons, they don't send out invites too much in advance.'

I'm not sure I want to be at this dinner. I don't see how sitting a few tables away from Prince Harry and the lovely Meghan Markle will enrich my life in any tangible manner. At best, it will give me some bragging rights with my friends and a hundred odd likes on Facebook and Instagram. On the other hand, I could write a column about them...Now that isn't bad material at all.

'So what do you think you will wear to the fundraiser?' my mother-in-law asks.

'I don't know. I have work to do. I'm going to Jaipur for a big Hollywood story soon. So I cannot think that far ahead about a dress,' I say smugly. This isn't true, of course, but right now I need her to know that I'm back to being a working girl and that she can no longer speak to me in her patronising ways.

'It's only a few weeks away. I think you should start planning,' she tells me.

As I put finishing touches to my story on Riyad, I check my phone several times for a message from him, with a prickle of guilt every time. Maybe tonight when Varun returns home, we can do something simple and yet fun, like drink wine and watch a movie, or have a proper conversation.

Varun already has plans for the evening and they definitely don't involve me. He's going to Nakul's to watch soccer. 'You know how it is with him Natasha. I need to be there for him. It's a difficult time for him,' he explains, when he realises that I'm not too pleased with this news.

Varun is constantly looking out for Nakul these days and making impromptu plans with him ever so often. I understand and obviously don't expect to be included but how will I ever reconnect with my husband properly if there is always Nakul or his work to form a little triangle between us?

'Varun, I know you are making sure Nakul does not feel left out, but how come you do not extend the same courtesy to me? I also wanted to talk to you about something important today, but no, you've made plans with your friend,' I say sourly.

'We live together. You have all the time in the world to talk to me. Think about Nakul. Think of this as atonement for your sins,' he chuckles.

'Well, I have a work offer, and I wanted to discuss it with you. But my career can wait. Nakul is more important. Oh, and do keep rubbing my nose in the dirt.'

'Nats, don't be upset. I didn't realise this was about your work. Tomorrow we'll go out for coffee or dinner, just you and I,' he says as if placating a small child.

'Sure, go ahead then.'

Nafisa rings me to inform me that she has slotted my interview with Riyad for her October issue. This means that she has assumed conveniently that Riyad will agree to the interview. I dash off an email to him.

Dear Riyad,

I forgot to mention to you when I met you at your office the other day that my friend who works for La Beau Monde knows that I did a story with you and now is chasing me for a story as well. Everybody knows that you shun the media and since I seem to have a foot in the door, I'm being pestered.

It's a personal story about whoever it is that you look upon as a role model. If you are comfortable with the idea, this can be done most conveniently over email. Do let me know and I shall email you the questions.

Thanks,

Natasha.

Note to self: I'm doing this very professionally. I'm proud of myself.

Later, while I speak to Nafisa about Priyanka's offer she tells me I will be a loser to turn it down. 'You won't get this opportunity again Nats,' she warns me.

Then she eagerly tells me about her dinner date in the evening with Nikhil Rikhye, a man she met at a big luxury marketing conference in Thailand last month.

'Is he hot?' I ask her.

'Very bright, funny and very handsome.'

'You are gushing.'

'Not at all. Just looking forward to the evening, that's all.'

'How are you so cool? For all you know you will be in love by tomorrow.'

'Natty,' she says with a pause, 'I'm not you.'

It's distressing to hear my suspicion about my ability to be easily enamoured, reconfirmed by my closest friend. Speaking of which, it has been twelve hours since my mail to Riyad, and he hasn't replied. I open my inbox with much anticipation each time in the hope of finding an email from him and feel sorrow on not finding one. This wretched pain of rejection is both unfamiliar and unbearable. Trisha is lucky that Guneet did not reject her. Sigh!

What if Riyad is thinking that I'm too keen to keep in touch with him somehow and finding reasons for doing so? This is a terribly disturbing thought.

I reflect on our last meeting over and over again and cannot think of anything that I said or did that might have led him into believing I was interested. What if he thinks I'm just an old, bored married cougar looking to flirt?

My cousin Sonia's call comes through just as I'm battling these terrifying thoughts. She tells me that Udit has been ringing her from NYC.

'Oh really? So that American babe, Clara, was she not his girlfriend?'

'I have not asked him about her. He calls and we chat, and he is interesting I must admit.'

'So, you like him?'

'It's too early to say. You know me, I'm slow. I take my own time,' Sonia says. 'But listen, not a word to Maasi, or she will get her hopes high and start printing our wedding invites as you know.'

Nafisa is being wooed by the dapper luxury marketing guy, Sonia is being pursued by an attractive banker from Manhattan and Natasha is raising her three children with her forever preoccupied husband and has been rejected by a hot filmmaker who she was shamelessly pursuing.

Oh, I feel old, hopeless and unwanted.

When Varun walks into our room after midnight, I'm still up reading. 'And why are you looking so downcast, may I know?' Varun asks me.

'Oh, it's nothing.'

'Then it's definitely something. Come on, tell me,' he says.

'We never do anything normal any more. No dinners, no movies, no Netflix, no car drives...'

'There you go again. Don't dramatise it please Natasha. We spend enough time together,' says Varun.

'That is like being a flatmate. What are you doing with me that a companion does?'

'Have you been reading one of those self-help books again Nats on "Ways to improve your marriage" or "How to bring the thrill back into your married life"?' Varun laughs as he pulls my cheek as if I'm a little child about to be dismissed by a busy parent.

No wonder I enjoy meeting Riyad. Unlike my husband, he is interested in listening to me and treats me like an individual. I check my mails one last time before going to bed and when I see an email from him, I nearly jump with joy.

Dear Natasha,

Apologies for taking an entire day to write back to you. I was up all night in the editing suite and then I slept through the day today.

So, about the interview. No, I will not do it over an email and miss out on an opportunity to have an enchanting conversation with you over coffee. Does tomorrow or day after at my office work for you, say post lunch? I'm going to be in the editing suites pretty much all the time starting the day after, hence, tomorrow works best.

About my reputation with the media, I prefer to let my work speak for myself, clichéd as it sounds. But you are not the media.

See you soon.

Riyad.

I go to bed with a smile on my lips and pretend to be asleep when Varun comes into the room and lies down next to me.

I write to Riyad as soon as I wake up in the morning.

Dear Riyad,
The day after tomorrow works well for me. Does 2 pm suit you?
Warmly,
Natasha.

I understand now how unfair it was for me to judge Trisha for wanting to see Guneet all the time. But I'm not Trisha. I'm not about to have an affair. I just enjoy Riyad's company, that is all.

Overcome with a sense of regret for having ignored her too long, I decided to ring Trisha. 'Guneet has found himself a fully furnished apartment in Bandstand,' she tells me cheerfully. 'Meet us today if you can Natasha? I avoid calling you too much because I know how you feel. Anyway, it would mean a lot to me if you and Guneet could have a friendly relationship with each other, in spite of your feelings towards him.'

'I'd love to meet him Trisha, and it isn't true that I don't like Guneet. The circumstances under which all this happened weren't the most ideal, and that is what I had a problem with,' I say.

I agree to meet them at his new apartment at 5 pm in the evening.

Things do have an extraordinary way of working out, I surmise. Trisha's twins are getting comfortable in their Hill Road flat and are spending weekends with their dad.

In the meanwhile, Nakul does not know about Guneet's Mumbai flat and believes that Guneet and Trish are through. 'His wife has him by his leash. That man was only interested in having an affair with her and she, like a fool, got played,' Varun told me recently with a glint of triumph in his eyes. Naturally, I didn't rush to correct him. Even though the worst is behind them, I do hope that Guneet and Trisha have the sense to keep it discreet for the next few months till things calm down on all fronts.

When I arrive at Guneet's unprepossessing dwelling in an old building at Bandstand, he receives me at the door with a warm smile even though I can sense a certain degree of restraint in him, as if silently apologising for his own existence.

Trisha rushes out from the kitchen and gives me a tight hug as soon as she hears my voice in the living room. She smells of spices instead of her usual intense Chanel perfume, a fragrance I associate only with her now.

The house is a pre-furnished cramped one-bedroom apartment whose only redeeming feature are the windows of the living room that faces the sea. It's sparsely done, with a small dining table that seats four and a tiny sofa set with a low budget coffee table. To me this is even more baffling than watching her cook in the kitchen – Trisha, the woman who has been passionate about home interiors is happy to spend time with her lover in this dump!

As we sit down to chat on the worn-out sofa of the living room, Trisha opens the windows to let some breeze in. Guneet clears his throat and starts our conversation with apologies for causing disruption in my life. 'I wish we had done this without hurting you and so many other people along the way,' he says regretfully.

I smile at him compassionately for the first time. 'I don't regret that Trish and I ended up together, but I do wish things had worked out for us in a less dramatic way,' he tells me wistfully.

Trish, in the meanwhile, leaves us both alone to fix me some tea. 'Can I make you a quick egg white sandwich with your tea?' she calls out from the kitchen. In Nakul's house, she would have been pressing a bell to summon her liveried staff to serve chai to me, but she seems to have slipped into this new avatar without any fuss.

'Guneet, I agree, the last few months have been unpleasant for all involved but what's done is done. I'm happy to see that contrary to everybody's expectations, you could take a stand with your own family and be there for Trisha,' I say.

Trisha arrives with my tea and asks me not to tell Varun about Guneet's pad.

'You know me better than that, Trish,' I tell her.

'I do Natasha. I know that hard as it has been for you, you have only looked out for me through this upheaval in our lives. I cannot blame you for being mad at me, I know how much Nakul means to you and I did fear that I might have lost that equation I shared with you as Nakul's wife forever. I know Varun will never forgive me, and that may complicate things between us, but I need you to know just how grateful I'm to have had your support over the past few months.'

Trisha's voice is choking with emotion as she says this.

'In a way, you are lucky that you are so satisfied with your life with Varun. Love complicates things. You can reason all you want, but I have come to realise just the one thing – the heart wants what it wants,' Trisha says wistfully.

'I did not go looking for Guneet, but truthfully, I realised within two years of my marriage that Nakul and I did not really have a connection...'

I used to think Trisha wasn't the sort to need a connection with a man when a credit card would have done just as well. I read it all wrong.

I take her hand in mine and tell her that I'm genuinely happy for her, and I mean it. I don't tell her that I'm just a wee bit sorry for myself, which I am after seeing all the tenderness between the two lovers.

Guneet, who had moved away to the other room to allow us space to chat I suppose, walks up from behind Trisha and bends over to drape his arms around her shoulders. She wipes her eyes and arches her neck and smiles at him gratefully. Sitting there, I sense their happiness in the midst of the storm that has been engulfing their lives. I understand for the first time that what these two people have is rare to find. I may find Guneet's sense of dressing ridiculous, but the fact is that he makes Trisha happy, and between the two of them there is enough love to make up for the lack of Savile Row trimmings and clipped accents that belong in the old money club.

***

My column about the hysteria surrounding the forthcoming Harry and Meghan visit appeared today. I hope one of my mother-in-law's awful friends will remember to send her a copy of the same.

I can, with great satisfaction, picture Maa's face grimacing when she reads it. Bubbles of sadistic joy are popping inside my chest at the thought of it. I conclude with faint regret that I will never evolve as a person because I'm always plotting revenge.

Priyanka has written to me to tell me how much she liked my maiden interview with Riyad for her magazine and that she hopes I will do an equally impressive job with Michelle Chung too.

The *Beau Monde* interview that I did with Riyad is also scheduled for today. I feel calm and in control for now, and I hope that my teenage-girl feelings for him do not get revived when I see him again.

Research on the human brain has shown that our brain releases dopamine in our body when we have just started liking somebody. That is how we feel that rush of excitement.

I wish there was an excessive dopamine-blocking over-the-counter pill that one could take, that would make things so much easier. Shouldn't we have a say with our heart when it comes to liking somebody?

The world needs a clinic like the one in *The Eternal Sunshine of the Spotless Mind*, where people go to get their memories erased after a heartbreak in the same amount of time that it takes to get a full body wax at the neighbourhood salon.

Enough about the heart. As mentioned before, I know I'm overthinking this. Literature and history are replete with women who have over thought their crushes and taken them to illogical conclusions in their own heads. But I'm no Anna Karenina or Madame Bovary. I have no reason to feel too worried about this.

In any event, this will be my last meeting with Riyad as I have no other professional reason to meet him after today and just as well. I ask for lunch to be served before leaving for the interview but when I see what is laid out on the table, I shriek in horror.

The fish on my plate looks and smells like it died of multiple organ failure long before it got caught in the net. Cook says he has a cold, which has incapacitated him from smelling the rotting fish. What my cook lacks in creativity in the kitchen, he makes up for by being creative with his excuses.

I decide to have mangoes for lunch instead – a fine idea to go smelling of tropical fruit to Riyad's office rather than dead fish.

Much thought has gone into keeping my look most casual. I'm wearing my distressed jeans and a T-shirt with white lace-up sneakers and hardly any make-up except a light gloss. Varun loves this preppy look on me. I'm suddenly reminded of how twisted it is to dress in a look that Varun likes on me for Riyad. The Bible would describe me as a fallen woman! Thank God I'm not Christian.

Once at Riyad's office, I see his eyes light up when he comes to the reception to receive me. Nice to know that I have this effect on someone other than my dogs.

Once again, I follow him to his cabin. 'Oh, we are almost identically dressed today,' he turns around and tells me cheerfully. He is right. We are dressed like twins today, same white lace-up sneakers, a white T-shirt, faded jeans.

'We are,' I agree.

'Except that my denim aren't distressed like yours. I avoid wearing ripped jeans because it turns on women too much. Best not to tempt anyone,' he says with a mischievous smile as he pulls the chair for me inside his cabin.

He then intercoms Martha and orders two black coffees for us. 'Hmmm, so how have you been Natasha?' he asks me.

'I have been good Riyad, thank you,' I reply politely.

'Won't you ask me how I have been?' he teases.

'How have you been Riyad? Excuse my poor manners please.'

'I have been thinking about you, Natasha.'

I'm stumped. I'm not prepared for this. As flattering as Riyad's attention is, he is making me quite uncomfortable.

'I know you are thinking I'm coming on too strong,' he says as if reading my mind.

'Oh wow, you're like Uri Geller,' I say trying to keep it light even though I'm feeling awkward.

'Ok seriously, I know you are here to interview me, and it's inappropriate of me to say this given that you seem happily married and all that, but I don't mean to say this in a wrong way.'

'Is there a right way to say this?' I ask without smiling. I don't want him to think I'm available. I like him, yes, but I want nothing from this interaction except this happy feeling of being around somebody you find attractive in so many ways.

'Oh, God! Don't panic. What I really meant when I said I was thinking about you was that just this morning I was thinking about how much I look forward to seeing you because I enjoy your company. Simple as that.'

'Ah,' I say, feeling relieved.

'I know I made it sound inappropriate. I was teasing you. Sorry. My bad. I shouldn't have.'

He gets up from his chair and walks towards the bookcase next to his desk, fixes the unevenly stacked books and turns towards me smiling impishly. 'Okay! Listen, let's do the interview. But let's sit on the couch casually and chat. That desk business is too stiff.'

I follow him to the well-worn leather couch laid across the room. The coffee table placed between the two sofas has a large abstractly shaped Lalique bowl on it and some old copies of the *New Yorker* magazine.

I clear my throat, switch on the voice notes on my phone and we get started. I love to hear him speak. Riyad has an animated way of talking and he is funny, interesting, witty and extremely well-read. Unfortunately, he is a compound of all the things that I like in a man.

There, I'm falling for him again.

'Okay, so shall we begin, please?' I ask, hoping to pour this nervous energy into my article.

'Yes ma'am, let's begin.'

He has so much to say that I don't have the heart to tell him I only came looking for 2,000 words. If only I weren't so attracted to him, we could have kept in touch after today and been friends. It's a pity that we have such a good time talking to each other, but we cannot pursue this friendship.

We are finally done, nearly two hours later. 'Are we done yet?' Riyad asks me with a smile.

'We are. Quite done.'

'No, I don't mean the interview. I mean are WE done yet?' he says clearly enunciating the 'we'. I look at him horrified.

'Shut up Riyad. Don't do this please.'

'Hahahaha,' he laughs gregariously. 'Gotcha. Just joking, again' he says as he continues to laugh.

'You are incorrigible,' I tell him.

'I enjoy it. We are pals now and I'm this way with my friends,' he replies. 'Okay, listen I don't know when I will see you again and I just don't want to not see you again. I mean at my age I rarely meet people I want to be friends with and then when you click so well…It's so hard to come across women like you, Natasha.'

'That is because you are hanging out with too many actresses. Maybe if you met some real women, you will realise that the normal world abounds with people like me,' I say.

'Don't try and be modest. It does not even suit you.'

Now it's my turn to laugh.

'Why don't we have you over whenever Varun and I organise a get-together at our house next?' I suggest.

'No, that wouldn't be the same. I'd love to meet Varun, don't get me wrong, but chatting like this won't happen at some party at your house. Can't you drop in here sometimes when you are passing by?'

'I will if I'm passing by and if you are free.'

'Hmmm…too many ifs there.'

'I must leave now, Riyad,' I say, quickly rising from the sofa.

He walks me to the door to see me off, and I'm reminded about how much I admire these basic courtesies in a man. As he places his hand on the doorknob, he unexpectedly turns towards me and says, 'Oh the pictures! I forgot to give you stills from my film, you wanted those, didn't you?' My heart starts thumping in my chest at this physical proximity. 'Oh no rush, you can send them to me via Dropbox or on a pen drive with your driver,' I manage to say. 'I completely forgot to mention that *Beau Monde* will coordinate directly with your office about the photo shoot to go with your story in a few days. Hope that is alright?' I switch back to my professional tone.

'Sure,' he says, opening the door for me.

He sees me off till the reception in uncomfortable silence and we say our byes without looking at each other.

Chapter 17

Having a severe crush is the same as being in a depression. The more you fight the feeling, the stronger it grips you. Even though I keep reminding myself that I'm not about to cheat on my husband and that Riyad is only just either being over-friendly or that he is a player, I cannot seem to stop liking him. Unable to concentrate on much, my thoughts have rarely strayed from him, and I have spent the past two days wondering how he is and what he might be doing. Just as well that I don't have to turn in a column – *City Reflections* needs extra space during the municipal elections for the next few weeks.

Mercifully my dear mother-in-law's presence at home and her ridiculous conversations are there to distract me from my mental preoccupations. She has been on the phone all day repeating the social history between the British royals and her family, ad nauseam, to her friends. 'Yes, yes, you know how it is. Dadabhaisa had to buy a table. It's our duty in a way. After all, our families have been friends for generations,' I can hear her say as I try and write some coherent sentences on my laptop.

'When we were very young, we met everyone from the family and then all those polo matches in London...'

I told Varun this morning as he was getting ready to leave for work that I worry his mother's health is at risk. He stopped buttoning his shirt midway and looked at me with horror. 'Why, what happened to her?'

'Oh, I just think she will pass out with too much excitement on the day of the dinner with Harry and Meghan Markle.'

He looked nonplussed and then when he finally realised that I was making fun of his mother, he was a little annoyed.

'You can be cruel sometimes, you know? These things make her happy Nats. Don't be mean,' the model son told me. I hope Sumer will be exactly like his father one day and defend his mother against the onslaughts of his wife. 'And now I get it, you had written that column about my mother, had you not?'

I flatly deny it. 'Of course not, would I ever do such a thing Varun? She had not even arrived in Bombay and demonstrated her excitement to me at the time I wrote it.'

'Alright, alright, I was only just asking. Why are you getting agitated?'

'Because you need to stop defending your mother all the time Varun. It's bloody annoying. She's human you know? Like you and me she has human failings too,' I tell him.

'Alright,' he says, raising his hands. 'I'm backing off.'

There has been radio silence from Riyad. It has been over a week incidentally. But this is perfectly fine by me. In fact, it's best that we don't keep in touch.

The universe decides to interrupt my stream of consciousness with a message from the man himself. I see his name and I can almost feel my heart leap out of my ribcage with joy.

'Hey…'

I cannot wait to write 'Hey…' back but I decide to count till a hundred.

One, two, three, four…twenty. I wonder if I'm too old to play games, though. Shouldn't I just be myself and write back tout suite?

Two whole minutes have passed; I can write back now without looking like I have done nothing all day except wait for his message.

'Hey…how are you?' I type and click send after reading it three times to see if it is sounding casual enough.

'I felt like checking on you. Hope you don't mind,' writes Riyad.

Do I mind? Of course, I don't. I have been meditating on you Riyad, I say to myself.

'I cannot mind that. It would be terribly impolite. It's very kind of you to check on me,' I write after careful consideration.

'Kindness wasn't the intention, I should clarify. Next, you will call me sweet, at which point I will quietly go and shoot myself with a "Goodbye, cruel world" note.'

A man who can write long messages…I must be dreaming. Oh, it's such an admirable trait, this ability to chat with a woman in full sentences is a greater virtue than chivalry, courage and honesty in today's times if you ask me.

'Hahaha. You are funny. And sweet,' I write.

'Goodbye cruel world.'

'Okay, don't do drama now. How come you aren't shooting?' I ask.

'Princess, I'm shooting. Was taking a break and thought that chatting with you might lift my spirits…'

I'm in love. I want to elope with Riyad and have a beach wedding in white lace in Maldives and waltz with him to Lara's theme.

My wedding on the beach is interrupted by the sound of Ria wailing. I rush to her room to find her sprawled all over the floor, blood oozing from her mouth. Sylvia picks her up while I stand there, frozen, a terrible sensation running up my spine. I can see a deep cut on her lip from where blood is continuing to ooze, forming tiny rivulets down her throat. My poor little baby girl! Sumer is standing in a corner, looking guilty.

I take her to the bathroom and help her rinse her mouth before pressing a cotton swab against her lip as Sylvia brings ice from the kitchen. With effort, we manage to calm her down, and I continue to dab her lip with betadine while Maa wipes her tears and promises her a trip to Hamleys the following Sunday.

As expected, it was Sumer's fault. Ria was playing with his Nerf gun, which he snatched from her so violently that she managed to land on her face. 'Thankfully, it was only just the lip, it could have been the eye,' Maa remarks. She is right. Sumer needs to learn how to treat girls. I speak to the doctor, and he says she has been given a tetanus injection and I need not worry as the blood loss hasn't been too severe.

I give Ria a spoonful of Paracetamol and it has a placebo effect on the child instantly. Within minutes she is asking me artfully to take her selfie with her bruised lip and send it to her father. I can hardly believe that Ria is using her wounds to gain sympathy and gifts from such a young age.

In the meanwhile, I have forgotten all about Riyad's message, as I rightfully should have.

'Sorry to disappoint you, I take the "sweet" back.' I write.

'That is very sweet of you,' he writes an hour later, by which time I'm so distraught with the wait that I look like I have had a death in the family.

I decide not to reply, and our conversation languishes.

Nevertheless, I'm thrilled by the fact that he decided to keep in touch with me.

Nafisa rings me to ask if my story with Riyad has moved forward. I tell her that I'm deeply anguished at the realisation that what is usually a mild flirtation for a man can be a whole story by itself for a woman. Oh well!

'I mean the story you were writing, not your story, you silly girl,' Nafisa laughs.

I have tried all the floor length pieces hanging in my closet in preparation for the fundraiser, and everything looks rather uninspiring. I don't feel like splurging on another expensive dress at the last minute. Perhaps I could wear my ivory white gown with black trimmings. It's a classic and just formal enough for the occasion. I try it on only to find that like everything else in my wardrobe, it doesn't fit me anymore. This is heartbreaking. I should have persevered with my kick-boxing classes and started having spoonfuls of cinnamon months ago to burn off the fat.

I'm in serious panic and ring Nafisa to share my woes with her.

'Is this urgent? Am just about to get into a meeting, Natasha.'

'It is, Nafisa, matter of life and death if you ask me.'

'You chipped your nail? My commiserations.'

'No, I have nothing to wear to the Prince Harry fundraiser.'

'You don't say! You never told me you were going. You wrote all those things about people who want to schmooze with the royals, little did I know?' Nafisa chuckles.

'But I only wrote about people who are getting hysterical about their arrival…'

'Yes, I remember, relax. Anyway, it should be fun,' she says.

'Fun or not, Varun's mama has bought a table. And we have no choice but to attend it. Anyway, I have gained weight, and nothing looks good.'

'Take something from me. Come over and have a look.'

'You are so tall Nafisa. I will have to walk on a pair of stilts under your gown.'

'Don't be funny! You can just wear your highest heels, and you'll be alright.'

'Do me a favour, just send me a bunch of clothes over in a bag. Shall try them at home. Please.'

'I will if you let me go now,' she says and hangs up.

This is exactly why I feel it's important to be friends with people your own size.

Varun rings to ask if the kids know that the Windsors are going to attend the polo match on Saturday morning.

I haven't heard of this, and I tell him that. I can bet Maa doesn't know either or all of India would have known about it by now. She has single-handedly created more awareness about this event than a fully staffed PR agency with an army of town-criers could have done.

Sofie jumps with excitement when I tell them that they will get to meet Harry and Meghan at the polo match. Sofie is obviously hoping she will gain more followers on Instagram after she posts her picture with the royals, this being the overarching purpose of her life lately.

She calls her friends to discuss her great good fortune with them. Hearing her gush over Harry and Meghan, I feel like a perfect hypocrite for writing the column jeering at the likes of my mother-in-law.

When I return to my room, I discover that I have a message from Riyad waiting for me on my phone. Be still my beating heart, I could get used to this.

He wants to know if I can meet him over coffee this evening. 'I'm editing all of tomorrow and day after. So please say yes, wanted to discuss something important. Sorry for the short notice.'

Coffee sounds quite innocent to me. I'd like to see him again, of course. 'But today is too soon Riyad,' I write back.

'So be a little spontaneous. I know it's a little hard, three kids and all.'

The bastard. He knows to strike where it hurts.

'You are trying reverse psychology on me but am not biting the bait. I don't meet anybody at such short notice.'

'Yes, because you are a princess. I get that. But can you not make an exception for humble subjects just this once?'

'Can we not meet next week? I'm a little busy today.'

'No, we are meeting today. 4 pm. My office? I want to narrate the story to you today. Reading it is no fun.'

The truth is that I don't want to see him in the privacy of his cabin, but is it safe to meet him outside and not have people presume things?

And so it is, that I find myself driving up to his office. I think am being paranoid about meeting him when it's only just a healthy friendship that is developing between us.

Later, we are both sitting on the couch in his cabin, and there is a fat script lying on the coffee table with the words *Jee Ley Zaraa* typed out on the cover of the script. I'm dressed in a teal blue cotton knee-length dress with sling-backs. Once again, I had to try to underdress, lest Riyad gets any ideas.

The peon arrives with two cups of black coffee and a half kilo chocolate cake on a cake dish.

'What are we celebrating exactly, may I know?' I ask Riyad.

'The fact that a busy princess like you overlooked protocol and agreed to see a humble subject like me today.'

He is so utterly and exceptionally charming. How can a woman not be in love with him?

'No, tell me seriously,' I still persist.

'Well, if you must know, today is my birthday, and a few cakes have been sent over to the office by my well-wishers who know that I'm allergic to most flowers.'

'Oh, I'm sorry, I did not know. Happy Birthday, Riyad,' I say, shaking his hand. 'But who is allergic to flowers?' I ask in disbelief.

'Next time, to prove it to you, I shall keep a pot of lilies around me. Then you can look at my face turn purple and be convinced,' he says, reaching for the cake with a knife and slicing two slivers from it.

The cake is dark chocolate and it hits the right spot.

'Oh, this is just too good,' I close my eyes to savour the flavour exploding inside my mouth as I moan in ecstasy.

He looks at me and chortles, 'You are like a child yourself. Look at you,' he says.

Sitting there, laughing with him, I realise I have no reason to be paranoid; we already feel like old friends. I take a few sips of my coffee and then setting my plate and cup aside ask him to take me through the script.

Riyad lets the script lie on the table in front of us and starts to discuss the protagonist's character in a very serious manner. His story starts from the anti-Sikh riots when the protagonist Sukhi, an eight-year-old girl, witnesses her mother's death in the lanes of her colony. Sukhi and her mother are walking out from their house in East Delhi along with her maternal uncle when armed men appear in truckloads unannounced and douse her mother and mama with kerosene and set them to flames. In the massacre that follows, nearly 320 Sikhs from that tiny East Delhi colony lose their lives.

Sukhi's father throws himself into work to cope with this tragedy and comes to terms with his loss in time. His small business begins to flourish and gradually he starts to build a business empire.

Sukhi is raised with much wealth around her and eventually gets admission in the London School of

Economics but her childhood trauma and the absence of a loving mother during her growing years scars her for life. Her fears prevent her from holding on to deep relationships due to the underlying fear of loss. But then a young businessman from India falls in love with her and moves the world around to win her confidence.

I'm listening to the story with complete attention and wondering how Riyad expects a story like this to resonate with me.

As if reading my thoughts, he stops his narration abruptly. 'What are you thinking?'

'Nothing. I'm listening to your story. Go on.'

'You are wondering why I felt the need to take you through this story.'

I smile at him. 'You are very perceptive,' I say.

'Sukhi marries this man, has a child from him and then realises that there is more stability in her life than she can handle. She ends up leaving her husband and moves to an ashram in pursuit of her happiness...'

'And you think this will resonate with me because...?' I ask.

Riyad turns to look at me and unable to suppress his chuckle he bursts into loud laughter. I stare at him nonplussed.

'You are very funny,' he says, still laughing.

'I like the story Riyad. It's engaging. I just wondered if you thought there were similarities between Sukhi and me for me to be able to provide you with inputs. I'm not about to leave my husband and move to an ashram for instance...' I trail off.

Riyad leans towards me and looks right into my eyes and says, 'I haven't been thinking straight since I met you and I guess...,' he pauses as if searching for words. Before I can react, he suddenly pulls me closer and presses his lips to mine. My pulse is racing, and every nerve in my body is asking me to let this happen. Before I know it, he is kissing me deeply, and I find myself kissing him back. The warmth of his unfamiliar mouth sends a delicious throng of sensations through my body.

This is wrong, my brain tells me. You are married.

But my body is disobeying my mind. I don't want this kiss to end. I will not meet him again, but this kiss...I want to be in the moment and allow it to go on.

Riyad puts his hand on my lower back and presses me closer. His eyes are closed and he is exploring my mouth, slowly and passionately. His spicy cologne smells seductive and exciting. I haven't been kissed this way in a long time, and even though I can feel an electric current run through my body, it all feels easy, familiar even. I run my fingers through his thick mop of hair as I return his kiss, an equal participant in this exchange. And then suddenly I picture Varun's face before my eyes and pull back abruptly. Riyad releases me immediately and looks at me for a few seconds before holding his head in his palms, elbows placed over his knees as if to regain his lost composure.

'Uh...I have to go,' I say as I get up from the sofa.

'No, wait. I'm sorry,' he mutters. 'Natasha, I hadn't planned it this way, don't be offended...I swear I have been fighting my feelings.'

I look at my watch, pretending to read the time, and then I tell him I have to rush.

'No, let me finish. I'm not some playboy who grabs every pretty thing that walks into his office. I know this is wholly inappropriate...'

'Don't worry, I shall see myself out,' I cut in as wipe my mouth with a napkin. 'You might want to wipe my lipstick off your face too,' I say as I shut the door behind me.

My mind is running in thirteen different directions. Maybe he does this all the time. How could I allow it? Why had my senses taken their leave?

I reach into my bag and spray some perfume on my palms before rubbing it on my cheeks. I surely don't want to be smelling of Riyad when I get home.

Ria and Sumer meet me at the porch outside the house. They have just returned from their respective classes at the Walrus Club, and even though I'm smiling while I speak to them, nothing feels right. I remind myself that this is my real world. They are my world. But I feel disconnected from this world.

Ria and Sumer are both talking to me at the same time as usual. Sylvia complains about Ria and tells me on our way up that she does not listen to her at all 'I only listen to my mummy,' Ria says proudly, hugging me. Once in their room, Sumer reminds me that I haven't purchased any provisions for the fete at school tomorrow.

I'm a terrible mother! I have completely forgotten about his school fete. I haven't even collected the icing cones I had ordered for his stalls a few days ago, nor have I purchased the disposable plates. Thankfully, the fete does not start until noon, and I will have time to get the requisite things in the morning tomorrow.

My mother-in-law comes looking for me inside the children's room and starts complaining about the cook. 'Shambhu is getting fat and lazy Natasha. You let him get away with anything. His hair is overgrown like a jungle. His cooking has become terrible. Anyway, I try not to interfere as this is your house, but you should have seen what he served me for lunch today. It was floating in oil.'

If this isn't interference what is, I wonder.

I summon Shambhu on the terrace to speak to him about his culinary transgressions. 'Badey madam bahut chik chik kartein hain. Unko mera khaana pasand hi nahin' he tells me with a sullen face.

I tell him to go easy on the oil, cut his hair and ignore badey madam. It's only a matter of another week after all and then she will head back to Jhalakpur. He looks relieved to hear that and makes no effort to conceal his joy as he smiles and takes my leave.

Later that night, I lie in bed next to the kids, reliving that kiss and being mad at myself simultaneously. What will Riyad think of me? That I'm a bored housewife? Is that why he narrated that story to me about the dissatisfied woman? And what about Varun?

The phone beeps just as I think of Varun and I see a message from him informing me that he will be home late as he needs to go over to Nakul's to discuss some contracts. This is a relief. I'd not have been able to face him so soon, not after my debauchery of today.

As usual, Sofie is up late, studying. Or so I think until I find her watching YouTube videos on her phone. I ask her to go to bed and dedicate her time and energy to something more constructive like watching the Discovery Channel. 'Speaking to the wrong child Mom!' she tells me. 'Tell your Sumer to watch alligators attacking wildebeests. Watching animals chase other animals isn't my idea of fun.'

I'm too exhausted mentally to argue with her and too guilt-ridden to sleep. I toss and turn in bed for over an hour, smarting with shame and disgust at the memory of the kiss.

There are no sleeping pills in my house to aid my guilty conscience. Sad that something so comforting cannot be purchased over the counter in India any longer, where the government is otherwise doing its best to kill you.

In hindsight, maybe the kiss wasn't such a bad idea. At least I got it out of my system, and since I already feel miserable with just one kiss, I will never have the nerve to embark on an affair with Riyad or anybody else for that matter.

Sadly, I cannot even tell Nafisa about what I have done and unburden myself – I have no choice but to suffer my shameful secret in a deafening but occasionally pleasurable silence.

I wake up a few hours later to find Varun's arm around me. You should be able to die of shame sometimes. This is my moment to do that. Slipping back into consciousness, I remember the events of yesterday and find my eyes, dry from the short sleep, stinging with tears. Varun does love me and how devastated he would be if he were to know that I had cheated on him. On us. As these thoughts play havoc with my mind, my silent weeping turns into a soft sob that wakes up Varun.

'Natasha, are you okay?' Varun asks me sleepily.

I continue to sob without saying anything. What can I tell Varun anyway? I cannot tell him what was going on inside my head. He sits up to look at me in the faint light that is filtering in from the porch through our blinds. 'Honey?' he says gently, 'What happened?'

'It's nothing,' I manage to say as I turn over to the other side. He then switches on the side lamp and wraps his arm around me and strokes my cheek with his long fingers.

'What is it hon, that is bothering you so much that you wake up crying like this?' he asks me.

Blowing my clogged sinuses into the tissue that he has so gently placed under my nose, I tell him that even I don't know why I'm crying. 'I just don't like my life any more,' I manage to say.

Varun holds me tightly against him and stroking my head, 'I know why you are upset. I may not say it but it isn't like I haven't noticed that you haven't been yourself lately. I blame myself for it though Nats. I have conveniently ignored your needs and let you fend for yourself.'

'No, it isn't you Varun,' I say softly as guilty tears find their way back into my eyes.

'Look, I have been wanting to say this to you the past few weeks. I know I used to tease you about it, but of late I've realised how hard you work as a mother. You are the force that keeps this family and home together. And I also know now that it isn't easy. I have never given you credit for it because I did not realise until I had to manage the children.

The Natasha I married was a lively girl full of spark, but over the years, you have sacrificed so much for all of us… And I have been too busy to appreciate – we haven't even had any time together since I started the hotel project last year. Tchah,' Varun says ruefully.

He then turns me over and cupping my face in his palms he looks into my eyes tenderly and says, 'But this is going to change. I promise. I'm going to make sure you find time to claim yourself back. I'm going to share some of your responsibilities with the children. I want my happy Natasha back.'

Listening to his words, I begin to feel sorry for myself, and some more tears spill out of my eyes. This is the man I fell in love with and married. This is that man I have been envied for by my friends. This is the man I cheated on yesterday. But if I were entirely happy with Varun, would I have wandered off into another man's arms so easily? Perhaps not.

I'm now both grateful and guilty. He leans forward and kisses my forehead. 'Tomorrow morning, first thing, I'll plan a short break for just the two of us,' he says.

***

In the morning, we are at breakfast when Varun receives a call from the captain of the Jhalakpur Royals polo team. He has been roped in for the polo match last minute because one of the younger players in the team hurt his elbow during the practice. Varun is the obvious choice under these circumstances. He has a good handicap, and with even just a little practice he will be in good form.

'This means I will have to spend the next four days practising at the race course Natty,' he says to me with an apologetic look on his face. 'But why are you explaining to me?' I laugh.

'Because I wanted us to go out on a date tonight. Those architects from Hong Kong are also here at the same time.'

'Let this match be over and get your meetings out of the way. You can take me out next week,' I tell him.

Around lunchtime, long after my morning routine has been observed, I have a message from Riyad.

Been meaning to text you. Have been feeling terrible about my misbehaviour. I don't blame you if you are mad at me. While I do apologise about what happened, I'm not sorry it happened, and I gave in to my impulses. I do understand, however, that it wasn't the right thing to do.

I read the message a few more times and then delete it.

❊❊❊

It's Saturday morning and we are at the race course for the polo match. I have worn a saree from Tayeb in emerald green with matte gold earrings to keep my look understated and sober. Ladies from the social set of Bombay have turned up in Outré hats and bright ensembles for the game. The paparazzi is busy snapping photographs as women in jewelled sunglasses, stylish fascinators, sky-high stilettoes, cold shoulder frocks and peplum dresses gladly pose for them along with their men in fine linens. Alisha Wazir, the peaches and crème complexioned daughter-in-law of an industry heavyweight, has decided to ignore the weather and wear high-heeled Hermès boots teamed with a ruffled white shirt and woven short skirt to the races. The walnut-sized diamonds in her ears are working as light reflectors as she strikes a pose for the paps, resting an arm over her diminutive husband's shoulder as she does that.

Meghan Markle and Harry are sitting right in the front with Tarini Sehgal, India's break-out star who has done well for herself in Hollywood. Tarini and Meghan have been friends from working in Hollywood together. Meghan's in an icy pink dress and a hat, with barely there make-up. With skin like that, who needs make-up? Harry is in a beige linen suit and Tarini, who is in a turquoise off-shoulder dress, is looking bedazzling. She is busy explaining India to the couple of the moment.

Varun's uncle, Dadabhaisa, introduces us all to the royals who agree to oblige the children by posing for photos with them graciously as their stern bodyguards look on vigilantly. Meghan ruffles Ria's hair and then speaks to Sofie.

I can tell my children are passing out with joy after shaking hands with a real princess, but Sumer – he couldn't be bothered with anybody who isn't a superhero.

A few minutes later, when it's announced that the game is set to begin, we all settle into our chairs. The match starts with regal flair with an army band as the players are introduced one by one.

And the umpire rolls in.

Varun is playing in the third position, and I'm sitting on the edge of my seat sending his pony good vibes from a distance. The Jhalakpur Royals are playing against the 62 Cavalry team, and in the next six chakkars, the fate of the winning team will be decided. Varun is looking like the prince that he is in his white breeches and his brown polo boots.

'This player Varun something Singh is just so handsome,' I overhear the woman behind me say to the girl next to her. I look back from the corner of my eye and I see the owner of that voice, a beautiful woman in bumblebee glasses with crystal detailing. I tilt my head in her direction to be able to eavesdrop better. 'I know, right? He is hot as hell. I have met him a few times. He is a prince,' the girl next to her says.

'You mean a prince prince?'

'Yes, from some place in Rajasthan. Blue blood and all.'

'No wonder he looks so regal. Is he married?'

The warm-up on the field in front of me has started, but I'm not looking. My ear is glued to this conversation. 'He is I believe. Has kids and all.'

'That is awful. All the good men are taken. Show me his wife. Is she here?'

'She has to be here. She is okay looking. I think I have seen her picture with him in a magazine. No great shakes. I think he could do with somebody better, like a tall model,' she chuckles.

'You mean someone like you,' giggles the other girl.

'So seduce him. You are single. What do you care?'

'Oh, how I wish, but I get the impression he does not cheat and all. You know Latika? She is very bold. I saw her flirting with him at a party in Delhi a few months ago. We were together when she saw him and went over to talk to him. He was the hottest man I saw in Delhi. At that time I did not know he was from Bombay. We were all ogling at him.'

'So then, anything happened?'

My heart misses a few beats as I prepare myself for what is to come.

'Latika told me she will sleep with him before the night is over. But I was with her the rest of the night,' she laughs.

'Serves her right for being so overconfident, haan!'

'He spoke to her, was polite and all, but did not show much interest in her because she gave him her card and came back to finish her drink with me at the table.'

'Oh, Latika Khosla, she can get any man she wants. I'd not write her off just yet.'

'She is a part-time chef too, did you know? If this Prince Varun were a normal man, he would have responded. Maybe he is secretly gay. No man is *that* faithful!'

Some more chuckling follows. I sit there processing all this information as I look blankly at the horses on the turf. I seem to have missed an entire chakkar in the process.

Game be damned. I'm dying to turn back and look at these women, and the only way to do it elegantly is to drop my sunglass case on the ground and bend forward to reach for it. As I do that, I manage to look at one of them from the corner of my eye, a dusky, big-lipped girl, a Bollywood aspirant or model, no doubt and her friend, a waif thin fashion influencer whose name I cannot remember.

'Mummy, Daddy is winning,' Sumer says, tugging at my chiffon in excitement just as I'm trying to make sense of the match. I wonder if the girls behind me have realised I'm Varun's wife. Life is indeed stranger than fiction.

The game has started off with Jhalakpur Royals scoring more than 62 Cavalry in the first three chakkars with Varun scoring a great goal with a short from the sideline on the right side in the third chakkar and two goals in the first two chakkars. My mother-in-law is sitting at the edge of her chair. I'm unable to contain my anxiety myself, but not all of it has to do with the match being played on the turf. My mind is reeling from that conversation I have overheard between those women seated right behind me. A fact only becomes a dignified truth when verified by a stranger. I have always known that Varun loves me and is faithful to me, but today suddenly that knowledge has gained arms and legs. It has become a thing of its own and not one that I can forget about even temporarily.

When my mind returns to the match, I discover that 62 Cavalry is quickly making good their losses and stealing a march over Varun's team in the final three chakkars.

I cannot decide who is more dejected at this turn of events, Maa or my children. To watch Varun's team lose in the presence of a prince and princess from England, I'd surmise, has crushed his mother's spirit and my children's in equal measure. Still, at least she will use this opportunity to exchange niceties with the Princess. In the grand scheme of things, Varun's losing isn't a loss at all.

I firmly forbid the kids from talking to their father about his team losing the match. Sofie is sensible enough to not rub it in, but the younger two, being ingenuous as they are at this age, I cannot trust.

At the after-party, I catch up with some of the other polo player's wives and Varun's mama and mami, who I will see again tomorrow night at the fundraiser dinner. Varun appears from nowhere and hugs them both warmly, apologising to them for not meeting them sooner. While Mamaji discusses his game with him, I look around the marquee and find the dusky model look in our direction appraising me – the 'no great shakes' wife of the man they have their heart set on.

'You were good, Varun,' I say, placing my hand on his chest. 'Haha. No, I have been better on the field Nats,' he laughs as he puts his arm around my waist.

'I did want that trophy for our team, but maybe next year,' he says wistfully and then smiling slowly he turns towards me and adds as an afterthought, 'Not that I'm without my trophy today. I have you, Natasha Singh.'

I feel the envious eyes of the models on me now as I bask in the glow of proprietorship.

Some of the other players from the team come by to greet me and to speak with Varun. 'Come, let's go and get a drink with the boys,' he suggests. How can I ever want another man when my own husband is this amazing person? I decide at that very moment to banish Riyad from my mind. I'm overcome with an instant sense of relief. I feel the strain dissipate from my bloodstream and serotonin take over my senses.

Varun and I may no longer share the compelling chemistry that new lovers enjoy, but is that not the way of every relationship? That exciting, enthralling attraction has been replaced by something more sublime and more permanent.

My mother-in-law interrupts my epiphany by asking me if I plan to go to the salon to get my hair done later because she wants to tag along as well. She can hardly conceal her disappointment at Prince Harry and Meghan not staying on for the after-party. 'I'm sure the heat got to them,' I hear her tell her sister-in-law, almost as if they would have gladly tagged along and shot the breeze with everyone else to the party if it weren't for the weather.

We are barely just home when I receive a panicked call from Sonia who tells me breathlessly that the tenants of my parents' flat in Greater Kailash in Delhi have threatened to kill my father if he sends them another legal notice to vacate the flat. I feel the blood drain from my face and my hands go cold as I hear this.

'Sonia, when did this happen? Is anybody hurt? Is my father alright?' I ask in a panic. I can feel my mouth going dry and my hands are shaking.

'A few minutes back. We sent out the first legal notice to the Chabbras a week ago. Today the bell rang and when Sunita opened the door, that Kishore Chabbra along with two goons barged into the house and straight away walked into the living room where Mausa was watching TV,' she says, quickly sounding terribly shaken up herself.

'I come across to borrow Maasi's saree and we were both in her room, and then we heard the sound of something breaking. We rushed out to see that Chabbra's goons were smashing the dining chairs on the floor as he was walking out.'

'Oh God Sonia, have they left? Is Daddy alright? Where is Mummy?' I feel my stomach contracting into a tight ball.

'They are a little disturbed, and they have asked me not tell you this happened. I will be staying the night with them, don't worry…I just wanted to inform you about what had happened.'

'Wait, I will just put you on the phone with Varun. I'm very frightened for Dad, Sonu.'

I go rushing to my bedroom, tears streaming down my face as I hand the phone over the Varun who is lying in bed, exhausted.

An hour later, Varun is on his way to the airport. 'Don't worry, I will not leave Delhi till Mom and Dad feel secure. By now the Trig Security man would be on his way to guard their flat. We will make sure that they have twenty-four-hour security, no matter what, from now on,' he tells me as he gives me a tight, reassuring squeeze of a hug before getting into the car. 'In Delhi, these things are all too common. Leave it to me now.'

Daddy rings me later, and he sounds decidedly composed. 'God bless our Varun. The security guard is here. We feel safer now. You please don't worry now beta. We are going to be fine. In fact, Varun need not have left Bombay at all.'

'Daddy, he wanted to be there and let him deal with the lawyers and the police etc. He said an FIR needed to be lodged first thing tomorrow. I just did not want you to go to the cops by yourself. This Chabbra must be having political connections. He would not have had the guts otherwise.'

'I'm just so disappointed with people beta. Kishore did not come across as a gunda to me. I thought he was a decent person. I never thought it would come to this,' Daddy says.

That night, I close my eyes and have a dialogue with the maker. I offer my deep gratitude to the universe for protecting my parents and for giving me Varun. I beseech the heavenly gods and deities for their forgiveness and promise never to look at another man again. 'I mean, I will look at other men, but I just will not do it in an inappropriate way,' I clarify, just in case the universe assumes I'm going to blindfold myself when I walk around men.

The next morning, after lodging an FIR, Varun calls to reassure me that all is under control. 'Maybe this Kishore Chabbra knows some major politician. One never knows in Delhi, but I have activated some of my Doon School contacts. My friend Kunal from school is the nephew of the home minister. If needed, I will speak to him, so the cops know not to mess with us,' he tells me. I find myself overcome with a sense of indescribable relief.

'You'll stay on for a few more days, will you not Varun?' I ask, hoping he will answer in the affirmative.

'Is that even a question, Nats?' he says. 'I will not leave till the lawyer has been hired, dealt with and Mom and Dad feel absolutely confident.'

'Thank you, Varun,' I say, unable to come up with anything else to express my overwhelming feeling of love and gratitude.

'Now that this matter with your parents is under control, I hope you will be coming to the party tonight?' Maa asks me with a polite smile. 'Dadabhaisa will be very upset if both of you don't show up.'

I don't wish to make a national issue over us cancelling on 'Dadabhaisa' last minute, and so I consent to attend the dinner without Varun. Moreover, I'm so relieved that he is taking care of my parents that I'm looking forward to going out tonight. 'I'll probably ask Nafisa to come along. I hope Mamaji won't mind?' I ask.

'Not at all, please bring her,' she says. 'She is your closest friend after all. And she is a decent girl.' My mother-in-law is implying that my other friends are trash, basically. Point taken.

That is a low blow, but I let it pass realising that there are too many good things in life to let my mother-in-law ruin my mood.

I immediately ring up Nafisa and coax her to into coming to the fundraiser in Varun's place. She agrees reluctantly. 'I'm only coming because you are a bully and because I can secretly laugh at your family at the table,' she giggles.

An hour later, my two girls are admiring my reflection in the mirror with Sofie giving me tips on how to make my eyes look like Kendall Jenner's.

Ria, on the other hand, wants me to change my lipstick to a deep red. 'Mummy, Taylor Swift always wears red lipstick. Put some for me also pleassssse,' she says, offering her pouty mouth to me cutely.

It's marvellous that my children want me to look like the love child of Taylor Swift and a Kardashian offspring. This is sure to impress the Windsors, especially Meghan.

My mother-in-law, Nafisa and I are finally on our way to the party. Maa is in a beautiful blue-and-silver Abu-Sandeep saree, Nafisa in a beautiful red cocktail dress and me in (her) borrowed white gown. 'White is your colour,' Maa remarks suddenly, looking in my direction before adding, 'Really Natasha, I must say, you haven't looked better.'

I nearly get a myocardial infarction on hearing these words of praise from her. Stupefied, I do my best to smile widely and thank her while Nafisa tries to suppress a giggle.

One often dismisses coincidences in a movie or a novel as too unlikely, blaming the writer for scripting in something that has little chance of taking place in real life. Truth though is truly stranger than fiction.

Of all the people in the world who do you think I spot as soon as I enter the venue after posing for the photographers along with my mother-in-law at the entrance to the ballroom? I spot Riyad Siddiqui who is being introduced by a gentleman in a tuxedo to his heavily bejewelled wife.

I wasn't expecting to see him at this sort of a dinner at all. But then any party worth talking about must have its share of Bollywood, and this party has invited almost everybody who has any association with the world of movies. There is, but naturally, a heavy smattering of big movie stars who have turned up in their finest tuxedos, sarees and ball gowns in honour of the grandchildren of our old masters. Given that I have spent the better part of the evening dressing up for this party, I'm myself in no position to mock anybody, I remind myself.

Maa excuses herself from our company to go looking for her family and I take Nafisa by her hand and navigate my way through the crowded room in the opposite direction from where Riyad is standing to avoid running into him.

We see Bollywood's biggest stars, all of whom are adding to the razzmatazz. There is also Sachin Tendulkar, Virat Kohli and several well-known Indian designers, each one looking pleased with himself to have made the list. Nafisa knows most of the celebrities personally and drags me along to say hello to some of them, including Amish Maheshwar, the designer who did a quick critical analysis of all of Meghan's looks during her India tour.

'This dress, I tell you,' he says, subtly pointing in the direction of the Windsors. 'Unlike Kate Middleton, Markle always gets it right.'

The Windsors have graciously been walking around the room pleasantly conversing with the guests. They are both looking, well, very together and very regal – he in a black tuxedo and she in a simple but elegant blue floor-length gown that makes her look like a Hollywood star instead of British royalty. I'm glad to see that she has held on to her identity. Meghan looks genuinely enthusiastic and exudes warmth as she shakes hands with the never-ending queue of people waiting to greet her.

We are chatting with bestselling writer Dhruvi Malhar when Maa comes looking for me and asks Nafisa and me to go along with her to greet Harry and Meghan. I say a firm no. 'How rude, Natasha!' she exclaims, her large eyes becoming even larger with annoyance, like a kathakali dancer's.

'But you met them already at the polo match yesterday. I did not think you would want to queue up to meet them again?' I venture.

'Oh but I do. They are our friends, and I have realised Meghan is quite a sweet girl,' she says, and Nafisa purses her lips to restrain herself from bursting with laughter.

Mercifully, Maa locates her dadabhaisa and bhabhisa shortly after and I hastily relinquish my mother-in-law-sitting duties to them and disappear to mingle with the crowd under the dim lights of the crystal chandeliers.

When the noise settles down, and we assume our seats at the table assigned to Mamaji, I find much to my consternation that Riyad is seated at a table right across.

There are two well-known industrialists on his table along with their wives, there is also Gita Ray the catty columnist and Shri, a statuesque model in a slinky but chic burgundy coloured silk dress seated near Riyad. Shri could just be a guest but may well be his date.

Maa has been placed right next to her bhabhi, and I find my place card next to Mamaji's friend – an avuncular Etonian, who has far too many stories to tell than I care to have the patience for tonight. Seeing that at least two other places on the table haven't yet been claimed yet by other guests, I quickly switch the cards in such a manner that Nafisa is seated right next to me.

'He is here,' she whispers to me.

'I know,' I say sotto voice. So discomfited am I by Riyad's unexpected presence that I reach for a glass of champagne floating past me and gulp down half of it straight away to calm my nerves.

While I wait for my anxiety to settle, I quietly feel grateful for Nafisa's presence this evening. Surviving my drunk-with-excitement mother-in-law at my table and Riyad two tables across from me might have been impossible without her and the bubbly.

'I must say, your Riyad is looking very debonair. How's your heart holding up?' Nafisa giggles.

'Shut up, don't look in his direction. You will make it obvious. And don't take his name either. People can read lips,' I warn her.

Nafisa violently rolls her eyes at me and says, 'Paranoid much?'

Etonian uncle, who would rather speak to me than my mother-in-law, starts telling me a tedious story about his recent trip to Vietnam. It's impossible for me to avoid looking at Riyad because our tables are placed adjacent to each other, and our eyes do meet briefly. He smiles faintly at me, and I acknowledge it with a polite reciprocal smile myself.

When I look in his direction a few minutes into my conversation with Etonian uncle, I catch him looking at me once again. His repeated glances are making me uncomfortable and also a little afraid – what if one of the family members sitting on my table has noticed it?

I break our eye contact abruptly and turn towards Nafisa to talk to her.

'Nats, his eyes are on you. Did you know he was going to be here?' she asks me.

I tell her I hadn't a clue.

I look around me. The room is abuzz with the humming of hushed conversations.

The British High Commissioner makes a welcome speech as does dishy Shah Rukh Khan after which there are some entertaining dance performances by well-known Bollywood glamazons in elaborate costumes.

Prince Harry makes a charming speech where he tells his admiring audience that when Meghan and he got married, she told him that the first place she wanted to visit was India. He then goes on to speak about his family's old association with our country, as if it needed reminding.

Everybody in the audience claps, the shutterbugs click and my mother-in-law, delirious as she is to be in the same room as the Windsors, cheers them on audibly with, 'How charming, how charming!'

'Did you hear that Dadabhaisa?' she asks without peeling her peepers away from the table where Harry and Meghan are seated as if Mamaji was deaf.

'Yes, yes. So elegant, so refined,' Mamaji says in agreement.

'Spoke from the heart,' she adds.

Nafisa and I elbow each other from under the table desperately suppressing our laughter.

'I like that girl you know?' Maa tells Etonian uncle.

'Which girl?' uncle asks.

'Meghan, who else. So gentle, so pretty. She was speaking to Shah Rukh Khan when I passed her by, but she remembered me from yesterday and acknowledged me with a smile,' she says. 'This is elegance.'

Oh, so this is why Maa's opinions about Meghan changed from a disparaging girl-with-black-blood comment to 'sweet girl'. Nafisa cannot take it any more, and she ducks down on her knees to laugh heartily under the table while I have to sit there and bear it with a straight face.

Soon the dinner service begins and our bouillabaisse soup is placed on our respective plates.

'What is going on? Why is he looking at you like that?' Nafisa asks me in a business-like tone a little later.

'Who? Harry?'

'Shut up. You know who I'm talking about.'

'Oh, maybe he is looking at you. Shall I introduce you two?' I smile.

'No thanks. Just deliver your story on time. That will be sufficient.'

Next thing I know Riyad gets up from his chair and walks purposefully towards our table. Walking up to my chair he greets me in a formal tone. 'Hi Natasha, I just thought I should come up here and say hello to you,' he smiles and says.

I turn my neck to look at him, doing best to appear impassive. 'I'm very well Riyad. Have you met Nafisa, my friend and the editor of *Beau Monde*?'

He shakes hands with Nafisa, and they say their polite hellos. Nafisa thanks him for the interview and tells him how keen she had been for years to have him featured in the magazine.

Maa, who is observing our interaction, seems impressed that her insignificant daughter-in-law is known to a famous Bollywood face. Sensing her desire to be introduced as well, I introduce Riyad to everybody at the table, one by one, finally stopping at my mother-in-law.

'And that is my mother-in-law, Rani Devika Kumari,' I say.

He goes over to her side to greet her politely, and they make small talk. Wasting no time at all, Maa cuts to the chase straight taway by informing Riyad about all her charities and requests him to visit one of the NGOs that she is a patron of. 'It would be my pleasure ma'am,' I overhear Riyad tell her earnestly.

'I never knew you knew Varun and Natasha. I'd have invited you sooner. We get the press to cover it too, of course,' she tells him as though Riyad might be offended for being overlooked as a potential chief guest at a Jhalakpur NGO's anniversary function.

'I'll be glad to come anytime. Natasha will have my coordinates. Do get in touch with me ma'am,' he says politely before excusing himself and heading back to his table.

I'm so annoyed with my mother-in-law's opportunistic tendencies. She talks about how impressed she is with his impeccable manners after he's gone back. 'It's rare to find people like that in the movie industry,' she tells Etonian uncle. 'I have been so keen to get some publicity for Balika with the help of someone famous. You never told me that you knew Riyad Siddiqui, Natasha,' she bemoans. 'Oh, now that you have met him, I'm sure he will be happy to help you,' I say with faux sincerity.

Maa, Mama-Mami, Etonian uncle and Mamaji's nephew, all head towards the royal couple to queue up for photographs shortly after the dessert has been served. Nafisa and I decide to stay behind. 'What happened to your crush?' Nafisa asks me as soon as we are alone at our table. 'I expected nothing less than a gushing blushing introduction from you, but you were really playing it cool. Everything okay with your new friend and you?'

'Of course, all is well. We are meeting at a formal party and he was being polite, that's all,' I say cheerfully.

'So your crush is still around, right?'

'The crush is history now. I got over it. You were right. It was nothing more than the thrill of a new interaction with an interesting person. But as you often remind me, how can I fall for another man when I have Varun at home?'

'You sound very sensible Nats. Now I'm worried,' Nafisa looks intrigued.

'We are all looking to be understood. I finally feel understood by Varun,' I smile.

The next day, as my mother-in-law leaves for the airport, I do all I can to conceal my relief.

Shortly after waving her goodbye, I write an email to Priyanka at *Vanity International*.

Dear Priyanka,

I have been thinking about our last conversation. As much as I'm enjoying working as a freelancer with you, I think I'm ready to come on board in the position of a deputy editor, as suggested by you.

Let me know when I could come across to your office to discuss this further.

Warmly,

Natasha.

❊❊❊

I'm waiting at the airport to receive Varun. He is returning after spending three days with my parents in Delhi. The extra security that is to shadow my parents for the next few weeks is making them extremely uncomfortable, but Varun insists on it. I cannot wait to tell him that I'm joining *Vanity International* as a deputy editor two weeks from now.

This leaves us with just enough time to recover from a romantic holiday in the Maldives that I believe his secretary has been working on. It was meant to be a surprise for me but since Varun is away, Cynthia had to ask me for my passport this morning and I managed to wheedle this information out of her. Of course, I will pretend to be spectacularly surprised when Varun announces this news to me. My acting skills have improved substantially over the past year.

Acknowledgements

I'd like to start by thanking the brilliant Faiza Sultan Khan for taking on and editing my book. This is my first attempt at fiction and she told me exactly what worked and what did not, and how to make my words crackle rather than simmer.

Special thanks to Ruchika Chanana for her invaluable feedback.

And to Divia Thani, for always, always being there for me and for believing in me, for her precious inputs and for suffering my manuscript twice, or was it thrice?

My special thanks to Aparna Jain for her moral support and constant encouragement.

A big thank you to my guardian, Shravan Shroff, for buying me a new laptop when an aquarium crashed against my old one, for thoughtfully offering me a cabin in his office to work from, and for patiently minding our children during our family vacation when I was overcome with an urge to rewrite my manuscript. But most of all, for asking me time and again in the year that followed if this book will actually be published in our lifetime.

I must also thank my wonderful children Zara and Rania for all the laughs and the love, and for vehemently declaring that they would never want to take up writing as a profession because writers made no money. It's heartening to know that I have been such an inspiration to you both.

Kaveri Khullar, thank you for always being optimistic about everything I do and for reassuring our mother that I'm alive and well, even when her calls to me go unanswered.

Saving the best for last, I want to thank my brilliant and beautiful mother Shobna, without whose boundless love, support, encouragement and prayers I'd be nothing.